THE
HUMAN
SEASON

THE
HUMAN
SEASON

A NOVEL BY
Sarah Rossiter

LITTLE, BROWN AND COMPANY
BOSTON   TORONTO

The characters, places, and events portrayed in this
book are fictitious. Any similarities to real places
or persons, living or dead, are purely coincidental
and not intended by the author.

Library of Congress Cataloging-in-Publication Data
Rossiter, Sarah.
The human season.
I. Title.
PS3568.08477H8   1987   813'.54   86-21463
ISBN 0-316-75759-4

RRD VA

*Published simultaneously in Canada
by Little, Brown & Company (Canada) Limited*

PRINTED IN THE UNITED STATES OF AMERICA

For
Ruth M. Murphy

I praise the fall: it is the human season
— Archibald MacLeish,
"Immortal Autumn"

Acknowledgments

I want to thank Ned, my first reader, and our children, Stephen, Jennifer, Lisa, and Kate, for their tolerance and encouragement. Lisa deserves special thanks for her reading of the final draft, and so does Jennifer, who not only read the manuscript for me, but typed the final draft as well.

I am especially grateful to my parents for their support, and to my friends Alison Travis, Lilla Waltch, and Mameve Medwed, who read and listened and advised.

I also wish to thank my editor, Fredrica S. Friedman, for the time and energy she has devoted to this book.

To Marian Young, my friend and agent, I owe a special debt of gratitude. I thank her for many things, but most especially for believing.

THE
HUMAN
SEASON

ONE

IT'S HARD to know where to begin. Should I start here, at the end, or should I go back to the beginning? But where is the beginning? My first year at Dunster, or before, at home? Did it start when I met Manning, or when I met his wife?

First there was Manning, then there was his wife. He called her Cate, I called her Mrs. Manning. Mrs. Oliver Austin Manning III. We met two years ago when she was twenty, and I was almost seventeen. Yesterday she was twenty-two.

Let me start with today. With now.

Right now I am sitting at my desk. I am sitting, staring out my window at the fountain in the middle of the school quad, thinking that this is the sixth year I've had to stare at the stone dolphin squirting water from its mouth, thinking that in two weeks I will never see it again, thinking about my Tragedy paper, thinking about last night, about Cate, when I hear footsteps coming down the hall. I hear a voice. "Is Peter Spaulding in his room?" I know that voice; I even like the person it belongs to. She is the last person in the world I want to see.

She knocks, a soft knock but insistent. "Peter?" she says. I take a deep breath, smelling wisteria, sun-warmed bricks. "Come in," I say.

Mrs. MacQuire comes in slowly. Too slowly. Maybe I should have guessed, but in the six years that I've known

3

her, I've never seen her hurry. She's always in control. Closing the door, she leans against it. "Peter," she says. She doesn't smile.

I do. I stand up, smiling. "So what brings you here?" She frowns, glides across the room, and sits, legs crossed, on the edge of my bed. The bed's unmade; she doesn't seem to notice. She sits, her back straight, and looks at me.

"I don't know how to tell you this," she says.

"Then don't," I say. I sit down too. I know all about bad news, what people look like when they pass it along. Even people like Mrs. MacQuire. "Perfect," I said to Judith once. "She's perfect." Judith laughed. "Sweetheart," she said. "Thank God there's no such thing."

Regal, then. That's what I thought six years ago the day I met her. My first day here at Dunster, and I was scared. Coach was my advisor so they had me down for tea. The house was cool and quiet. So was she. She served me iced tea in a frosted glass, a sprig of mint, a silver straw. "Oliver brought these," she said, "from Europe." She smiled. I didn't know who Oliver was, but I smiled too. I sipped slowly through the silver straw. "It's good," I said. She smiled. "Home-made," she said.

I thought of home, my mother at the airport just that morning. At home iced tea was always Lipton's Instant. At home I made it, not my mother. My mother left me at the airport. "You'll be all right," she said. The way she said it it sounded like a question. "Sure," I said because what else could I say. She smiled, and her hands moved, fluttering, to her hair. Beyond the glass doors I heard Robert honk the horn. I saw him, sitting in my mother's car. "The girls," my mother said, "we've left them home alone."

"Sure," I said again. I put my hands inside my pockets so she wouldn't see them trembling. Her lips brushed my cheek. "Darling," she said. I closed my eyes so that I wouldn't have to see her walk away.

"Peter," said Mrs. MacQuire. Her voice was firm, both

soft and strong. She wore a blue dress, and her hands were quiet in her lap. "It's always difficult the first few days." Her hair was dark gold, and her face was smooth. "Before you know it, it'll feel like home."

She said it as if she really knew. I didn't believe her, but I liked her. "Sure," I said. I even smiled.

"Peter," she says. She's sitting on my bed; her eyes are on me. She's wearing a dark green sleeveless dress, a dress I remember from before. I don't know why. Maybe because my mother had one like it once, the same color anyway.

I don't know what happened to my mother's dress. After I came Dunster, I lost track of things like that. It's just as well. When she married Robert, she threw out everything, including clothes.

"I want to tell you, Peter," says Mrs. MacQuire, "before you hear it announced."

"Sure," I say. I take a deep breath. "Fine." I lean forward to make it easier, trying not to crack my knuckles, a habit of mine when I get nervous. My father cracks his knuckles too. An awful sound. Like bones breaking, says Judith, my stepmother, who's lived with him for five years now.

Mrs. MacQuire doesn't tell me anything. She looks away, around the room. Old posters, books, ripe-smelling clothes. I don't think she's seeing it, though. I look at her. She's good-looking for someone who must be almost forty. I said so once to Manning, and he told her. Peter thinks you're well preserved is what he said. When I was there.

Mrs. MacQuire clears her throat.

"Peter," she says. Her voice is soft. "She's dead. Cate, Mrs. Manning, is dead." She waits for me to say something. "She killed herself," says Mrs. MacQuire.

I don't move. She blinks. Her eyes are on me. I am very careful to stay still. I feel like a puppet I had once, my body carved from wood, held up by string. His mouth curved in a smile, and he always made me laugh until Bets, my youngest sister, fouled the strings. I tried to fix them, but I couldn't.

5

All I could do was cut them, and when I did he fell, in pieces, on the floor.

I don't move. I sit, with my hands on my knees, and feel the sweat collecting. My skin prickles. On the floor I see a strip of sunlight. Spring sunlight, lemon-colored. The color of Cate's hair.

I see a beetle with shiny wings move slowly, inside the light. I watch. The beetle crawls, across the boundary, into shadow, then scuttles back. I watch the light slide slowly across the floor, the beetle moving with it. I feel her watching me.

"Say something," says Mrs. MacQuire. "Please."

I clear my throat. "Does he know?" I say. "Manning?" My voice is husky.

"Yes, of course." Her fingers pleat the sheet, working it into small tight creases.

"I thought you should know," she says. She says it softly.

"Thanks," I say. "Thanks for telling me."

Her eyes are on me, bright and burning. I'm afraid she's going to cry. I start to crack my knuckles. I hate the noise, but I can't stop.

"Peter," she says. "Don't."

I stop. I watch the strip of sunlight, moving slowly up the wall. I can't see the beetle anywhere.

Mrs. MacQuire doesn't move. She sits, waiting. Waiting for what? For me to ask a question? Not a chance.

"Listen," I say, "I'm really sorry, but I've got this tragedy paper to write."

The minute I say it I wish I hadn't. But it's too late, and I know she knows who I have to write it for.

"Oliver and his tragic flaws," she says. Her voice is quiet.

She stands up. She stands, staring down at me. I stare at her feet. Her feet surprise me. They're wide and sturdy.

She's wearing sandals, and where the straps cross over, skin bulges out on either side.

"Peter," she says. "She was found this morning. Down by the river."

I stare at the feet. They look like they belong to someone else. Her ankles are thicker than they should be. So are her legs. Have they changed, or is it that I've never looked before?

"I thought," says Mrs. MacQuire, "it would be better if you weren't taken by surprise."

I don't say anything. I watch her feet, moving away toward the door. When they reach the door, they stop.

I like Mrs. MacQuire, but I have to clench my fists to keep from hitting her, from shouting at her to go away. Judith is always telling me to let my feelings out. As if she knows. She doesn't; she doesn't know what would happen if I did.

"You should know," she whispers. "There's going to be an autopsy." The door opens, and I hear kids coming back from practice, cleats and soccer balls banging against the floor. When the door closes, I'm alone.

Cate's dead. That's the story. I wait to feel something. I hear the chapel bell strike five. Someone is playing hand-ball down in the cloisters. I hear the hard thwack of rubber against stone. Against the rules, but someone else can stop them.

All I can do is get down on the floor, and start looking for that beetle. I look under the bed, along the walls. I shake my socks. I open drawers, and close them.

I go back to my desk. The chair's so damp you'd think I'd wet my pants. I used to, used to wet my bed, back when I was a First Former, and before, at home. I didn't mean to; it just happened. Some things do.

I didn't lie to Mrs. MacQuire. The paper I have to write is right here, in front of me. "The Nature of Tragedy in

Shakespeare." We've been working on it for six months now. Supposedly. I've got the title page. I even typed it. I've got the title, my name, and down at the bottom, "Sixth Form Honors English, Mr. Manning." Maybe I won't have to write it now. Maybe no one will.

Outside, the light is really something. It's like a green grape. Translucent. There is no wind at all. It's the best time of day for the river, and the best time of year too when the water is high, still running fast from winter snow. There are blackbirds in the cattails, and the late sun turns the water gold.

I have some choices. I could take a shower, go to evening chapel. Chapel is voluntary now, but back when I was twelve, it wasn't. The only thing I liked about it then was the way the stained glass turned my hands to color, different colors depending on where I'd sit. Red or gold. When it was sunny, that is. Otherwise the chapel's so dark you can't see to read the hymns.

We always sang a lot of hymns. On clear days, especially in the fall, we sang hymns like "Onward, Christian Soldiers," and the Head gave sermons on what he called the Football Field of Life. In winter, in January, when it was dark, we sang the sad ones. You know. "Time like an ever-rolling stream." "There is a green hill far away."

I'm beginning to feel something. I wish I wouldn't, but don't know how to stop it. My hands are shaking. I hear a rattling noise, and for a moment think it's me. A piece of paper quivers on my desk; I lift the paper, and there's the beetle.

Carefully I lift him, and leaning across the desk, nudge him through a small hole in the screen. For a second he falls, and then his wings flash fire as he rockets up. All things considered, I saved his life. . . .

There's no getting away from it though I could keep on trying. There are facts I could consider. For instance. I am eighteen years old, nineteen in November, and on the desk in front of me a letter reads, "It gives great pleasure to inform you . . ." The letter is from Yale. Also on the desk is the first draft of my graduation speech. Another fact. Peter Spaulding, Senior Prefect. Senior Prefects always speak at Graduation, or should I say Commencement.

Commencement means beginning, something I'd never thought about before until Cate gave me the idea. Just last week. Just last week we sat down by the river, the Maple River, and talked about endings and beginnings.

Actually, she was sitting and I was standing. I stood behind her so she wouldn't have to see me slip the worm on the hook. She doesn't like fishing, but I do. Even with nothing much to catch, I like it. Judith thinks I'm crazy. It's good, I said; it's doing something while you're doing nothing. Like being pregnant, I suppose, said Judith. I suppose she might be right, but what do I know. What does she know; she's never had a kid. She never will. She's never wanted one, she says. Anyway, she says, I have one; I've got you. She smiles when she says it, but I think maybe she might mean it. I think of Judith. I want to call her. But I can't.

Last week Cate sat by the river. The grass was green, and wet. I saw it shining. "You should sit on my jacket," I said. She didn't answer; I don't know if she even heard. I watched her pull a strand of hair between two fingers, rubbing it against her skin. Her hair is long, below her shoulders, though usually she wears it up. Last week she wore it down.

"I've been thinking," she said. The worm wriggled, and the barb caught my finger, a sharp jab beneath the nail. It's surprising how much a small thing like that can hurt. I sucked my finger, tasting blood. Her back was to me. "Commencement," she said. "Why do they call it that? It's more an ending than beginning."

I looked above her head across the water, fast-moving water, the color of smoke. I cast the line out as far as I could, feeling the tension as the current carried it downstream. The rod bent; I held on tight. "You haven't changed your mind," I said. I said it lightly, as if I didn't care.

She knew. She had to know. She didn't answer right away. "I've just been thinking," she said.

Because her back was to me I couldn't see her face. "You're right," I said. "It's the ending that comes first."

I stood there, fishing. She was quiet, and so was I. The sun was setting, and the new leaves of the poplars spun like silver coins. Commencement. I'd never thought of it like that before.

I crouched down by the water's edge. "Here," I said. I handed her a small green sprig. She looked at me.

"What's this?" she said.

"A present," I said. "Go on. Taste it. It's not poison."

She nibbled the small edge of a leaf. She smiled. "Watercress," she said. "How did you know?"

I smiled too. "I planted it. Four years ago. It's really taken off."

"Peter," she said, "the things you do!"

I shrugged. "Survival skills," I said, but I was pleased. "We're going to make it, aren't we?" I said. "We're going to be all right?"

She kissed me. I tasted watercress. "What do you think?" she said.

I stand up so fast the chair tips over. I hear it hit the ground. Not just my hands, my whole body is shaking now. Even my teeth are chattering. I have never been so cold.

I let the chair lie where it's fallen. Out in the hall I hear the bell ring, the dinner bell. I look at the bed; where Mrs. MacQuire was sitting there's a depression in the wrinkled sheets. She came to tell me. That's a fact. The question is, what does she know?

The bell rings again. Out in the hall, I hear doors banging, and footsteps heading down the stairs. I hear a thrush singing, liquid notes that sound like rain.

Cate kissed me. I tasted watercress.

"Sometimes," I said, "I can't help it. I get scared. If someone knew."

"No one," she said. She touched my forehead with her finger. "Our secret."

"OK," I said.

She smiled. "Cross my heart and hope to die." She crossed her heart. "Trust me," she said.

"I do," I said. "I do."

TWO

I SKIP DINNER. Sixth Formers are allowed to, but I'd do it anyway. I need to think. I hold still until the dorm is quiet, then sprint down the hall to the showers. I stand, shaking, under freezing water. It feels like needles against my skin. When I can't take it anymore, I turn to hot. Scalding. It helps. Then I start scrubbing. I scrub so hard, it hurts. The more it hurts, the better I feel.

The room is thick with steam, so thick it's hard to breathe. It's hard to see. The mirror above the sinks is clouded over. I wipe my hand across the glass, one small circle so I can see my face. Wet, my hair looks straight, and darker than it really is. My eyes are bright. I don't know who that face belongs to, or what I'm looking for.

I think of Timothy.

I dress quickly. With everyone at dinner, the hall is quiet. I watch my shadow move along the wall, down the stairs, past the main desk, toward the basement. My feet don't make a sound. There is only my shadow, and the smell of chalk and sweat, a sweet smell, like dying or death.

The year my father left, I'd get up early. The house was so quiet the air seemed alive, as if the walls were breathing. My mother's door was closed. I watched my shadow move along the walls as one by one I woke my sisters. I didn't talk. What could I say? I gave them breakfast. In silence we stood around the kitchen table. The others ate, but Bets

12

sucked her Sugar Smacks, and spit them out. She couldn't
swallow. "You're gonna die," I said. Bets was three. When
she tried to swallow, she'd start to gag. Sucking the sweetness
from her thumb, she'd stare at me. I was eleven, and felt as
if I'd lived forever.

I turn the corner, and hear the voices, coming from the
dining hall.

"Spaulding! Just the man I want to see."

The Head stands at his study door.

"You're not at dinner, sir?"

Frowning, he sucks loudly on his pipe. "And you?" he
says. He doesn't wait for me to answer. He beckons with
his finger. "We need to talk," he says.

Turning, he marches back into his study. There's nothing
to do but follow him. "And close the door behind you," he
says. I close the door, and stand there, waiting. Spencer,
pipe clenched between his teeth, looks at me. "Sit down,
boy, sit!" As if I were a dog.

I cross the room, and sit. He sits too, his desk between
us. "Well now," he says. Smoke billows from his pipe.
Through the smoke he peers at me. His fingers tap the desk.
I look away, around the room, a large room centered by his
desk, with past headmasters on the walls.

"Well now, Spaulding. I assume you've heard the news."

I nod. Rumor has it Spencer's leaving too. Or was.

"Terrible business," says Spencer. "Terrible."

On the walls the gold frames glisten. The walls are crowded.
They'll have to take one down to make room for him.

"Spaulding," he says. "I need your help."

I turn to look at him. His hands are clasped together,
fingers laced. Here's the church, here's the steeple, open
the door, see all the . . . His forefingers point to heaven.
Spencer's a minister; before that he was a soldier. He spreads
his fingers in a gesture of despair.

"Do you hear me?" he says.

"Yes, sir."

13

His pipe's gone out, but he doesn't seem to notice. There's not much Spencer seems to notice, but I didn't know that when I was just a kid. When I was just a kid, he frightened me. He has a temper. He just erupts, his face turns red, the words pour out, and then it's over.

This isn't over, though; it's just begun.

"Your pipe, sir."

He frowns, at me, then at his pipe. "Ah," he says. He cups it in his palm, and strikes a match. Smoke rises, forms a screen; I feel better.

"Now then, Spaulding, here's what I think. I think it's a question of responsibility."

"Yes, sir."

"We are all responsible, but you, of the student body, more than most. Do you understand me?"

"Yes, sir. Actually, no, sir. Not quite, sir."

He leans toward me. His face is flushed. Sweat beads his forehead. He's wearing tweeds, dark heavy tweeds he wears the year around.

"As Senior Prefect, Spaulding, you are responsible for the attitude of the entire student body, most particularly responsible in moments of crisis. It is imperative that talk of this, um, affair be kept to a minimum. Do you understand?"

"Yes, sir."

He leans back, sucking on his pipe. Through the smoke he looks at me.

"I'm glad to hear that. I have been here for thirty-five years now, Spaulding, twenty-five of them spent sitting behind this very desk, and it has been my experience that nothing is more damaging to a school of this kind than the vicious circulation of unfounded rumors and unwarranted gossip. Do you hear me, Spaulding? The future of this school depends upon the continuing goodwill of our benefactors, trustees and alumni both. Am I making myself clear?"

"Yes, sir. Only . . ."

Spencer raises his eyebrows. They're white now, but still

14

bushy. They used to make me think of caterpillars; they used to frighten me.

"I just don't understand, sir, exactly what it is you want me to do."

"Talk to them, boy!" His fist hits the desk. A pen rolls off onto the floor. "Nip each rumor in the bud before it has a chance to flower. I will do my part. I expect you to do yours."

I get up. If I don't I'll start to crack my knuckles. I walk over to the windows, and stand there, looking out. Spencer is behind me. I hear his chair swivel as he turns. I hear him sucking on his pipe.

Out the window some kids are playing Ultimate Frisbee. Sixth Formers, I think. I see Thurston, reaching high, bending back, laughing. Thurston. Old buddy. The grass is so green it's blinding. Pollen dances in the air. I press my forehead against the glass.

"When I talk, sir, what do you want me to say?"

Behind me I hear papers shuffling, then a steady tapping as he lines their edges. Tap, tap, tap. When he's under stress, his army training shows. He fought in World War II, and, after, liberated a concentration camp. It was Manning who told me that. Spencer's never said a word.

I hear him sigh. His chair creaks as he rises, and comes to stand beside me. We are the same height now. "Stick to the facts," says Spencer. "The simple facts. She's dead. A dreadful waste. She was only twenty-three."

"Twenty-two," I say.

He doesn't hear me. His hand is dead weight on my shoulder.

"A tragedy. Manning is devastated, naturally. Apparently her childhood was most difficult. Manning said nothing, but I remember Melissa, Mrs. MacQuire, once made mention of an orphanage."

"No," I say. "If I could be excused, sir."

I move backward, toward the door. Spencer's hand drops

15

from my shoulder. His other hand rises, pipe aimed at my chest. "One more thing," he says. I stop. "Regarding Mr. Manning. I'm sure it's not necessary to mention how much he would appreciate your calling on him."

I hold my breath.

"I don't think, sir . . ."

"No, no, no. Pay no attention to my announcement made in chapel. I said that to protect him. From the others letters of condolence will suffice. But from you, Spaulding, I know he would appreciate a visit."

"I can't, sir."

"Of course you can. As representative of the student body, it's your responsibility."

"I'm sorry, sir. I can't."

Spencer frowns.

"There's no such thing as can't, Spaulding. I'm giving you an order. Is that understood?"

"Yes, sir."

"Good boy," says Spencer. "I'll tell you something. You're too sensitive. Always have been."

"Yes, sir."

"I've said the same to Manning. Don't coddle that boy, you'll do him harm. That's what I said. And his reply, Spaulding, his reply?" His eyebrows twitch. "He said, 'The harm's already done; it's up to us to undo what we can.' "

"Yes, sir. If you don't mind, sir." I edge away. He follows.

"Spaulding, you owe him something. Do you understand?"

"Yes, sir. I reach the door. My hand is on the doorknob.

"Any more questions, Spaulding? Before you go?"

I open the door. The hall is empty. I look at Spencer. "If they ask, sir, about the autopsy . . ."

I've never seen him move so fast. Lunging past me, he shuts the door. He's breathing hard. "I don't recall," he says, "any mention of that in my announcement."

"One of the kids, sir. I heard him after chapel. Talking."

He stands, thinking, tapping his pipe against his teeth. His teeth are yellow. "In strictest confidence then, Spaulding. Not a word to anyone, you understand? The fact is, Spaulding, after suicide, autopsy is routine. A necessary precaution, you understand. There's no doubt, of course. Not the least suspicion of foul play. A most unhappy woman, Spaulding. But law is law. We can only comply, and hope that the whole sorry, and, yes, untimely business can be forgotten before too long."

"Yes, sir."

Spencer smiles. "You're a good boy, Spaulding," he says. "Run along."

I do run. As soon as I am out the door, as soon as I hear it close behind me, I run, as fast as I can down the hall and past the dining room, past the classrooms, to the basement stairs. The stairs are dark, but I take them two at a time, and I don't stop running until I reach the other end, where Timothy's chair sits by the furnace.

The chair is empty, but I'm not surprised. He's still upstairs. Above my head I hear water running through the pipes, the roar of dishwashers in the kitchen. I crouch, next to the chair, hugging my stomach, trying to catch my breath. I'm soaked with sweat. When I wipe my face, I feel the trembling in my hands. Waiting, I rock. My sweat dries, slowly. The basement is warm and clean. There are no windows, and the light is dim.

I told Judith once about the basement. I didn't mention Timothy because I thought she might not understand. How could she when I don't myself? She smiled. "Big deal," she said. "You like the basement. What's wrong with that?" I shrugged. "Maybe it's weird," I said. I was thirteen, and didn't know her then.

"Weird!" said Judith. "To want to be alone?"

"The basement," I said.

"Kiddo," said Judith, "I used to use the crawl space. I couldn't even sit. I spent hours, lying flat."

I wasn't sure if she was kidding. "Why?" I asked.

"Like you," she said. "It made me feel safe."

The air is warm. I don't feel safe. I feel sleepy. Behind me, the furnace starts its throbbing. The pipes connected to the furnace start to rattle. Large metal ducts, they snake across the ceiling, and out of sight.

I think of hearts, hearts pumping, beating, all connected. My heart. Cate's heart. Only her heart isn't beating anymore.

Am I the only person who knows why?

THREE

TIMOTHY'S EYES were what I noticed first. They made me think of Bets, my sister, when she was still a baby. When she was still a baby I'd pick her up when no one was around. And hold her. She smelled of milk and powder, good smells, but it was her eyes that got to me. She looked so wise, as if she knew things I couldn't hope to know, and never would. But when she learned to talk her eyes turned cloudy.

Timothy's haven't changed at all, at least not in the last six years. Not since my first term here, when I was twelve, and I first met him. My first term here, and I was scared of everything. Especially the dining hall.

The dining hall is huge, a stone floor, vaulted ceiling and tall thin windows sealed shut. When Judith saw it she told me all it needed was strewn rushes, and giant mastiffs crunching greasy bones.

Back then, when I was new, the tables were assigned. We moved daily, on rotation basis, around the table from chair to chair. The chair I dreaded reaching was the end one on the left-hand side. That chair cleared the table. I was tall for twelve, but skinny. The trays were heavy. When my turn came I knew I'd drop it, loaded with thick white plates, cold lumps of mashed potato. Saltpeter, someone said. Twice a week they served us mashed potatoes. No one ate them. I didn't know what saltpeter was, but I didn't eat them either. I scraped, and stacked. The noise was awful, glasses, plates, and silverware. The tray was heavy, and my tie too tight.

I moved away, across the floor, feeling it slip beneath my shoes. I felt eyes on me, watching, waiting for the crash.

It never came.

I pushed through the kitchen swinging door. Boys passed behind me, emptying plates and glasses into plastic bins. No one talked. In they came, and out the other door. I slid my tray onto the counter, and hands reached out to take it.

I saw his hands before I saw his face. White hands, fingers wrinkled by the water. Then looking up, I saw his eyes. The steam rose up, thin wisps rising from hot plates, drying. I couldn't help it; I stood there, staring. I thought of Bets, of Lake Michigan on a still blue day when, holding still, you look down and see clear to the bottom. To minnows, pebbles, grains of sand.

His hands reached out to take my plates. He smiled. "Good," he said. At least I thought he did. His lips moved, but it might have been the sound of steam.

I didn't know then that he hardly ever talked, that the others in the kitchen didn't either. I didn't know, and by the time I learned it was too late to make a difference. By then I knew his name, and found the basement, and every night I could I'd sneak into the kitchen to help him wash, and afterward to sit in silence beneath the school.

Kids call them retards, that is if they call them anything. Mostly it's as if they don't exist. Spencer calls them "the unfortunates," and says that were it not for Dunster they would be locked up in the local institution. As it is, they live down by the river in the old mill, with bars on the windows, and the doors locked every night. "They're people, sir," I said to Spencer just last year. He glared. "Good God, boy, did I ever say they weren't!" But I bet he doesn't even know their names. I bet he's never heard them laughing, something they only do when they're alone, a ripple of sound, like leaves in wind.

It was Manning who found me in the kitchen that first

year. Someone must have told him where I was, but I never found out who. Someone must have seen me sneaking in or sneaking out, though I was always careful to wait till no one was around.

"So this is where you get to, Peter," Manning said, taking me completely by surprise. I hoped the steam would hide my blushing. Timothy stood there, washing dishes, not looking up. Manning beckoned with his finger. "You'd better come with me." I had no choice. I dropped my dishtowel on the counter, and left without a word.

Our footsteps echoed. My head came only to his shoulder then. "Aren't you supposed to be in study hall?" he said. He knew I was. We walked, out of the dining hall, down West Wing, and I thought he was taking me to the Head. "I didn't mean to break the rules, sir," I said. "It's just Timothy. He's my friend."

Maybe my voice was trembling. Manning stopped, and took me by the shoulders, and turned me so I faced him. His dark hair glistened, and his eyelashes were fringed with steam. When he blinked, drops of water fell like rain. He shook me gently. "Listen to me," he said.

I stood still, listening. I felt his hands, one on each shoulder, a careful weight, a balance. He was a master like all the rest. Like all the rest, he scared me. "Peter," he said. He was the only one who called me that; the others called me Spaulding. "I've been watching you," he said. "You're worried. Tell me why?"

How could he tell? I never knew. It was enough that he had asked.

"My sisters, sir. I miss them." I swallowed hard. "Bets is only three."

"Ah." He nodded as if he understood. "It's to your credit that you care." He paused. "I want you to believe me, Peter," he said. He said it slowly. "Everything." He paused again. "Everything will be all right."

That's all he said. And I believed him. There was some-

21

thing in the way he said it, in the way his hands felt on my shoulders. He squeezed my shoulders. I wasn't used to that; my father wasn't big on touching. I ducked my head, and he let go, smiling. As if he knew.

I hear Timothy before I see him, hear the shuffle of rubber soles against cement. The shuffling sounds like breathing. He walks with his head thrust forward, his shoulders hunched. He walks as if he's old. He is old. Very old. His hair is white.

He smiles when he sees me. Slowly he sits. The chair creaks. Settled, he plants his feet and starts to rock. The air stirs, smelling of Ivory Soap and rusty pipes. Hands clasped in his lap, he looks at me, eyes open, waiting.

And I wait too. With Timothy there's never any hurry. He's different, but I don't know how to put it into words. It's like he's all there, complete already, his own beginning and his own end too. I get the feeling when I'm with him that he could wait forever because there's nothing that he's waiting for. Does that make sense?

He sits, rocking.

I rub my hands against my face. "Timothy," I say. "I'm in trouble." Rocking, he looks at me. He doesn't speak.

"She's dead. Mrs. Manning, Cate. She's dead." The word echoes off stone walls. I say it loud to make it real. "Dead," I say. To Timothy. "Do you understand?"

His eyes are open, but if it's not real yet for me, how can it be for him?

"You met her," I say. "Remember that?"

He looks at me. "Fireflies," he says. I nod.

He does remember. I do too.

The night last winter I brought her down so they could meet. I'm not sure why. His blessing maybe. That's what I wanted. He was the only one who knew. I'd told him everything though there's no telling what he'd understood.

I brought her down, and she was scared, scared of everything, the banging pipes, and Timothy, and me. I held her hand. I held it tight, afraid that if I didn't, she'd run away. "Cate," I said, "this is Timothy. Timothy, Cate."

She smiled. Or tried to. She looked at me. "Peter," she said. "If someone finds us." Her face was pale. I felt the trembling in her hand. There was nothing to do but let her go. "I'm sorry," she said. I watched her leave, hugging the walls, almost running toward the stairs. When she was gone, I turned to Timothy. "What do you think?" I said.

He looked at me. I wanted words. I wanted something. And finally his mouth moved. "Fireflies" is what he said.

When Timothy talks, I always listen, but I don't always understand.

"You mean the ones I brought you?"

"Fireflies," he said again. His voice is soft, not feather-soft like Cate's, but soft like the kid gloves my grandmother used to wear. Words, when they come, come slowly. Smooth polished pebbles. He raised his hand, pressed thumb and forefinger together, and apart. A firefly blinking.

What did he mean?

Six years ago I brought him fireflies. My first year over, and somehow summer sounded like forever. My mother was married, and my father too. School felt like home. But Timothy was old, and sometimes, with no warning, his eyes would close, and I'd get scared. It was the way my grandfather died. His eyes just closed, and he was dead; I never got to say good-bye.

I couldn't say good-bye to Timothy. Maybe he knew. I brought him fireflies instead, hundreds of them in a clean glass jar with holes pricked in the lid so they could breathe.

He smiled when he saw them, and reaching up, he pulled the light string. We sat in darkness. He held the jar cupped in his hands. We sat watching a galaxy of tiny stars, so bright they made his hands glow too.

I get up quickly, and start to circle. I need to move. "Oh

Jesus, Timothy. I'm in trouble." I reach up, hit the light bulb with my hand. Not hard, but hard enough. It starts to swing. "I hate him, Timothy. Oh God, I hate him!"

My voice cracks. I keep on moving. Timothy sits; he could be dead except his eyes are open. He follows me with his eyes, eyes that make me think of Bets, Bets as a baby. Eyes that are clear, but they aren't empty.

And Cate thought he was sweet! Sweet! But it was my fault, because I asked. When she didn't say, I had to ask. It was the next day, down by the river. By the time she came, the fire was going. The shelter smelled of pine and smoke. Her cheeks were red with cold, and when she pulled her gloves off I smelled wet wool. She held her hands toward the fire. Her hands were white, her fingers pink, the nails chewed to tiny moons. "Sweet!" I said. "I thought you'd understand." My voice was loud. She looked at me. I turned away.

"What's wrong?" she said.

"Nothing," I said, because I didn't know.

The fire smoked. My eyes were stinging. I looked out toward the river. The river was frozen, the same gray color as the sky. Smooth as glass and strong enough to walk on, yet in a month or more the thaw would start.

I thought of telling her of how when I was still a kid at home I'd stand up on the bluff above the lake, watching late winter sunlight strike the ice. I'd stand there, waiting, hoping to catch the moment when the ice gave way.

I didn't tell her how much it scared me to lie in bed at night, knowing that out there in the dark some change was taking place, ice going soft in secret, a silent rotting I couldn't see.

I didn't tell her. I looked at her instead. She knelt beside the fire, hands held to the flames, her fingers spread. The tips were red, and wrinkled. Cold. She looked at me, and smiled. I didn't smile.

"If you'd wear mittens," I said, "not gloves, that wouldn't

happen." I heard my voice; my voice was angry. She stopped smiling.

"Peter," she said. "What's wrong?"

I didn't know. I didn't answer.

"You sound like him," she said. "You sounded just like Oliver."

She sounded scared.

I stop circling. I stand, looking down at Timothy, who looks at me.

"Timothy," I say. "He killed her."

I hear the sound of someone crying. A jagged sound, like breaking glass. It comes from me.

Kneeling, I press my forehead against his leg. My face is hidden. "What am I going to do?"

I can't stop crying. I can't stop; and then I feel his hand. His hand is on my head. I don't know how long it's been there, but when I feel it, I go quiet.

Listen. His fingers talk. They stroke my hair. They're talking to me, and I listen, trying to understand.

FOUR

I DON'T KNOW how long we stay like that. When he leaves, rising slowly, stiffly, I walk with him to the basement door. My knees are sore from kneeling. It's dark now, and cold. Through the open door I see fireflies flickering above the playing fields. I think Timothy might say something, but he doesn't. I hear his chair still rocking on its own. I stand, waiting, until the darkness swallows him. Then I leave too.

The dorm is quiet, and except for the light outside the bathroom, dark. As Senior Prefect, I'm responsible for all First Formers; for all First Formers, it's lights out at nine. I could check behind closed doors, but I don't.

I don't bother to undress. I close my door, and fall across the bed, shoving books onto the floor. I sleep hard, and wake, just as the sky begins to lighten. I wake up suddenly, my heart pounding, the way it sometimes does when I've been dreaming. I try and remember a dream. I can't. What I remember is that Cate is dead.

I close my eyes again. There is a whirr of wings outside the window, and then a thump. I lie still, listening. It comes again, thump after thump. The window rattles. I don't have to open my eyes to know.

"You dumb shit bird!"

I get up so fast I feel dizzy. At least I know what woke me. Moving to the window, I pound, hard, against the glass.

"Give up, you dumb shit. Give up, God damn it!"

She's at the glass again before she sees me. Eyes bright with fear, she thrusts backward, but it's too late to stop. Her chest hits the window, and she's gone.

I hope for good.

I have my doubts. Three years in a row now she's come back, so maybe I should take it as a sign. The question is, a sign of what?

When I told Cate about the bird, she cried, or anyway her eyes filled up with tears. Then, too late, I wished I hadn't told her.

It was the first time we'd been together by the river. I came down through the trees, and found her standing by the shelter. It was the first time we'd really been alone. She was Mrs. Manning then, not Cate.

"I hope you don't mind," said Mrs. Manning. The light came yellow through the leaves, fall leaves, the color of her hair. Her hair was up. "But when you told me, about this place of yours, it sounded so perfect. I wanted to see it for myself." She smiled, blushing. A faculty wife. "I hope you don't mind," she said.

Her voice was so soft I had to lean to hear.

"I don't." I said. I didn't. Except I didn't know what to do. I heard the whisper of her breath. I slid my hands into my pockets. She was so close. She smelled like morning. "I'm surprised you found it, though. It's not exactly easy to find."

"That's why you like it. Isn't it?" She looked at me. I couldn't think of anything to say.

"That's what you told me," she said, "last year when you helped me with the garden. Did I ever thank you for the garden?"

"Yes," I said, even though I wasn't sure. I wasn't sure just what I'd told her, either. I did remember telling her about the river; I never told her how to get here, though.

27

She seemed to know what I was thinking. "You mentioned the cemetery," she said. "On the hill. Melissa and I were walking yesterday, and we found the path."

"Melissa?" I said.

"Mrs. MacQuire," she said. I nodded, and she smiled, as if she had a secret to tell. "She's my best friend," she said. The way she said it, she sounded like a kid. The way she said it made something in my heart turn over.

"Yeah," I said. "Well." I smiled. "I like her too."

She turned toward the shelter. "We didn't see this, though," she said. She ran her hand across the top. The pine boughs quivered. "It's so snug," she said. "Safe and hidden."

"I like to be alone," I said. It sounded rude. She didn't seem to notice. She stroked the needles.

"It's like a nest," she said. "The way it's shaped. A nest that's upside down."

A cup is what I'd always thought. I didn't say it, though. I sat down, hoping she'd sit too. She did. Not close, but close enough, almost close enough to touch.

"There's this bird," I said. She looked at me. She looked as if she wanted to hear. She leaned forward, her chin resting on her knees. "Up at school. A robin. She lost her nest a couple years ago. It fell. But she keeps coming back."

I stopped, waiting. "Go on," she said. And so I did. And when I'd finished, her eyes were full of tears. At least that's what I thought. Maybe they weren't. Maybe it was just the river I saw reflected in her eyes.

"That's sad," she said. "Banging. She could hurt herself."

"I wish," I said. "I mean, all she has to do is build another nest," I said. "It's like she's blaming me or something."

"It's not you," said Mrs. Manning. "She just wants to get inside. Maybe she thinks her nest is there."

"Maybe," I said.

Maybe. I didn't know. I don't know now. There is so much to be considered. So many things.

*   *   *

Morning comes with bells. The rising bell's at six-fifteen, the breakfast bell at seven. I sit, waiting, watching the sky brighten, considering my options. I know what I would like to do, only now I can't. I lost my chance.

In March I went to New York to talk to Judith. I went then because my father was away. I tried to tell her, but I couldn't. I hoped that maybe she might guess.

"What's up?" she said.

The weekend was almost over. Outside I heard a New York Sunday morning passing by. A quiet hum. The sound of traffic slowly building up. All weekend I'd been trying to tell her.

"It's complicated," I said. I rubbed my hands against my face. She drank her coffee, French coffee, hot and strong. She looked at me above the rim.

"You want the benefit of my wisdom," she said, grinning, "you'll have to tell me more than that."

I shrugged. Now that I had my chance, I couldn't. She shrugged too. "Your loss, kiddo," she said. Rising, she walked past me to the kitchen. Her legs are long, her walk easy without being slow.

"How's Manning?" she said. Her back was to me. I heard her grinding up more coffee beans. I swallowed.

"What's that have to do with anything?" I said.

She poured the beans into the filter, lifted the kettle from the stove.

"Nothing," she said. "You just don't talk about him anymore."

"Big deal," I said. "I haven't for years."

I heard the water trickling as she poured.

"I know," she said. She turned to look at me. I looked at her. She looked the same as when I met her, the same sharp face, tight curls. That's Judith, sharp and tight, but open too. It still surprises me my father married her. You wouldn't think she'd be his type. When I first met her I didn't think that she was mine.

29

"Do you remember," I said. To change the subject. "When we met?"

She looked at me, as if she knew, and then she laughed. She has a husky laugh; her voice is husky too, from smoking. She smokes a lot, more than she should. I wish she wouldn't, but there's nothing I can do. She laughed.

"Remember!" she said. "As if I could forget."

If I close my eyes, I see her, six years ago, stepping out of my father's car, her first visit to the school. My father's first visit too. Not that I cared.

"My God," she said. She looked around. Her hair was brass, and there were freckles on her face.

"Judith," said my father. "Please."

I couldn't call her Judith. "How do you do," I said.

She looked around. She looked at me. "In shock," she said. "And how are you?"

"Fine, thank you." I tried to smile, and for the first time I heard her laugh.

She turned toward my father. "David," she said, "has he been cloned?"

The coffee made, Judith brought it in, set it on the table. She sat down on the sofa. I sat on the floor. I looked at her.

"You were godawful," I said. "Rude."

Judith laughed. She poured the coffee, some for her and some for me. "The shock of seeing two hundred boys dressed in the same blue blazers. I didn't think a place like that existed, except up here." She tapped her forehead, then reached for a cigarette.

"When I'm not there," I said, "I feel that way too." She lit her cigarette, and leaned back, peering at me through the smoke.

"Kiddo," she said, "you better tell me."

"You were better at lunch though," I said. Stalling.

"You weren't," she said. "Your poor father! Yes, sir. No, sir. No dessert, thank you, sir. No dessert!"

I see it. I see Judith still eating her lobster, sucking on

30

the claw. Her face was greasy, her eyes hidden behind dark glasses. My father sat beside her, his knuckles cracking.

"I'd better get back, sir," I said, and she leaned toward me, across the table. "Tell me," she said.

"Yes, ma'am," I said, waiting.

"Tell me," she said. "Tell me, do you ever FART?"

She said it loud. She said it, so that people all around could hear.

"Judith!" said my father.

I couldn't help it, I had to laugh. When I laughed, she did too. "What's so funny?" she said, grinning.

"Fart," I said, but not as loud as she had. I didn't dare. I kept on laughing, though. It was the first time I'd ever heard a grownup use the word.

"Thank God," said Judith. She wiped her hands, and lit a cigarette. She grinned at me. "You're young yet, but at least you're still alive."

My father's laugh surprised me. He turned to me. "Don't listen to her," he said, but it was too late. That's when I started.

"Listen," I said to Judith.

"I'm listening," she said.

"There nothing to tell," I said. "It's just that sometimes life gets a little complicated. Up here." I tapped my fore-head. "I can't stop thinking."

"*You* listen," said Judith. "Your father worries, you know. He worries about you."

"Bullshit," I said. "He's never worried about anything but work."

"He worries," she said as if I hadn't spoken. She sipped her coffee. "You're very much alike."

"Don't say that!"

"It's true," she said.

I hardly ever talk to Judith about my father. She's married to him. I find that more surprising than my father marrying her.

"He's not so bad," she said. She grinned. When Judith grins her freckles spread across her face. "When you get to know him."

"Know him!" I said. "I've known him eighteen years. You haven't."

She studied me. I drank my coffee.

"Do you know," she said, "that he writes poetry?"

I started choking on my coffee. "Come off it," I said when I could breathe.

"It's very good," said Judith. "He's got enough for a collection now."

What could I say? She doesn't lie. And if she says it's good, it's good. She's an editor at Blake and Day. But poetry! My father!

My father is a criminal lawyer. He deals in facts, twisting them to suit his case. He uses words like rocks. I've heard him. When he talks, his hands talk too, slicing the air, each slice another severed head. His hands are dangerous. He always types his briefs himself; when I was just a kid, I'd hear keys clicking like machine-gun fire.

I tried to see his fingers curled around a pencil, words sliding silent onto paper. I shook my head.

Judith leaned forward. "Listen to me, sweetheart." She lit another cigarette. "People are like onions. They've got layers. Peel one off, there's another underneath. The older you get, the more there are."

Onions. I tried to think, to see it her way, but thinking of unknown layers made me dizzy. And tired. I yawned. With Judith I've never had to worry about covering my mouth.

"You know, kiddo, when your father left . . ."

"Forget it. OK? Let's just forget it."

I lay down, flat on the floor, behind the coffee table, and stared up at the ceiling.

"Kiddo, you want to see someone? A shrink. My shrink."

"I did that number." Looking up I saw the ceiling had been painted over. A white so white it hurt my eyes.

"Once."

"Twice. Anyway, you're better than a shrink. Cheaper."

"I hate to tell you this, kiddo, but stepmothers don't . . ."

"Then don't. Don't tell me. Listen."

I closed my eyes to block the ceiling out.

"When I was a kid, my father, he'd always come home late. My sisters would already be in bed. Asleep. I wasn't. I'd hear him coming, walking down this long hall we had. My bedroom was at the end of it, and I had my door open. I hated the dark. I really hated it. Anyway, with the door open, I could see him coming. He was always wearing black, that's what I remember anyway. Black suit, black shoes, black hair, but his face, his face was the color of this ceiling. He'd come home on the train, and he smelled like the train. Smoke and soot and ashes. Dragging himself along that hall. When he'd get to my room, I'd pretend to be asleep."

My eyes were closed. I couldn't see Judith, but I heard her listening.

"How old were you?"

"Sometimes," I said, "he'd lean over, and straighten my sheet. Awkward, like he didn't know what else to do. Sometimes he'd touch me, by mistake, and when he did, I'd get a shock. You know, static from the rug, only I didn't know that then. Those shocks, they always felt so big. They really scared me. He sent someone to the electric chair; I read about it in the paper."

"Go on," said Judith.

"That's it," I said. "That's it. Zeus. You know, hurling thunderbolts, lightning flashing from his fingers. One touch. And zap."

Judith was quiet. So was I. I liked lying there, listening to slow Sunday traffic. With Judith I felt safe. But school was waiting. So was Cate. If I told anyone it would be Judith. But lying there then, I knew I wouldn't. Somehow something had been set in motion, a snowball rolling down a hill, and nothing was going to stop it now.

33

I know now I didn't want to stop it. I know now. Too late.

"Remember the onion, kid," said Judith. "All those layers." I opened my eyes. She stood up, stretching. "If he's Zeus, I'm Athena." Eyes opened, I looked at her, tall, bony, hair springing from her head like rusty wire. I grinned.

"Medusa," I said.

She gave me the finger. "Growing up, kid. It's not easy." She smiled, but her eyes were sad. I rolled over on my stomach.

"I grew up a hundred years ago."

"It's not that easy." She dug her toe into my ribs. "I hate to tell you. You've got to find those layers first."

Her toe dug harder. I grabbed her ankle, felt the bone.

"Hey, cut it out. That doesn't tickle," I said.

"The layers," she said. "That's growing up. You hear me?"

"Jesus," I said. "I'm not deaf."

She tried to get me in the ribs again, but this time I was ready. Holding her ankle, I pulled up. Hard. She lost her balance, falling backward, onto the pillows on the floor. "You shit," she said. She laughed. "You shit."

"You're a shit, Spaulding," I say to myself in the mirror. The bells have rung, are ringing. I smooth my hair down with my hands. Outside the door, the kids are up, and running. The last day of classes before Study Week, before exams. To look at me you'd never know that anything had changed, same eyes and nose and mouth.

No one knows. Or do they? Just what a shit I really am. Except for Cate. But Cate doesn't count. Not anymore.

There's a knock on the door, and I turn fast. Expecting. But it's Snickers who opens it before I say a word, comes scuttling in, sideways, like a crab. Behind him, I smell breakfast, hot coffee, bacon, eggs. My stomach turns over. "Hey, kid," I say. I throw a fake punch, and he ducks, grinning.

34

God, how he's grown since fall. His legs are skinny, but his feet are huge.

He sits on the bed.

"Peter." He starts rocking. The bedsprings creak. "You think maybe you'll be back to visit?"

"Nope." I push books aside to find my shoes. They smell ripe, too ripe. When I leave I'm going to throw away the works, and start again. The way my mother did. The creaking gets louder. "You're going to break that bed, kid." The creaking stops.

"I don't blame you," he says. "I wouldn't either."

His voice goes high, the crackle gone. When I look at him, he smiles, or tries to. His face is thin. His eyes are chocolate. His eyes give him away.

I look down at my shoes. "You're not going to get rid of me that easily, kid. I'm going to keep tabs on you."

"Oh, shit!" says Snickers. His voice squeaks even higher. With relief.

I wink at him. When he grins, his braces glitter.

"You been studying?" I say.

"You kidding!" he says.

But I know he has. He's a smart kid, a lot smarter than I was at his age. But I still worry. Sometimes I think that when you start out worrying, it's hard to stop. I started the moment I laid eyes on him last fall when I found him, quivering, on the school steps where the cab had let him off. He sat, perched on his trunk, surrounded by his fancy luggage. The trunk was bigger than he was. He sat, clutching a wrinkled paper bag. All bones and eyes and silver-colored hair, he looked like a half-formed baby bird. "Hey," I said, wondering how long he'd been there and he blinked, fast, trying not to cry. "I'll bet you're a First Former," I said. "I bet I even know your name." He stopped blinking, and looked scared. "Jamie," I said. "Jamie Renolds. Right?" He nodded, looking more frightened than before. I could tell he wanted to ask me how I knew, but didn't dare.

I knew more than his name, but I wasn't going to tell him that. From his clothes, I knew he was a city kid, and rich. I knew his parents were divorced, because there's never been a First Former whose parents aren't. "The other kids are here already," I said. "That's how I know you." He looked at me. "There're twelve of you this year," I said. "Let's get your stuff upstairs."

He turned and looked up at the building, four stories of dark brick, a three-sided fortress built around the quad. I remembered how big that building looked on my first day, late afternoon and all the windows turned to gold. I pointed up. "That's your window. You've got the cubicle next to mine."

Thurston leaned out my window. "Hey, buddy," he called.

"Buddy," I said. "Come on. We need a hand."

We waited for him on the steps. The steps were warm; the sun felt good. I was tired, and the kid didn't look strong enough to carry anything except the bag he was clutching in his hands. Waiting, I closed my eyes. I heard the paper rattling. "What you got in there?" I said, not sure the kid could talk.

"Snickers," he said. Actually he whispered.

"Great. Quick energy," I said.

He gave me one, half-melted, but I ate it anyway, and licked my fingers. "Thanks," I said. He tried to smile. "I'll tell you something," I said. I saw him waiting. "It's gonna be OK." You could see him wanting to believe me. I rapped my knuckles against his head. "I promise," I said.

"You promise?" he says.

"Promise what?" I walk over to where he's sitting, and rap his head. He shakes it, but doesn't smile. "Come on," I say. "Let's get to breakfast." He doesn't move.

"Promise you'll see me in New York."

"I said I would."

"Just wondering," he says. Standing, he slides his hands into his pockets. He blinks. "Oh, shit," he says. "Manning came by last night. You weren't here. He said to give you this."

He pulls a crumbled envelope from his pocket, and holds it out. I don't want to take it, but I do.

"She was pretty," says Snickers.

"Yeah. Take off now. Scram."

He doesn't budge. He looks at me. He shakes his head.

"I don't get it," he says. "She was pretty; she wasn't even very old."

I take him by the shoulders, and turn him round, toward the door. "March," I say.

He marches, slowly, toward the door, and turns.

"It's hard though. I mean, dying. It's so . . ." He closes his eyes, tight, then opens them. "I didn't know what to say. To him."

"Don't say anything."

"He's my teacher. I wanted to. He's a good teacher!"

"You're going to miss breakfast."

He doesn't move; his face is red. "Some people," he whispers, "some people say he killed her."

I take a deep breath. "Don't listen."

"It's hard," he says.

I take a step toward him, frowning.

"I'm not kidding, kid. Take off."

This time he hears me. He blinks, and scuttles out. The door closes.

I take my time. I look down at the envelope in my hand. *Peter*, it says, in black ink, strong letters slanting to the right. The note inside is short.

Dear Peter,
  I am sorry to have missed you. It is imperative that we talk. Please come by after Monday classes.

As for my class, if circumstances prevent me from attending, you are in charge. They may work on their papers.

O. A. Manning

I read it once, then shred it, and drop it in the trash. Another piece of evidence destroyed.

FIVE

I'M STILL NOT HUNGRY, but I go to breakfast anyway. It's better than doing nothing. That's what I think until I reach the dining hall.

Usually breakfast is quiet. No one's awake, and no one talks. Today is different, the place humming like a swarm of bees. "Spaulding, hey, Spaulding, over here!" Faces turn, hands waving. I ignore them. Spencer, at the head table, glowers. To hell with him.

Thurston stands in line for coffee. "Hey, buddy," he says. His hair hangs in his eyes. He shakes his head so that his hair swings sideways. He smiles. I smile too. "Buddy," I say. He always makes me smile.

"You want company?" he says.

I shake my head. "Thanks anyway." He shrugs, still smiling, turns away.

"Thurston?" He looks at me. "I'm sorry," I say.

"For what?" says Thurston.

I fake a laugh. "I don't know. For everything. This year."

"Don't sweat it," he says. "OK?" He sounds as if he means it.

"OK," I say.

I take my coffee to an empty table by the windows. Holding the mug in both hands I take slow careful sips. Coffee doesn't do much for an empty stomach, but it's hot and strong.

It makes me think of Manning. I look around, but I don't

39

see him. That's not surprising. Not many masters come to breakfast except when they're on breakfast duty. The coffee stinks.

Not like the coffee Manning serves at Burke House, real coffee served in cups the size of eggs. Cups so thin the light shines through. Like eggshells really. He always serves his coffee black. Otherwise you lose the essence. That's what he said my Second Form year. I didn't know what essence was, but I believed him. I learned to like black coffee too.

I sit, my back to the window, sipping slow. It's only seven, but already I can feel the heat. Around me people ebb and flow. I sit alone while kids move in and out. No one bothers me. It's what I want. I see Mrs. MacQuire standing in the door, and for a moment figure I'm mistaken. Faculty wives don't come to breakfast, at least not often, but I see it's her all right. She's looking for someone, her head turning from side to side. Her hair is thick. She always wears it up. When her head turns I see the clasp that holds it glinting. Her dress is the same amber color as her hair.

Most of the faculty wives are dogs. The ones that aren't inspire lust. Except for Mrs. MacQuire. Regal. If she inspires anything it's awe.

I see Coach at the far end of the hall. His face is red; his shoulders shake. I know he's laughing. She sees him too. Then she sees me. She lifts her hand and starts toward me, and if I wasn't backed against the windows I'd get away.

She comes closer, stopping now and then to talk. She seems to glide across the floor, smiling, moving on. Spencer beckons. He talks, she listens, then pats his shoulder, pat, pat, pat, the way you pat a baby. Behind her, Coach looks up, and waves. She doesn't see him. She reaches me.

"Well," she says. "How are you."

"Coach," I say. "He's waving."

She turns, and lifts her hand. Not a wave exactly. A brief salute. Without asking, she sits down.

"Where are the kids?"

She smiles as if amused. "Where do you think?" she says. "At home. They're old enough."

"Sure," I say. Because they are.

Dana's twelve and Daphne's ten. Rufus is their afterthought. That's what she calls him anyway. He's only five. Daphne is Bets' age and Dana's the same age as Celia, my middle sister. You might think Dana was a girl, just from the name. He's not. Once I asked her why she did that, gave a girl's name to a boy. "Actually," she said, "my father's name was Dana."

Dana was seven then, a nice kid who hated sports. Coach had him jogging every day, and lifting weights at night. The night I asked, the kids were sleeping, and we were having supper. The three of us. Coach grinned at me.

"Her brother's name is Dana too."

"God forbid," said Mrs. MacQuire.

"Hell," said Coach. "He's not so bad."

She looked at him and shook her head. "You like anyone," she said.

Coach scratched his head and then he laughed. "You're right," he said, "I guess I do."

I guess he does. Or so it seems. But everybody likes him too, at least the kids, his students. He'd rather play with them than teach. In Ancient History all we talked about was Vietnam. He'd spent two years there, and from the way he talks you'd think that was the high point of his life, after college football anyway. At Harvard, in the sixties, he was a star, and trophies line the bookshelves in their hall. He keeps them polished, and everytime we're in the hall he glances up. "Those were the days, all right," he says.

There's something about him that makes me sad.

"I thought," says Mrs. MacQuire, "I'd just check in, see how you're doing."

I shrug. "I told you. Fine."

41

It sounds rude but she doesn't seem to notice.

"Suicide is a terrible thing," she says. "Terrible for everyone. For those closest, it's the worst."

"How do you know it's suicide?"

"Oh, Peter," she says. Her voice is sad.

She touches my arm. "I know you're angry."

"Not with you."

"With her."

"No," I say. "Him."

"Peter," she says, "suicide is an act of anger too."

"It wasn't suicide."

"I'm trying to help you, Peter. Won't you let me?"

I nod, but I can't look at her. Outside, I hear the mower starting up. "I have to ask you something," I say. I swallow, the bitter taste of coffee in my mouth. Turning, I look out the window. I take a breath, a deep breath.

"What did she tell you?"

The words hang. She doesn't answer. I watch Ernie on his mower riding back and forth across the grass. Sweat glistens on his round bald head. The engine hums. My heart is hammering in my ears.

"Tell me," she says. "Have you seen him yet?"

I wait a moment. "No," I say.

Her hand is on my arm. "A word of advice from an old friend," she says. When I look at her, she smiles. "Don't." Her voice is coaxing.

I hook my legs beneath the chair to lend them weight. I hear it creak. A fly buzzes in slow circles above our heads.

"I wouldn't, but Spencer's ordered me."

She sighs. "He would." She glances off in his direction. "I suppose he lectured you on obligation."

I start to shred my napkin. "Responsibility," I say. Bits of white paper flutter to the floor.

"Responsibility," she says. She says it softly. "You're not the one he should be talking to." She rubs her forehead, sees me watching. "Headaches," she says. "I get them some-times." Her skin looks tight between her eyes.

I nod. Migraines, Manning told me once, but I wasn't sure what migraines were. I'm not sure now.

She stops rubbing, puts her hand back on my arm.

"It seems to me the less talk there is the better."

"You sound like Spencer."

I try to pull my arm away, but she holds tight as if afraid to let me go.

"He has a point," she says. "But I meant talk between you and Oliver. And not for his sake. Yours."

"You don't think I can handle it? Is that the problem?"

The mower comes closer. I hear the drone.

"Of course not." She pats my arm. "But should you?" She lowers her voice. "I do know what he's meant to you, and I would hate to see you hurt."

"I know that."

"Good," she says. "I've seen him, you know. Last night." Her eyes flicker. "I'm afraid he has some rather unpleasant things to say."

She doesn't say what, and I don't ask. "I'll bet," I say. The mower throbs outside the windows. The windows rattle. I smell cut grass and diesel fuel.

"Well, so do I."

"Peter," she says. Her voice is sad. "It won't do any good, you know. You're upset. I know that, and I don't blame you. I am too." She looks at me. A hard look. "I had no idea this was going to happen. I want you to believe that." There's something in the way she looks that makes me nervous.

"I know that," I say.

It's only now that she relaxes; it's only now I notice she was tense.

She straightens, sits, her hands clasped in her lap. "I'm glad to hear you say that. I'd feel badly if you were in some way blaming me."

"You! That's crazy! You did everything you could."

"For better or worse," she says. Softly.

"What?"

"Never mind." She looks at me. "I wanted to help."

"You did help," I say. "You made her happy." Mrs. MacQuire frowns. "She told me once . . . she said, you were the best thing that ever happened to her."

She presses her fingers to her forehead, and holds them there.

"Listen," I say, "it's not your fault he married her."

She hesitates. "No," she says, "or yours."

"I never said it was!"

She strokes my arm. "I know, I know." Soothing, as if she's talking to a kid. I pull my arm away.

"I know he's a friend of yours, but I can't help it if I hate him."

"You're angry," she says.

"You're God damn right I'm angry," I say. "She's dead!"

"Shhhh," she says. "Shhhh."

She looks around and I do too. The hall is almost empty, and I know the bell's about to ring. First period is Manning, the class that I'm supposed to take.

"I've got to go."

"Not yet," she says. "I want to help you."

"I don't need help."

"She's dead, Peter. She killed herself. There's nothing anyone can do. It's over, Peter."

"Oh no it's not! It's just beginning!"

"She's gone, Peter." Her voice is firm. "She's gone, and nothing you can do will bring her back. The sooner you forget, we all forget, the better."

I have to laugh.

"Can you forget?"

She looks at me.

"What?" she says.

"The day she came."

She rubs her hand across her forehead. "I remember," she says, "being taken somewhat by surprise."

Now I'm surprised. "You didn't show it."

"Didn't I?" she says. She covers her eyes. "You did."

My face goes red. Her eyes are closed.

"It's not as if he gave us any warning."

"No," she says. "It's not."

I look around. The hall's completely empty now. We're all alone. Remembering what we wish we could forget.

A day two years ago, the end of summer, the beginning of my Fifth Form year, and I came out of Main to find her on the school steps, waiting. I thought for me.

"Hey," I said, and Mrs. MacQuire hugged me, smiling. "You've grown!" she said. I had. I was taller than she was now, much taller, and she looked up and laughed. "I suppose," she said, "change is inevitable and sometimes welcome." She held my arm. "Have you seen him yet?"

I didn't have to ask her who she meant. I shook my head and looked away. "He called," she said. "He said to tell you he's brought us a surprise."

I shrugged. "I don't like surprises much."

She took my arm. "Look," she said. "He's coming." I felt her fingers tighten on my arm.

I looked and saw him, walking up the drive. The way he walks reminds me of a swimmer, each step a stroke. Watching, my heart began to pound.

"I've got to go," I said and tried to pull away. She held on tight.

"Don't be silly. He's dying to see you."

I could have told her that wasn't true. But if I did she'd ask me why.

"You," I said.

"Silly," she said, but smiled at me. Her eyes were sudden green, the color of spring, and I remember thinking that maybe forty wasn't very old. I thought of her, of her and Manning. Of how when I was just a kid, a new boy here, I used to watch them, joking, laughing with each other. How it used to make me feel good. Some people just seem to fit together, and others don't. I used to think that they were perfect. No one's perfect, Judith says. She's right, but I didn't know that then.

We stood there watching him stride up the drive, striding as if the air was water and he was swimming. "There's someone with him," said Mrs. MacQuire. "I wonder who."

Whoever it was was having a hard time keeping up. Every so often he stopped and waited. Together they started up again. Together we watched, and I was glad that she was with me. I could never have waited there alone.

They came closer, and I saw the person was a woman, the woman a girl. She looked that young but maybe it was just the way she walked. Her legs were long, and there was something awkward in the way she moved, toes turned in and elbows sticking out.

"Who can that be?" said Mrs. MacQuire. Her voice was soft.

Whoever it was was pretty, tall and thin. Her hair was honey-colored. She wore it up. She wore a pink dress that fluttered when she moved.

We didn't talk. When Manning was close enough to see us, he stopped and smiled, a slow smile spreading like sunlight across his face. "The two people I most want to see!" he said.

I tried to smile, but there was something sticking in my throat. I coughed instead. He stood there, smiling, as if he were standing on a stage.

He held his arms out, but Mrs. MacQuire was the first to move.

"Don't you look splendid!" She smiled when she said it, and walked toward him down the steps. Arms out, he hugged her, kissed her cheeks. Both cheeks.

"Clearly England suited you," she said.

"And you?" he said, to her but looking at me. "How was your summer?" I looked away.

"I survived," said Mrs. MacQuire. Smiling, she turned to Cate. "And who is this?"

He didn't answer. He looked at me. I felt his eyes. "How's my boy?" he said. His voice was soft. My legs were shaking. I shrugged.

"Oliver," said Mrs. MacQuire. "Don't leave us in suspense."

And he turned slowly, to her, to Cate. "Cate," he said. "Catherine, my two dearest friends. Melissa MacQuire and Peter Spaulding. Shake hands, my dear."

She shook hands, first with Mrs. MacQuire and then with me.

"Hello," she said, her voice a whisper. I felt a trembling in her hand.

I didn't get it, didn't get what was going on.

Manning touched Cate's shoulder. "Melissa's been after me for years," he said. He turned to Mrs. MacQuire. "I'm afraid I couldn't wait for your approval."

Mrs. MacQuire blinked. She didn't get it either; but I was just beginning to.

"My wife," said Manning. "Cate and I were married last week." He smiled at her. He smiled at me.

We stood frozen. At least I did.

"I'm speechless," said Mrs. MacQuire. She lifted her hands, and let them fall.

"With pleasure, I'm sure." He smiled at Cate. "What did I tell you?" he said softly.

Her cheeks burned pink. Her eyes were bright. She nodded, shy. "Oliver said you'd be surprised."

"Surprised," said Mrs. MacQuire, "and delighted." She glanced at me. "I'm sure Peter is delighted too." There was something in her voice. A note of warning? Blushing, I shifted my weight from foot to foot. Mrs. MacQuire turned back to

Cate, but Manning didn't. He looked at me. I looked down. "I hope he will be," Manning said. Near my foot, I saw an ant.

"You're lovely," Mrs. MacQuire said. "Where did he find you?"

The ant was staggering, carrying a load a hundred times too big. Lifting my foot, I squished it flat.

"On the street," said Manning's wife.

"As a matter of fact," said Manning, "she was looking quite lost."

I saw another ant. I squished it too.

"I *was* lost," said Mrs. Manning.

"I asked if I could be of some assistance."

"He helped me," said Mrs. Manning. "The person I'd been traveling with, he'd had an accident, and had to go away, and . . ."

"One thing led to another," said Manning. "And here we are." His smile embraced us all.

"Tell me," Mrs. MacQuire said. "Are you older than you look?"

"Twenty," said Mrs. Manning.

"Cradle robbing," said Mrs. MacQuire. She smiled when she said it. "Oliver, how could you?"

"Quite easily," said Manning. "But dear Melissa, she'll need your help."

"I've never been to boarding school before," said Mrs. Manning. "So I don't know." Her hands fluttered up. She caught a strand of hair between her fingers, and tugged on it. She smiled at Mrs. MacQuire. The way she smiled she looked pathetic. A little kid. Maybe Mrs. MacQuire thought so too.

"Oh, Oliver," she said. She sounded sad.

"She's yours," said Manning. "I told her that you'll teach her what she has to know. There's no one who knows more. Isn't that so?"

48

"Is it?" said Mrs. MacQuire. She looked at him. She wasn't smiling.

"I'd like that," said Mrs. Manning. "Please."

Manning laughed. "How can you refuse?" he said.

"And Peter." He turned to me. "I'm sure Peter will help too."

I shrugged, my face burning. What could I say?

"Give him time," said Mrs. MacQuire.

And Manning smiled. He spread his hands. "That's what I've done."

I hear bells ringing. It's time for class. I glance at Mrs. MacQuire. Her eyes are closed.

"Hey," I say, thinking maybe she's asleep. "I've got to go." I stand up.

Her eyes open, and she blinks. "Peter," she says.

I look at her. "Don't listen . . . to him."

"Don't worry," I say. "I won't." And walk away.

SIX

THERE ARE ONLY EIGHT of us in Manning's Sixth Form Honors English. The intellectual elite, supposedly. Bullshit. No one believes that except for Spencer. Last spring I wrote to Spencer requesting transfer to another class. Spencer wrote back, "Request denied."

There wasn't any point in arguing, and anyway, what could I say? Spencer thinks the best of everyone, including Manning. Especially Manning. I'm not the only one who knows he's wanted Manning to replace him. At least he did.

I hear voices coming from the classroom, one voice louder than the rest. "Is this a dagger that I see before me." I stop outside the closed door, listening. "Come, let me clutch thee." I take a deep breath. As soon as I open the door, heads turn, and voices stop. Edwards stands in front of Manning's desk, arms wide, mouth open, a one-man act. "Dear Spaulding," he says. I ignore him. The others are seated; I turn to them. "He's not coming," I say. Feet shuffle; there's a low moan, half disappointment, half relief. Edwards sits. I walk to Manning's desk, trying not to look at it.

But of course I do. I have to. I look for change, but nothing's different. A white ceramic jar for pencils, another jar for pens. The pencils are freshly sharpened. A pad of blank white paper lies on the blotter. The blotter's clean, the pad is centered. There is nothing that gives him away. The drawers, I know, are locked. I know because I've tried them.

"So what's up, Spaulding?" says Barnes. "So what's the

50

scoop?" When I look at him, he grins, a friendly grin. Ingenuous. Barnes is OK.

"We're supposed to work on our papers," I say.

"Not that," says Barnes. "You know."

The last thing I want to do is sit at Manning's desk. Not that he sits there often. Usually he's on his feet.

"I don't know any more than you do," I say.

The one thing Manning knows is Shakespeare. I have to give him that. All year I've had to sit, listening to him recite chunk after chunk. From memory. All year I listened, waiting for him to forget a line, to falter. He never did. He's good. He could have been an actor. Actually, that's what he is.

"You guys can take off. He's not coming."

But no one moves. I didn't really think they would. I look at Thurston, who sits in back, his chair next to mine. His head is down, his fingers poised on the edge of the desk as if the desk's a keyboard. His face is hidden by his hair. Who knows if he's listening? Edwards coughs. Heads turn. It's what he wanted. He looks at me. "Spaulding," he says, "tell us about the autopsy."

"Jeez," says Barnes. No one else says anything. They're waiting. Edwards smiles; he's having fun.

I keep my face straight. "What would you care to know, Edwards?" I say.

"Anything, Spaulding. Anything at all."

"How about autopsy being standard procedure in a case like this?"

"I know that, Spaulding. As a matter of fact" — he smiles — "I know more than you think."

"Edwards," says Thurston. Thurston isn't much of a talker, which means when he does talk, people listen. Even Edwards. He turns to Thurston. Thurston doesn't lift his head. "Shut up," he says. He sounds tired. Who can blame him? Edwards affects everyone that way. He's like a black hole, a specimen of imploded power. So says Thurston, who's

51

really into space. The origins of the universe, the Big Bang theory. Stuff like that.

"Thurston's right, Edwards. Why don't you just shut up."

My voice sounds tired too. There's something about Edwards that sucks the energy from the air. Thurston's fingers start to move against the wood, a tuneless tapping.

"But what do you mean, Spaulding, 'a case like this'? You surely don't believe that it was suicide? Surely you know better than that?"

There was a time when I tried hard to feel sorry for Edwards. He was my roommate First Form year. First Form year, I even tried to like him.

"Even Barnes, Spaulding, doesn't think it's suicide."

"Hey, come on, Edwards," says Barnes. His face flushes. He twists in his seat, looking at me instead of Edwards. "I only wanted to know what was going on. I wasn't talking about . . ."

He can't say it. I can see he's hoping I'll help him out.

"Murder," says Edwards. "Of course you weren't. Your mind is far too pure."

It takes a lot to make Barnes angry. Fists clenched, he glares at Edwards. I hope he'll hit him, but he doesn't. He shoves his books together. "And yours is filthy," he says. He leaves the room.

"Bravo," says Edwards. "Quite a retort for old Barnes."

A few minutes of Edwards is enough for anyone. The others leave too. I guess I should be grateful. Except that Edwards hasn't left. Thurston hasn't, either, thank God.

Edwards leans toward him. "Hey Thurston," he says, "you can take off now." But Thurston doesn't answer. Shoulders hunched, he plays his music, his fingers raindrops against wood. Within the rhythm I hear the tune. The Secret Life of Plants. I have to smile. Edwards doesn't like this.

"Your friend," he says, "is fucking out to lunch."

"If you say so, Edwards. You can take off too, you know."

He sits, eyes gleaming. "Too bad you can't handle things that way," he says.

The trouble with Edwards is that he's not dumb; in fact as far as IQ goes, his is the highest in the school. That's what he says, and I expect it's true. It's also true that except for brains, he's got nothing going for him. His parents, he says, are dead. They're not. Judith knows his mother in New York. When he was born his parents got divorced and neither of them wanted him. A great-aunt raised him, but she didn't want him either. She has blue hair, and lives on Beacon Hill. He took me in to tea my first year here when we were roommates. Her apartment smelled of dogs and money. The dogs, four pugs with pop-out eyes, ate with us off china plates. When she spoke to Edwards she called him Boy.

He leans toward me. I move behind the desk, Manning's desk, and sit, to keep the desk between us. "Take off, will you," I say, knowing he won't until he's ready.

"How does it feel, Spaulding? Sitting in his chair? Do you feel Banquo's presence?"

His laugh is as high-pitched as six years ago. A juicy laugh. I close my eyes to block him out. I shouldn't. Manning is suddenly everywhere. The smell of him, Old Spice and sunlight. I open my eyes quickly, thinking he may have slipped inside.

"OK, Edwards. You've got something to say, say it. Let's get it over with."

Thurston is still playing. His fingers don't sound like raindrops anymore; they sound like bones.

Edwards smiles. "Surely, it must have occurred to you, Spaulding, that under the circumstances Mrs. Manning could not possibly have taken her own life. Surely, given your knowledge of the participants, you are aware of this."

The sound I heard comes from me, my knuckles cracking. I clench my fists.

"I don't know what you're talking about."

"Surely, Spaulding, I don't need to tell you, you of all people, that Manning's marriage was a disaster from the start."

His tongue makes a clicking noise.

"You make me sick," I say.

Edwards laughs as if nothing could please him more. "You know far better than I that Manning was not the marrying kind. You know that, don't you, Spaulding?"

He giggles, rubbing his hands together, the way he did as Iago in last year's play. He was good in that role. He stole the show. "The essence of evil," Manning said, "is a hard act to follow." He smiled at Edwards when he said it.

I make myself smile. "If you say so, Edwards."

"Are you saying that you agree with me?"

"You haven't said anything yet. Or have you?"

"Oh, far be it from me to sully his good name," says Edwards. Crowing.

"I'll say it for you then." I lean forward, hands folded on the desk. "Manning is a fag."

Edwards blinks. He's always preferred undercover operations, the sneak attack, to a head-on confrontation.

"If you say so, Spaulding," he says. Sulky because I've taken away his ammunition.

"I'm not saying anything but what I've heard. Rumors, Edwards. You ought to know. You're pretty good at starting them yourself." Edwards stares at me. "Unless of course Manning made a pass at you." Edwards licks his lips. "Did he, Edwards?"

"Maybe," says Edwards.

"Bullshit," I say. "He can't stand the sight of you." Edwards flinches, then he smiles.

"That's quite unlike you, Spaulding."

He's right. I close my eyes, and wave my hand, hoping he'll disappear.

He giggles. "But now, shall we discuss the murder?"

"No."

54

"Does it offend you, Spaulding, to think of Manning as a murderer?"

"Why should it?" I get up, and walk over to the window. Anything to get away from him. I push my hands against the shade. The shade is hot. "Fine," I say. "Manning killed his wife. Now bugger off, why don't you."

"Oh, Spaulding, but *why* did he kill her? That's the question. Such a pretty wife, such a perfect wife. For him."

I hear Thurston clear his throat.

"Come, come, Spaulding. There's no point pretending that you're not involved. Your intimacy with certain members of the faculty is not exactly a secret, is it?"

"Oh, secrets. Precciousss secrets," says Thurston in his Gollum voice.

"I saw you this morning with Mrs. MacQuire," says Edwards.

"So what?" I say, careful to keep my voice light.

"Don't play dumb, Spaulding. It doesn't suit you. Do you really think you're the only one who knows that Mrs. Manning was carrying on all year behind his back?"

I am careful to stand still. "Is that so, Edwards?" My voice cracks. I hear it, but Edwards doesn't. He's too excited. "Why don't you tell me all about it?" I even smile. Maybe the smile fools him because he frowns.

"You're playing games, Spaulding. I don't like games."

"Curse the Baggins," says Thurston. "What has it got in its pocketses?"

Edwards looks at Thurston, then back to me. Sweat glistens on his forehead. He claps his pudgy hands together. "I do believe," he says slowly, "you don't know, do you?"

"Just get it over, Edwards, OK?"

That's what I want. To get it over. But Edwards is having too much fun.

"Can it be true that I am privy to information withheld from the inner sanctum?"

"It has its secrets," says Thurston. "Slimy sneaking secrets."

Edwards doesn't look at him; he looks at me. He smiles. "Mrs. MacQuire," he says.

My hands are shaking. I shove them in my pockets. "She told you all about it, did she?" I say.

"Don't be an ass," says Edwards. "Tell me that she was getting it on with Mrs. Manning? Now why would she do that? Especially now?" He smiles, waiting.

I lean against the window, feeling the weight of it behind my back. It is all that holds me upright. I close my eyes.

"You're the ass, Edwards."

"Poor Spaulding. Another precious illusion shattered."

I keep my eyes closed. I don't say anything. He does.

"Shattered," he says. "And after all she's done for you. All these years. Tea and sympathy. Just like a mother. And all this time to think you never knew that she was otherwise inclined."

"You don't know it either, Edwards."

"Oh, but I do, Spaulding. I have eyes. I use them. I see things, Spaulding, that others don't."

It's quiet when he stops. Very quiet.

"Imagine, Spaulding," says Edwards. "Imagine Manning when he learns of this betrayal. Can you imagine he was pleased? His wife, Spaulding. Mrs. MacQuire, who had pandered to his needs for years. All his needs, Spaulding. Such as they were."

I force myself to open my eyes, to look at him.

"Your mind is a cesspool, Edwards."

"Your voice is shaking, Spaulding. Why is your voice shaking?"

It's all I can do not to hit him. But I don't. I look at Thurston. Pleading.

"Hey, Edwards," says Thurston, drawling. "I suppose you've got proof." His fingers play the desk.

"Proof," says Edwards. "Well, let's say I'm not completely

56

unprepared. On some matters, at any rate. On others, it's a simple question of observation."

Eyes half closed, Thurston starts to sing. " 'We all live in a yellow submarine.' "

Edwards frowns. He turns back to me. I start singing too.

"You better listen to me, Spaulding."

I keep on singing. Off-key, but it doesn't matter. Thurston carries the tune. We sing together, drowning him out, just like the old days. Thurston. My old buddy.

Edwards doesn't like it. "For your own good, Spaulding." We keep on singing, the same words over and over. Edwards stands, fat fingers plucking at his tie. "Bastards," he says. I see his eyes flickering when he turns.

"It's only just begun, you know," he says. He licks his lips. "You don't have a prayer."

I close my eyes, and keep on singing. When I open them he's gone.

I stop singing. "Give thanks," I say. My voice is shaking.

Thurston stops singing too. For a minute he holds his fingers, hovering.

"Don't let him get to you," he says.

"Thanks."

He shrugs. "No sweat."

I move across the room, toward the door.

"So take it easy," I say.

Head bent, he leans into his music.

"Peter," he says. He says it softly. I turn to look at him. Head down, he doesn't look at me. His face is hidden by his hair, blond hair, shaggy, streaked by sun. "You didn't do it, buddy," he says.

I stand, frozen. "What are you talking about?"

But he doesn't answer, and he doesn't turn around. He sways, fingers moving, to music only he can hear.

SEVEN

IT'S EVENING when I start off down the drive to Burke House. I walk slowly. Very slowly. I'm in no hurry.

The air is like glass. That clear. That still. A weather breeder. I move against it, imagine a shield, an invisible shield, surrounding, protecting. It doesn't work. Glass, as we all know, breaks.

The house I grew up in was mostly glass. My father had it built, according to his specifications, built for the view.

The house sat on the bluff above Lake Michigan. He kept some trees up for protection, but through the trees we saw the water. A huge expanse of shining water. He said he liked it because it made him feel small. I never understood that. He may have felt small, but he didn't act it. In the house, when he was home, he seemed to fill it. I liked it best, we all did, when he wasn't there. That's what I used to think, until he left. Before he left, for good, we never knew when he was coming home. He never called. My mother waited, looking out the windows. She always looked toward the lake. She'd sit, not moving, and I'd sit watching her look out across the water as if she thought that any minute she'd see him, walking across the lake toward her.

That last winter I remember best. It grew dark early. She'd sit, in darkness, not speaking, not doing anything. Bets sucked her thumb. I was eleven. My sisters watched me turning on the lights. I turned on every one. My mother didn't notice. Wind hit the house. The windows rattled, and he was home. She turned to him. His face was pinched, with cold and anger. "God damn it, Cecily," he said. "Every God damn light is on." Moving through the house, he flicked the switches. One by one, the lights went off. Just one was left. "It's my fault," I said. He didn't hear me. He was looking at my mother. "Cecily," he said, his knuckles cracking. "What's happening?" The light shone on my mother's face. Her eyes were empty. "I'm sorry," she said, as if she thought the fault were hers. I hated her for that: she should have hated him. Maybe my father thought so too. "That's what I mean," he said. He sounded sad. "I'm sorry," my mother said again. "It's no good, Cecily," my father said. He left the room. He left. I heard the door close, banging in the wind behind him. He left us there. My mother sat. The wind hit against the house. The windows shook. My mother shattered.

There's no wind now. Over my head the branches meet. In full leaf now, the branches hide the sky. I like it this way. I like trees. I always have.

There's one tree here that I like better than the rest. My first year here I used to climb it, clear to the top, even though it was against the rules. I hadn't found the river yet, and it was the one place I could always be alone.

The tree is much older than the maples, much older than the school. At least two hundred years. A copper beech. The trunk is silver, smooth as skin, the leaves, in June, the color of blood.

It stands, near the drive, outside the chapel. I see it, glimmering, and walk across the lawn toward it. The branches, circling, reach the ground. I press my ear against the trunk, listening, the way you listen to a shell.

"Trees have hearts," I said to Bets. We stood in woods, thick woods, some birch but mostly oak. "Listen," I said.

59

She put her arms around a tree, and held on tight. She wore a knapsack just her size. She was six. I wore one too, a larger one. I was fourteen. She pressed her ear against the trunk, and listened. I watched her listening. She smiled. "I hear!" she said. When she smiled I saw a tooth was missing. "When did that happen?" I said, poking my pinkie in the gap. She turned her face, pressing her cheek against the tree. "I like trees," she said. "They don't run away."

"It's not my fault, Bets. I couldn't help it."

She didn't look at me. "Nice tree," she said. She patted the trunk.

"I'm here now. Camping, the two of us. Just like I said."

She turned then. "Forever?" she said. "Forever?" I should have told her then. I couldn't. It was the way her eyes looked, clear, not cloudy, the way they'd looked when she was just a baby. "We'll see," I said. I couldn't help it.

I can't help it now. I push off from the tree, and feel my legs carry me, out from under, and across the road, and up the hill to Burke House. I see the chimneys first, four red brick chimneys, two at either end. "Elegant," said Judith when she saw it. When Burke, whoever he was, died, he gave it to the school. "Tell me," Judith said to Manning, "if you don't mind my asking, how you get to be the one to live here?" Manning smiled. He didn't seem to mind. I'd told him Judith wasn't one to beat around the bush. "As Assistant Head, I do a great deal of entertaining. It fits the bill."

It does. And he does too. Even now. When I think of him, I think of Burke House. They fit together.

The roof is slate, shining like water in the light, a steep roof that throws a shadow on the drive. The house is stone, the color of flint.

It's been a long time since I've been here. The drive circles, small white pebbles crunching underfoot. They make me think of fairy tales, the ones I used to read to Bets.

60

Even before I reach the door, it opens.

"Peter," he says. "You're just in time."

What gets me is how the same things happen time after time. I look at him, to see if he remembers. He turns, starts down the hall. "Close the door, please," he says, turning briefly, back to me.

I close the door. The house is cool. Up here, even on the hottest days, there's usually some kind of breeze.

It blows now, gently, through the back doors that open to the garden. Cate's garden that I helped her plant. I cross the hall. The floor is marble, chessboard squares of black and white. I turn right, into the kitchen.

The kitchen is bright, white walled, with yellow curtains, and a round wood table in the middle of the room. There are flowers on the table. Cate's flowers. Sweet peas in pale pink and white. I smell them. I smell herbs and wine. A pot simmers on the stove. Manning holds a decanter in his hand. His other hand holds a glass. He pours. "Here," he says.

"No, sir." He holds it out. "Take it," he says. When I don't, he sets it on the table.

"Sit," he says. I shake my head.

"That's not an order, Peter," he says. "A request." He smiles. His voice makes me think of butterscotch.

I sit. He puts the sherry on the table. "Spencer told me, of your reluctance, Peter. Believe me, I appreciate your coming."

"I didn't come for you," I say.

He waits a minute before he speaks. "I know that," he says. His voice is smooth, unchanging.

Nothing has changed. I could be twelve, sitting here, in this kitchen, for the first time. Maybe I am. If I am, then none of it's happened. Yet.

"Here," he says. He sets a bowl of snow peas on the table. "You can fix these while we're waiting."

"I'm not hungry. I only came because . . ."

"You came because you had to," he says. He turns back to the stove.

I look at the peas. I remember when she planted them. I remember her. I wait for him to say her name.

He doesn't. He stands, his back to me, stirring. He wears a tan jacket, and a pinstriped shirt. The collar's white. He smells of mint.

"I need to talk to you," I say. My voice sounds thick.

"Later," he says. "After we eat."

He stirs, briskly. A pinch of herbs, a squeeze of lemon. He doesn't measure. He knows exactly what he's doing.

On the table in front of me is a knife, a fancy kitchen knife with a curved blade, and a smooth wooden handle. The blade is sharp. Carefully, I slide my fingers around the handle.

There is no sound but the flicking of the whisk against the pot, a steady rhythmic clicking like a clock. There are clocks all over Burke House, different clocks, all of them ticking, all chiming uneven hours. He collects them, among other things.

I've always hated them. They make me feel time has stopped.

Up here time does stop. His back to me, he bends above the stove. He looks the way he looked six years ago. He's fifty-five. He could be any age.

"You're quiet," he says, not turning.

I don't say anything. I finger the handle of the knife. Let him talk. Let him say her name. He doesn't. He cooks. The chicken simmers. His hands move, holding, folding, stirring. I drink my sherry, without thinking. His hands move with sure precision. Whatever they touch becomes defined.

"You must be hungry," he says.

I shouldn't be. I shouldn't be sitting at this table.

"Relax," says Manning. "Eat."

He sets my plate down. I eat. He sits, eating too. He eats slowly. I eat fast. I'm hungry. I want to get this over with.

I want to leave. I'm done before he's hardly started. He pours himself a glass of wine. "Where do we start?" he says.

He doesn't start. And I don't either. He clears the table.

He puts the plates in the sink. His plate's still full. He brings a bowl of lettuce to the table.

"You need to know I don't hold you responsible," he says. "For anything."

He pulls the leaves apart. Spring lettuce, Burpees' Early Green. Last year I helped Cate plant it; this year she did it by herself. "Come look!" she said. She looked so happy. She took me by the hand. "Close your eyes," she said. I closed them. She led me to the garden. "Open!" she said. I did. The whole garden had come up overnight. She looked so happy. "It's like a miracle," she said.

"Responsible for what?" I say.

He sighs. "Peter," he says.

"Peter," she said. A week ago. "I love you. Will you remember that?"

She held my hand. "Remember?" I said. "Why would I forget?"

"Peter," says Manning. "I'm only trying to help."

I look at him. "I'm not the one who needs help."

I wait. He stands.

"I'm not the one who killed her."

"I never said you were." He sets the kettle on the stove. Gas flares up, hissing.

"I've been remembering," he says, "the first time you ever came to dinner. The things you told me."

The silence settles. I feel its weight, the weight of all these years. Six years. Out in the hall a clock begins to chime. "Do you remember?" he says. He glances at me. "You told me about sledding, with your father."

I don't remember. But I remember sledding, riding my father's back, clinging, as the sled gathered speed. My arms around his neck, I held on tight.

"You sat," says Manning, "right there, where you're sitting now, and you told me, not in so many words, that you'd never felt so close to him before. All arms and legs and eyes. You talked, but everything you weren't saying was in those eyes."

I close my eyes. I hear the kettle begin to shake.

"Hold on," my father shouted. I tried. My fingers ached. With each bounce, my body lifted but my fingers held. The runners screamed, sparks flying beneath us like blue fire.

I felt the fire. My fingers parted. I flew, suspended in the bright cold air. And then I fell. Fell hard. It hurt. I remember how it hurt, my father standing over me. His gloves were off, his knuckles white. His fists were clenched. "Didn't I tell you to hold on!"

The kettle starts to scream. I open my eyes. Manning looks at me. "I remember," he says, "listening to you that night, watching you, and what I felt was the promise of things to come." His hands rise, shape the air.

He takes a step toward me.

"Don't," I say. He stops, hand out.

"You killed her. I know you did!"

He looks at me. "Do you?" he says. He turns away, lifting the kettle from the stove. The screaming stops.

"Everyone does," I say.

"Everyone?" He pours the water. Steam rises. I hear the water dripping through the filter, smell fresh hot coffee.

He glances at me. "You disappoint me. I'd always thought of you as someone separate from the common herd. Perhaps I was mistaken."

I watch the coffee drip.

"It's me," I say. "It's what I think."

"That's better," he says. The pot is full; he takes the filter to the sink.

He brings the coffee to the table, and then the cups, those same cups, white, thin as shells.

"She knew how to swim," I say.

64

He pours the coffee. The way his hands move, it's like a ritual. A secret rite.

"Does that matter?" He slides my cup across the table. I look at it, but I don't touch it.

"Of course it matters. You don't drown, in a river, if you know how to swim! Not by yourself, you don't."

He doesn't touch his coffee either. Holding the cup to his lips, he blows gently. The steam drifts sideways. "If it helps you to imagine that I . . ."

"I'm not imagining!"

"Aren't you?" he says. He takes a careful sip. "Were you there?"

"You found out. You found out about us. That's when you killed her."

Manning closes his eyes. He opens them. He looks at me. I lean forward, across the table.

"You were jealous," I say. "Jealous! You couldn't stand that she loved me. Not you. Me!"

"Peter."

"She loved me," I say.

He says nothing. He doesn't have to.

"She did!" I say. "She did!"

"Peter," he says. He says it quietly. "She did not know the meaning of the word." He separates his words so that they hang, suspended in the air.

"Do you?" I say. He looks at me. That look. "You didn't love her! You never loved her!"

He hesitates. "No," he says. "I didn't."

"I did."

He nods. "And I hold myself responsible."

"You! It didn't have anything to do with you. She was leaving you."

"Peter," says Manning.

"She was!"

"I'm sorry, Peter."

"Shut up!" I want to kill him. My fists are clenched.

I stand, pushing the chair back, hard. He stands up too.

"There's something I have to tell you," he says.

"No." I keep on moving.

"The autopsy's due tomorrow. You should know, Peter. Perhaps you do." He clears his throat. "She was pregnant, Peter."

I stop moving. I stop breathing too.

"I didn't think you knew." He says it softly.

"Did she tell you that?"

He doesn't look at me. He rubs his hand along his face. The light carves shadows on his cheeks. He looks, suddenly, older. "No," he says. "She didn't."

"Who?"

"Peter," he says. "It is a long, and rather dreary story."

"Mrs. MacQuire," I say.

He looks at me, startled. "You talked to her?"

"Why shouldn't I?"

"Listen to me, Peter. Listen carefully. She is not to be trusted."

"That's a laugh. And you are, I suppose." He looks at me.

"Tell me something," he says. "You talked to Mrs. MacQuire. Did she tell you Cate was pregnant?"

"Maybe she thought I knew."

He doesn't say anything. He just looks. I hate that look.

"She told me to stay away from you."

He smiles. The bastard smiles. "She would," he says.

"I hate you," I say. He stops smiling. I move toward the door.

"And I," he says, "would advise you to stay away from her."

"You think I'm going to listen to you?"

"I wish you would." He moves so quickly that he takes me by surprise. He puts his hand on my arm. I feel his fingers, digging in. "Peter," he says.

66

"Let go of me!" I'm shaking.

Maybe he feels it. "I'm sorry if it hurts you, Peter," he says. He says it softly. "She didn't care about you, and Mrs. MacQuire doesn't either."

"Let go," I say. "I mean it."

He lets go.

EIGHT

"SPAULDING!" says Coach. "Come on in!" He kicks the screen door open.

"I know it's late, sir."

"Late? Late for what? It's never too late. Come in."

He holds the door open with his foot. His feet are bare. He smells of beer. "I could use some company," he says. Grinning, he slaps me on the back. There's a red pencil stuck behind his ear. "Company's better than correcting papers. What do you say? Coke? Beer?"

"Actually, sir, I came to see Mrs. MacQuire. If she's around."

"She's around all right. She's up in bed. One of her headaches."

"I'll come back tomorrow." I take a step backward, toward the door. Coach stops me with his hand.

"No, you don't." He slams the door shut. The windows rattle. Plaster falls like snow. "Damn house," says Coach. He stoops, grunting, picks up a piece of plaster from the floor. "You watch. We'll wake up some morning and find it's fallen down around us." He laughs, his belly shaking.

"What do you say, Spaulding?"

"Not much, sir." I watch his belly shaking. He's got a big one now, big enough to hide his belt. Actually, he's big all over, all that muscle turned to fat. His laugh turns to a chuckle.

"Something, Spaulding." Chuckling. I can't see the joke,

68

with Coach it's always hard to, but I smile, to keep him company.

"I like this house, sir."

"So do I, Spaulding," he says. "So do I." He winks, rocking backward on his heels. "What'll it be, Coke or beer?" Turning, he starts walking down the hall.

"If she can't see me, sir . . ."

"She'll see you," he says. "She said to tell you."

Tell me what? There's nothing to do but follow him.

The house is old, and big, but I wasn't kidding when I said I liked it. A school house, just like Manning's, but they've made it theirs. Especially the kitchen, a big room with white walls and yellow molding, and a wooden honey-colored floor. There's a wood stove, and hanging plants, and most of the work they've done themselves.

Coach turns on the kitchen light, stands, blinking. "So," he says, "what'll it be?"

"Nothing, sir."

He shakes his head. "It's a damn shame, isn't it?" he says. He walks over to the fridge, and pops a Carling. "You sure?" he says. When I nod, he walks over to the table, and sits. "Sit down, Spaulding. Take a load off." He watches me until I do, and then he turns, looks up at the photos on the wall. Tipping his head, he drinks his beer. "What's it all about, Spaulding?"

"I don't know, sir."

I look up at the photos too. The ones above the table are all of Coach. Coach as a kid, as captain of the Dunster football team, Coach at Harvard, gripping the League Trophy in his hands. Coach, the Green Beret, holding a gun, proudly, the way he holds the trophy.

"Me neither," he says. "But I'll tell you something." He reaches up, taps his finger against the glass. The Green Beret. "Those days." He shakes his head.

"You knew the enemy, and all you had to do was . . ." He lifts his finger, aiming at the glass. "Pow." He stares at

69

his finger. "I just can't figure why she'd do it." He looks up, at the photos, as if he thinks he's going to find some answer there. And then he sighs.

"Go on up. She's waiting for you."

I leave him there, and go up slowly, and stand outside the bedroom door. I don't even have to knock.

"Come in," she says. "Don't turn the light on."

I come in slowly. The room is dark except for light shining from the hall. She lifts up on her pillows. "Sit there," she says, pointing to a chair beside the bed. My eyes adjust, and I can see the shape of things. Two bureaus against one wall. The big bed, king size. She lies in the middle, looking small, her eyes dark smudges in a pale face. She eases back down, slowly. The room smells of apples, a sweet, slightly sickish smell.

"What did he say?"

"That you wanted to see me."

"Peter. Please. I am not talking about Logan." Her voice is tight, as if her teeth are pressed together. "Did you see *him?*"

"I saw him. I came to talk to you." I did, but now that I'm here . . . I don't know. Maybe it's being up here, in the bedroom, in the dark. Maybe it's having her lying down. Everything is different. Is it different because Cate's dead?

I don't even have to close my eyes to see her standing by the river, her hair blowing, watching me run down the hill. "Catch me," I called, but she shook her head so I caught her, lifting her off the ground. She was so light. I felt so strong. "Three weeks," I said. "Three weeks!"

"I suppose," says Mrs. MacQuire, her voice coming from far away, "he told you it was all my fault."

"You were her best friend," I say.

She says nothing. She doesn't have to. I see them standing, side by side, yellow leaves falling. The sun shone as I ran down the field with the ball. I heard Coach shouting from

70

the bench, "Way to go, Spaulding." I went, I flew, and they were watching. Their arms were touching, and they smiled. At me last fall.

"She loved you," I say. Saying it, I think of Edwards, think of telling her what Edwards said. But I don't; it's not the kind of thing I'd say to Mrs. MacQuire. Which is funny when you come to think of it. I always feel I can tell her anything, and yet I hardly ever do.

"Tell me," Judith said after she met her. "What is it that turns you on?"

"That's a stupid way to put it," I said. Mad because I wanted Judith to like her, mad because I hoped that they'd be friends.

"You're right," said Judith. "It was." She grinned. "Sorry." When she grins her freckles spread. She took my hand. Her hand is freckled too. "Tell me," she said, in her husky voice.

I shrugged. "It's little things," I said. "Like birthdays."

"That's not so little."

"She bakes me cookies. Whenever I've been sick, she visits. She brought me this book on Tolkien once. I hadn't even told her that I liked him. Dumb things, you know. Like that."

"Not that dumb, sweetheart," Judith said. "In fact, not dumb at all. They all add up."

"She didn't love anyone," says Mrs. MacQuire. "Anyone. The sooner you realize that, the better." Her voice is tight, with pain or anger. She slides up against the pillows. I hear her wince. "Go look in that box," she says. She points to a dark corner of the room. I can't see anything.

"Go on," she says.

It's so dark I trip against it before I see it. A cardboard box, not very large, and square. "Look inside," she says.

I can't look. But I can feel. I kneel, and slowly slide my hand inside. "Clothes?" I turn, but can't see her on the bed.

"Cate's," she says. "Her way of saying good-bye."

71

Cate's clothes. Pulling a sweater from the box, I hold it to my face. I smell lilacs. I smell Cate. Tears prick my eyes. I squeeze them shut.

"She brought them over the afternoon before she died. I was out, and when I came back, there was the box. She left it in the kitchen. She told Daphne she'd been cleaning out her drawers for summer. And the worst is, I believed her."

I rub the wool against my cheek. "How do you know it wasn't true?"

"The truth is, she killed herself. That night."

"Have you ever thought," I say. I say it slowly. "He might have killed her?"

"Oh, Peter," she says.

My face is hidden in the sweater.

"She was pregnant," I say.

I hear the silence.

"I was afraid," she says, "he'd tell you."

"Why shouldn't he? Don't you think I have a right to know?"

"I told you, before. The less you know the better."

"Why? Because you think I can't handle it?"

"I thought we were friends," she says. "Why are you angry with me?" Her voice is quiet, laced with pain.

"I'm not. I'm sorry. It's just that . . . I don't know what to do."

"You've done it. You've seen him. You're seeing me now. Maybe," she says, "you have to make a choice."

"I made it," I say. "A long time ago."

"In that case . . ." She stops. "Come here," she says. "Over here."

I walk, slowly, to the bed. "Sit down," she says. "Here." She pats the bed. She takes my hand. Her hands are cold. "When someone dies," she says, "kills themselves, we feel responsible. We can't help it. We can't help it, and it hurts."

It hurts.

I picked Cate up, and swung her round. "Put me down," she said. I put her down. "Did I hurt you?" I said.

"No," she said. Her head was bent. "Peter," she said. "I can't."

"What?" I said.

"I can't do it," she said. "I can't leave him."

Time stopped. "What?" I said again. She looked at me. "I know it hurts," she said. She kissed me. I let her kiss me. I tasted watercress.

"Peter," says Mrs. MacQuire. "Where are you?"

"You don't have to feel responsible," I say. "That baby wasn't yours."

"No," says Mrs. MacQuire. She sucks in her breath. "But she was."

And she starts to cry. Mrs. MacQuire. Her shoulders shake. The tears slide down her cheeks. She doesn't make a sound.

"Hey. Don't. Please! Are you OK?"

She shakes her head. I hand her a Kleenex, and she wipes her face. "I'm fine. I'm better."

Her voice is thick but she sounds more like herself. We sit in silence. Downstairs I hear the TV droning, Coach watching a Red Sox game. I think her eyes are closed. I stand up, quietly.

"Don't go."

"Did she tell you everything?"

"Everything?"

"About us. Cate and me."

She's quiet. So quiet. Not even breathing. "She didn't have to," she says.

"That was my baby."

I hear her breathing, in and out.

"You don't know that, Peter."

"I know him." I take a deep breath. "He was a shit to her."

Again the silence. "Peter, that doesn't mean . . ."

73

"She told me!" I say it louder than I mean to. I hear her wince.

"She didn't tell you she was pregnant, though. Did she?" I don't answer. "Peter," she says, "she didn't always tell the truth."

"She told you the truth. She loved you."

"She needed me. She needed more."

"Me?"

"And Oliver. She needed all of us."

"You're angry with her. For that?"

"I'm angry. Yes. I'm very angry."

"But if he killed her . . ."

"When you do everything in your power to help a person, and that person . . . lets you down. You ought to know about that," she says.

I don't say anything.

"You're angry," she says. "Instead of blaming her, you're blaming him. Actually," she laughs, a harsh short sound, "with some reason. He did marry her, didn't he? And he's blaming me. So we're all happy, aren't we?"

"Happy!"

"It's called displacement." She leans back, against the pillows. "This is making me tired. My head's better. Maybe I can sleep."

"I'm not blaming you."

The TV goes off downstairs. I hear the quiet.

"That's good," she says.

"But why did you tell him she was pregnant?"

It's quiet. The house creaks, the way it always does when the weather's changing.

"Is that what he said?" Quiet.

"That's what I figured. You thought it was his. You must have thought he already knew."

She's quiet.

"Peter," she says. Her voice cracks, then steadies. "I don't think I could bear it if you blamed me too."

74

"Don't worry. I won't. But you've got to understand about Manning. How it is with him. What he's like. How I know he couldn't . . . it wasn't . . . his."

I'm glad it's dark. My face is burning. But she can't see.

"I thought you might have known already," I say. "Guessed."

I hope she's going to help me. "Guess what?" she says.

She's not. I take a deep breath. "He doesn't like women," I say.

"Really," says Mrs. MacQuire. I swear she sounds amused.

"What I mean . . ."

"I know what you mean. You don't have to spell it out."

"OK."

"He's perfectly capable, you know."

"Capable?"

She doesn't answer right away. "Is it possible," she says, "that I have brought this on myself?" Her voice trembles. "All my life I've taken care of people. Who's taking care of me?"

I back away.

"I'll get Coach."

"Don't bother," says Coach. "I'm here." He stands in the doorway, filling it. He stands with Rufus in his arms. "I've brought a friend. He's scared."

Rufus rubs at his eyes with the back of his hand. "I heard thunder," he says. His legs dangle. His arm is loose around his father's neck. He reaches out to touch me. He smells of sleep. He smiles. Sleepy. "Peter," he says.

"I'm fine," says Mrs. MacQuire. "Just fine."

Rufus leans toward me, both arms out. Without thinking, I reach out too. Coach lets go, and Rufus wraps his legs around my waist, his arms around my neck. I think of Bets.

"Darling," says Mrs. MacQuire. Her voice soft.

When Coach turns on the light, she smiles. At Rufus. She holds out her arms. I carry Rufus across the room. He's solid for a six-year-old, all of a piece. I put him on the bed next

75

to his mother. He lies there, grinning up at me. His hair is dark; his eyes are too. He grins. She smiles. She strokes his cheek. "You," she says. "Since when have you been scared of thunder?" He giggles. "Tonight," he says.

"You," she says. She laughs too. Softly, she kisses his cheek. Something in my heart turns over.

"I'm off," I say.

I think maybe she might stop me, but she doesn't. "All right," she says. She nods. "Thank you for coming," she says. Cool and formal; as if she's forgotten who I am, and why I came.

NINE

IT RAINS in the night. The thunder wakes me, but I'm not sure I've been asleep. I lie, listening. When lightning flashes, the sky turns purple. The wind whistles against the screen. I smell the ocean even though it's miles away.

Cate loved the ocean. That's what she said. She'd only been there once, with Mrs. MacQuire, just last year. They took a picnic to High Island, wine and chicken and deviled eggs. The best day she'd ever had is what she said. "The sun, and the ocean, the way it held me up. It felt like magic. Floating. We went way out. I wasn't frightened."

"I'll take you to the ocean," I said.

"I'd like that," she said. But did she mean it? Did she mean anything she said?

The room goes white. A loud crack, and then a moaning. The hiss of leaves, and I hear something scratching at the door. I hold my breath.

"Peter," says Snickers. "Are you awake?"

I catch my breath. "No."

"Oh." He hovers in the doorway, poised on one leg, like a stork. His hand is on the doorknob. "I thought I'd check," he said. "Just checking."

"Right."

"There's a storm," he says.

"You're kidding."

"Nope." He slips into the room, closing the door. The

77

room goes dark. "A big storm." He moves like a shadow across the floor. "It's raining hard."

"You better close the window."

He scuttles to the window, slams it down. Lightning flashes. He freezes, flinching. "See!" he says.

"Watch for the thunder," I say, counting. One, two, three . . . Thunder rumbles, echoes, fading. "It's passing by."

He inches across the room toward the bed, and leans against it. The casters squeak. "There was this loud noise," he says. His voice squeaks too. "Sometimes it feels like morning's never going to come." The bed shakes with his shivering. "It's just that I'm cold," he says.

"I know," I say. I push over, against the wall. "Get in. Before you freeze to death."

He scrambles up, and under. His feet touch my leg.

"Jesus! You're a bloody piece of ice."

He giggles. His breath smells of chocolate. He knots himself into a ball, head down, knees up. His knees dig into me. "Roll over," I say.

He rolls over. "You were too awake." His voice is muffled by the blankets.

He's so damn young. He makes me feel very old.

"Go to sleep," I say, and slowly his shivering stops, his breathing steadies. I lie still, listening. Listening, I remember Bets.

How Bets sang. Under the trees she sang. "Poor babes in the wood, poor babes in the wood." Her voice was high. Overhead wind stirred the leaves. "Do you remember the babes in the woods." She stopped singing. Only the leaves, and far far away the sound of a train. Our sleeping bags were side by side. "Peter," she said, so close her breath tickled my ear. "Why did they die?"

"They got lost."

"Are we lost?"

"Of course not."

78

"I can't see."

"Because it's dark."

"Will we stay here forever?"

"Go to sleep."

"You promised."

"We'll see."

"Peter?"

"What?"

"Is dead forever too?"

I didn't answer.

She slept.

Snickers sleeps.

And I sleep too.

"Marvelous!"

I know who it is without opening my eyes. I open them anyway. Edwards stands by the foot of the bed. In the hall the bells are ringing. "I was hoping to find you in."

The light is gray. Fog presses against the window.

Edwards flips on the light. The overhead bulb is bare. Blinding. "For Christ's sake, Edwards." I shield my eyes with my arm. "Get out."

"You don't know why I've come!" He smiles.

I start to sit up. My leg rubs against . . . I stop moving. I lie still. Very still.

"As a matter of fact," says Edwards, "I came by last night, but you were, unfortunately, otherwise engaged."

"Out."

If I don't move . . . He must be under covers.

"To make a long story short." Edwards pauses. He's never had such fun. "It's Spencer, dear boy. Spencer would have a word with you."

"You bastard, Edwards."

He laughs.

"Get out."

"If there's anything I can do."

79

"You can get out."

"Your wish, dear boy." And under the covers, Snickers whimpers in his sleep.

"What's this!"

Before I can move, he's pulled the blankets back. Snickers sleeps, curled in a ball. He sleeps with his mouth open. His thumb rests by his mouth, wet and wrinkled.

"How charming!" Edwards presses his fingers together. Beaming. "What a pleasant surprise."

"It's not what you think."

"Isn't it, Spaulding? What do I think?"

Snickers twitches in his sleep. His eyelids flutter. I pull the covers over his head. I look at Edwards.

"One word, and I'll kill you."

"My, my," says Edwards. Smiling. Uneasy. He takes a step backward.

"I mean it."

Maybe he knows I mean it. "Don't be a poor sport, Spaulding." He edges back toward the door. "Spencer," he says. "After breakfast." And he's gone.

I lie down, slowly, carefully. I try to think. The second bell begins to ring. I press my pillow to my ear. The bell rings, muffled. Something rattles.

I hold still, listening. The beetle, I think. I listen, but I don't hear it. I feel it. I slide my hand inside the pillow case. I feel paper. I pull it out, a blue book, the kind we use to write exams. I open it. I see the writing, small letters crouching against each line. I know that writing. For a moment my heart stops beating. I turn the page. I turn all the pages. Writing, writing everywhere, except the last page. The last page's missing, ripped out along the binding. Back to the beginning. My hands are shaking. On the inside of the blue binding, I find what I am looking for.

Dear Peter,
*   I'm sorry. I hope maybe this will help you understand.*

That's all. She didn't even sign her name. A journal. Cate's journal. I didn't know she kept one. I don't know when she brought it here. I'll never know.

"Hey!" Under the covers Snickers starts to thrash. I slip it underneath the mattress just as Snickers comes up for air. Gasping, eyes wide and frightened, he looks around. "Where am I?" he says. "What happened?"

I could tell him, but what's the point. He'll find out soon enough.

"There was a storm last night. Remember?"

His eyes focus. Then he nods.

"Ah," says Spencer. "Fresh air!"

He strides down the drive. The fog is thick. My shoes are soaked. Spencer wears walking shoes of thick brown leather. We both wear yellow slickers that shine like beacons in the fog. We walk in unison, like soldiers marching. Halfway down the drive I stop.

"God!"

I point, to the right, toward the chapel. Spencer grunts, then follows me across the grass. He taps his pipe against his teeth.

"A direct hit, Spaulding. More's the pity."

A pity. Half the copper beech hangs lifeless, the heart exposed, white wood glistening. I place my hands against the trunk.

"I used to climb this tree."

My voice cracks, and Spencer looks at me. His eyebrows furrow. "A pity, but a tree, Spaulding, is a tree. Nor should I have to tell you that climbing them's against school rules."

"It was a good place to be alone, sir."

He shakes his head.

"It's not healthy, Spaulding. I said the same to Manning, more than once. Not healthy, I said, the amount of time young Spaulding spends alone."

"I liked being alone, sir!"

81

"Precisely. And I like to think we've cured you of that habit."

I don't answer. He doesn't seem to care. He marches back toward the drive.

"As a leader, Spaulding, one must always strive for the common good. I trust you know that."

"Yes, sir."

"I'm glad to hear it. I must tell you, Spaulding, that certain matters, delicate matters have recently been brought to my attention. Matters that, unfortunately, must be discussed."

Silence. I hear water dripping from the trees.

"Yes, sir."

"We'll do the Loop," says Spencer.

At the end of the drive we follow the road that curves downhill to run above the river. The river is hidden by the trees, the trees by fog.

His breath whistles through his teeth. He leans toward me. "This is not the army, boy. Relax."

"Yes, sir." My hands are cold. I slip them in my pockets. His nose is red. He sighs.

"When I was your age, Spaulding, I believed myself to be immortal."

I try to imagine him my age. I can't.

"Was that before the war, sir?"

He doesn't answer. Head down, he marches, pipe in his teeth, and I march with him. The road curves along the bluff, above the river, heading toward the falls.

"I don't suppose you know where she was found?"

What would he think if I said yes?

"No, sir."

We hear the falls, but we can't see them. We see Mill House though, rising above them, a dark building made of brick. Mill House where Timothy lives. The windows are barred and nothing moves. Spencer looks up too.

"Precisely," he says. "They were questioned, last night.

The police insisted. I told them it was no use, but they insisted."

He stops by the edge of the road. His short hair bristles, beaded with wet. He chews his pipe. Behind him the iron bridge rises, floats through fog. I hear the falls.

"If we start with the facts," he says. "The facts, at least are clear. But in strictest confidence, Spaulding. Do you understand?"

"Yes, sir."

We reach the bridge. His boots ring out. The bridge is old, no longer used, the first bridge built of iron in the state. He stamps his feet. The whole bridge vibrates. "It's not safe, sir."

"Nonsense. Just watch your step."

I watch my step. Through rusted holes I see bright water dancing. On either side are railings made of wood. Old wood, rotting, in places broken through.

"Yes, sir." I wait. The water dances.

"The coroner's report. I heard last night. Death by drowning. Self-inflicted. She jumped apparently, from this bridge. The height, Spaulding, is insignificant, but there are rocks. She was found some yards down the river. Drifting."

Around us the fog is lifting slowly. Under the bridge the water slides, a sheet of silver, into the pool below. A drop of ten feet maybe, fifteen at the most.

"Apparently, Spaulding, she was pregnant." He clears his throat.

"Yes, sir. Manning told me."

He blinks. "Did he? Did he indeed. Well then. Very good. Perhaps you know the rest."

"The rest, sir?"

He nods. "Precisely, Spaulding, precisely!" He bends to his pipe. Hand cupped around the bowl, he tries to light it. His hand shakes. Match after match flares up, hissing, goes out. The fifth try does it; smoke billows from his pipe. "Ah," says Spencer. "Small pleasures, Spaulding." He smiles. I look away.

"Pregnant. Yes. And did Manning mention her acute distress, concerning her condition?"

"No, sir."

"Most distressed. So Manning told me. Her childhood, Spaulding. Her childhood was no preparation for such responsibility."

"I don't believe it."

He frowns.

"Thanks to this school, Spaulding, your needs have been attended to, as hers were not. He did everything in his power, Spaulding, to calm, to reassure. Now, unfortunately, he blames himself."

"I don't believe that either, sir."

"Precisely! I told him that he should in no way hold himself responsible, that he had done all that was possible. You must help me convince him of that fact, Spaulding. The fact is, I feel the responsibility as mine."

"You, sir?"

"Guilt, Spaulding, guilt! Man's driving force. Which is why, as headmaster, I have tried to instill in all of you, a sense of honor. Not guilt, Spaulding. Honor!"

"Yes, sir."

"With you, I feel I have had some small success, but there are others . . ." He squints at me. The sun is stronger now, almost hot. Sweat catches in the creases on his neck.

"Yes, sir."

"There are some, Spaulding, for whom nothing can be done. Mrs. Manning. A troubled soul, Spaulding. May she rest in peace."

"No."

Spencer shakes his head. "I know you, Spaulding. It is in you to think the best of everyone, but there are times when one must face the facts, however unpleasant the facts might be." He straightens, shoulders back. "In Manning's case, I blame myself. It was at my suggestion that he married. Perhaps, if I'd let well enough alone . . ." He stares down at the water. The pool at the bottom of the falls is dark, and still. A cloud drifts across it.

"He didn't have to listen, sir."

"He didn't," says Spencer. "But he did."

He opens his hand, and the pipe falls. It hits the water. The surface shatters, cloud broken into bits. The current carries the pipe downstream.

I glance at Spencer.

"An offering," he says. He shakes his head. "I confess I find this spot depressing."

He looks at me.

"This school, Spaulding, has been my life."

"Yes, sir."

"Thirty years. A long time." Pause. "Perhaps too long. What do you think, Spaulding?"

"I don't know, sir."

"Of course you don't. Pay no attention. Pretend I am talking to myself. Let us be off."

I start back the way we came, Spencer a step or so behind. I slow down, match my step to his.

"Thirty years, Spaulding. A lifetime."

He walks, head forward, hands clasped behind his back. He frowns. "Spaulding, have you ever had a dream?"

"Dream, sir?"

"I have, Spaulding. This school. This . . ." He looks up, as if expecting to see the school surrounding him. He shakes his head.

We walk in silence. When the trees shake, the leaves drop diamonds.

"The war, yes, and afterward, such chaos, such devastation. You can't imagine, Spaulding. This school was nothing but an empty shell, a shadow of its former self. When I arrived, they gave it a year or two at most. What do you think of that?"

85

"I don't know, sir."

"Nor did I, Spaulding. Nor did I. But I knew I'd found a refuge. A refuge, Spaulding. Then a dream."

"I had a dream," said Cate. She smiled. I saw clouds floating in her eyes. I smiled too. "A good dream?" I asked. We lay in the sun on the edge of the river. The water whispered; the ice was gone.

"Very," said Cate. Whispering.

I lay above her, feeling the sun above me, her weight below, weight shifting slightly. "Once upon a time," I said. "Long long ago."

"Not a fairy tale," she said. "A dream." She smiled. "I dreamt I had a baby."

I looked at her. Her face was soft. "You said you couldn't."

She touched my cheek. "It was a dream."

"Not that I care." Gently I rolled off her, onto my back. "We can always adopt one."

She was quiet. The sky was pale, the ground was damp. It smelled of spring. "I used to think I was adopted," I said. She said nothing. "It was like not being connected, to anyone, to anything." I rolled over. She was looking at the sky. "I used to have this dream," I said, "that someday this person would show up, someone I'd never seen before, but right away I'd know . . ."

"She had the sweetest face," said Cate.

"Who?"

"The baby. In the dream."

She sat up then. Arms round her legs, legs up, she rubbed her cheek against her knee. "She was all there," she said. "All there. And her name was Cate."

"Spaulding!"

We stand in the middle of the road. Spencer's hand is on my shoulder. "Have you heard a word I've said?"

"Yes, sir. Dreams, sir. You were talking about dreams."

"Not dreams, Spaulding. Not dreams. *One* dream!"

"The school, sir."

"Precisely." He peers at me. I feel dizzy. I pull away.

"I hope this is not too much for you, Spaulding," he says. "For thirty years I have made it a practice not to involve students in adult affairs."

I keep quiet. He leans toward me, fumbling in his pocket for his pipe. "Where is my pipe?"

"In the river, sir. You dropped it."

He glares. "You should have stopped me."

"I didn't know you were going to drop it, sir."

"Ah," says Spencer. "And you don't know why I've brought you out here, either, do you?"

"No, sir. I do have classes."

"Classes, yes. It is Manning we must discuss." He turns left, starts up the hill. "Thirty years, Spaulding. This year has been my last."

"Yes, sir."

"You're not surprised?"

"Rumors, sir. No one knew if they were true."

"Rumors, yes, precisely. Precisely why I wished to keep the whole procedure under wraps."

He frowns at me.

"Tell me, Spaulding. Those rumors. Have you heard who is to take my place?"

"Manning, sir."

"I see. And what do you think? Of Manning as head?"

"I don't know, sir."

"Of course you know. You of all people, Spaulding."

"I'm sorry, sir."

"Loyalty." He shakes his head. "I confess to a sense of loyalty myself. Does it help you to know he has long been my personal choice? He has been here a long while, Spaulding. Twenty years. A dedicated man, Spaulding, a committed teacher. A man who knows what he's about!"

Spencer slows down. Thank God he slows down. We're

almost to the top of the hill. His cheeks are mottled, like cottage cheese. I see him falling, toppling suddenly like an uprooted tree.

"I don't mind telling you, Spaulding, the Board had approved. It was to be announced at Graduation."

I stop.

"He knew?"

"Of course he knew. He's made no secret of the fact that he wished to succeed me, Spaulding. I admired him for that. I have always admired Manning. Now more than ever. He came to me last night to tell me that under the circumstances perhaps he should withdraw. For the good of the school, he said."

Spencer stops, swaying. I imagine him falling, imagine dragging him, step by step, up the school drive.

"I need to sit down, sir." Without waiting for an answer, I sit by the road.

"I've surprised you, Spaulding?"

I look away from him, down the hill. At the bottom the stone lions guard the gates.

"It was just a rumor, sir. About his being Head. I wasn't sure if it was true."

If it was true. I close my eyes. Would he have killed her, if he wanted to be Head? Not only wanted, but knew he would be?

"Now that you know, I need your help."

Spencer lowers himself to the grass. The grass is wet; he doesn't seem to notice. "Tell me, Spaulding, what do you think of Edwards?"

"Not much, sir."

"The feeling, I'm afraid, is mutual."

"Yes, sir."

"He came to me with stories he claims are true," says Spencer.

"What stories, sir?" As if I don't know. Spencer pulls a blade of grass, spinning it between his fingers.

88

"Stories about Manning, Spaulding. Manning and students. You in particular."

"Edwards is jealous, sir."

"Are you telling me there is truth to these stories then?"

His voice is quiet. I shake my head, and turn away. "Manning hates him, sir."

"And you're not lying to protect Manning?"

"I wouldn't do that, sir."

"I'm glad to hear it. Loyalty is a virtue only when not detrimental to the common good."

"Yes, sir."

"It has been my experience, Spaulding, that nothing is more damaging to a school of this nature than rumors, particularly vicious rumors of the sort Edwards is spreading. Do you understand me, Spaulding?"

"I think so, sir."

"Buggery, boy, buggery."

"Yes, sir."

Spencer laces his fingers, and stares at his hands. His knuckles are a nest of wrinkles.

"We must stand behind Manning, Spaulding. Where we lead the school will follow. We must not lose him."

"Yes, sir. No, sir."

"I need a hand." He holds out his hand. I stand up first, and then take hold. I pull him up. We start, slowly, down the hill. "You should know, I suppose," says Spencer. "It is not the first time Edwards has come to me."

"I didn't think so, sir."

"You are a leader, Spaulding, a natural leader, but I must confess it was some time before I recognized the fact. Your first offense, as I recall, was fraternizing with the kitchen help."

"Yes, sir."

"There have been others. Yes. Edwards, I grant you, is clever as well as persevering, but until now either I, or Manning, have managed to serve as buffer."

"I suppose I should thank you, sir."

"Perhaps not. Perhaps if we had dealt openly . . . This time, unfortunately, he claims proof."

"What proof?"

"I've no idea." His hand pats my shoulder. "But you've nothing to fear. It's Manning who requires help. I feel, as I've said, somewhat responsible. First his wife, now this. It was I who suggested he might marry."

"He married because he wanted to be Head! That's all he cared about. He didn't care about her."

Spencer's hand drops from my shoulder. He looks sad, not angry. "Such cynicism does not become you, Spaulding."

"It's the truth, sir."

"The truth, Spaulding, is that Manning has enemies."

"Edwards, sir?"

"Edwards. And others. Power breeds envy. As Senior Prefect you ought to know that."

He waits for me to say something. "Not really, sir."

"I am afraid, Spaulding, that soon enough you will."

TEN

December 3

Oliver says I should keep a journal to improve my writing skills. But what would I write about, I said. I don't have anything to say. He closed his eyes, the way he does when I make him cross. All the more reason, he said. Will you want to read it, I said. He opened his eyes. God forbid, he said.

I have been married for three months. I am very happy. But it is hard to write about happiness.

I asked Melissa. She is beginning to be the best friend I ever had. I've never had a best friend before.

What about you, she said, do you want to keep a journal. If he wants me to, I said. Oh Cate, she said, Oh Cate. I love the way she says my name. It can sound hard, but when she says it, it sounds soft. Do it for yourself, she said. I told her I didn't know what to write about, and she said how about your childhood, start with that. You never talk about your childhood. There's nothing to say, I said, and she said, don't be silly, of course there is, go back to the beginning, to your very first memory, and start there. "What was it?" The wind, I said, and she smiled. There you are, she said.

I remember the wind. Blowing and blowing. The earth was flat, and I lay flat, on the playground, to keep from blowing away. To hide from Willie Joe. He was ten, and I was five. He couldn't see me. He was blind with eyes like moons. He shuffled when he walked, feeling his way toward me. If I cried

91

he'd hear me so I didn't. He found me anyway. He put his hand on my head. A dirty hand. I was dirty from the dust. Then I cried. He took a sourball from his pocket, and gave it to me. Eat it, he said. I didn't want to, but I was afraid. So I did. It tasted sour. How did you find me, I said. You're a hole in the wind, he said. He watched me with his empty eyes. Aunt Effie watched me from the car.

" 'Some say the world will end in fire,' " says Thurston, settling on the couch beside me.

"Jesus!" I slap the blue book shut. "You scared me."

Thurston grins, waiting. " 'Some say in ice,' " I say, but maybe he knows I'm not in the mood because he stops. Closing his eyes, he strums the air with his fingers, and sings. Lucy in the Sky with Diamonds. He opens one eye, and looks at me. "Spencer," he says, and settles back into the song. His way of telling me that if I want to talk, he's here to listen. When I shrug his eyes close again. I slip the blue book inside my notebook. Still singing, he slips his hand into his pocket, pulls out a letter that he hands to me. "Sukie," he says, without missing a beat. "I got one too."

I look down at the envelope, the familiar writing, large and loopy. It's been so long. As if she happened to someone else. Thurston swings into "I Get By." His voice is deep; Sukie calls it sexy. He's got perfect pitch. He slouches beside me, singing.

He's the only one who could have found me here, this small room behind the library. It's part of the library actually, but no one ever uses it. There're no windows, just dusty stacks of books, and an old sofa with the springs gone. When we were younger, Thurston and I used to come here all the time, to get away, to be alone. The walls are thick, and on the ceiling is a mural painted years ago by Willard Gilbert, '31. The paint's gone dark but it's still possible to see what looks at first like your typical jungle scene. Leaves, and grass, and twisting vines. It's only after a while you see the snakes, winding through the grass, and elves with pointed hats inside the flowers. In six years we've spent hours looking for things we might have missed. We've found them too.

Sukie's letter is short.

> *P.S.*
>   *Do you still exist, or did I dream you? What happened? Do I have bad breath? Smelly feet? Please tell me. I'd like to know.*
>
>   *S.*

Last year, when she came up for Fifth Form Dance, I brought her in to see the ceiling. Thurston was with us; they've been friends for years, grown up together. That's how I met her, and then we both did Outward Bound.

She loved the ceiling. She even climbed the stacks to get a better look. Sat up there, swaying, braids and bluejeans, while Thurston and I did what we could to keep the bookshelves from going over. She loved it because she'd been studying Freud. "Phallic symbols!" she said. "Everywhere." Grinning down at us. "Repressed sexuality."

"He must have spent six years here," I said.

Thurston and I grinned, quickly, at each other.

I stuff the letter in my pocket. When I think of Sukie, I miss her. In the last year I've hardly thought of her at all.

"What did she say to you?"

Thurston swings into "You Know How Much She Loves You."

"Bullshit."

Thurston shrugs. He stops singing. "She's going to Yale."

I didn't know. When you come right down to it, I don't know much of anything.

"You could do worse," he says. "I mean, she's alive."

"What's that supposed to mean?"

His eyes close. " 'Things fall apart,' " he chants. I don't say anything. I hear him sigh. "Look at it this way," he says.

"The universe is expanding. Every minute." He wiggles his fingers. "Like all the time there's more space between the stars, more darkness. I mean, infinity! Jesus! Think of us moving out *forever!*" Awed, he shakes his head.

"But you said if there's enough density . . ."

"Who knows." He opens his eyes, and looks at me. "That's not the point. The point is Sukie likes you, asshole. God knows why." He grins. "All you'd have to do is snap your fingers, and . . ." His fingers come together. "So why not?"

"Thanks for the advice."

"Don't mention it." He stands up slowly. "So stay out of trouble," he says.

"Too late." I try a laugh. With his foot, Thurston nudges my Shakespeare book that's lying on the floor.

"You done this yet?"

I shake my head.

"Edwards went to Spencer," I say.

Thurston goes still. His hair hangs over both eyes. He gives his head a shake. One eye appears. "Murder?"

"Buggery," I say.

His one eye widens. He laughs. He has an easy comfortable laugh.

"He's serious," I say, but I can't help smiling.

"The common good!" he says. "For the common good you must confess." His face contracts. He looks like Spencer. His voice is Spencer's too.

"To what?" I say.

Thurston, losing interest, shrugs.

"Take it easy," he says. He walks to the door. "There's the meet," he says. "Don't forget."

The wind comes up in the afternoon, blowing hard from the north. The air turns cold and clear. Along the lower field the leaves of the poplars turn belly-up.

The meet starts at three. Waiting for the whistle, I jog in

place. I can't keep still. Down the line, Thurston catches my eye, smiles his sleepy smile. He stands, slouching, wearing a red headband to keep his hair from his eyes. Coach's orders. He thinks Thurston needs to see to run. He doesn't. He could run with his eyes closed if he wanted to, and win. He's the best runner Dunster's ever had, but to look at him you'd never know it. To watch him running you wouldn't know it either. He lopes, a free and easy style, and never looks as if he's pushing.

When the whistle goes, I'm ready. I start fast, something I don't usually do. "Go for it, Spaulding!" A voice shouting from the sidelines. Maybe Snickers, but I don't look. The wind comes pushing from behind, and runners fan out across the field. I stick to the edge. In the tall grass daisies shine. I see them, and I think of stars.

"For God's sake, Spaulding! Save yourself!" Coach stands on the bank, arms waving, his face flushed and beefy. "Three miles to go, boy." I know that, but I don't slow down. The last race of the season, and there is nothing left to lose.

The woods approaching, we pass from one field to the next. Against the bright grass, in bright sunlight, the uniforms dazzle, bursts of gold on green, silver on red. Running, I feel the earth give, springing back, springing as we spin through space, as the wind carries me beneath the trees.

Save yourself, said Coach, and running, I am trying to do just that. As if by running I can get away.

Ahead, through green leaves, a needle of light. I run toward it, and the needle widens, becomes the sky, as the wind lifts me over rough grass, across the stone wall, along the hill. Up. The hill rises, and I rise too, bending to the curve of the earth.

My feet take the ridge, shaping grass and rocks and stony soil. The hill is mine. Running, I am the hill. I am the wind. I am the bright earth spinning into darkness.

I am all things; and there is no escape.

*　　*　　*

"What got into you?" says Thurston. He grins, pleased.
He finished right behind me, but he's hardly out of breath.
I feel sick. As soon as I crossed the finish I felt sick. I wanted
to run forever. I still want to run forever. But I can't. I'm
soaked with sweat, and shivering. My insides feel like broken
glass. I can't feel my legs at all.

Coach claps me on the back. "Keep moving," he says.
"You'll keel over."

I keep moving. Mrs. MacQuire stands by Spencer. Spencer beams. "Splendid, Spaulding, splendid!" Mrs. MacQuire
doesn't smile.

"He's tired, Chauncy. Let him go." Her voice is soft. She
looks at me as if we share a secret. "I'll see you later," she
says.

The shower feels good. The water beats against me, stinging. My legs ache, coming back to life. I won the race. But
what good is it going to do?

"I want to know everything," I said. "All about you."

Cate smiled. Shy. "You don't," she said.

It was fall, and leaves were falling in the river, yellow
leaves against the brown.

"Everything," I said.

"What do you think?" she said.

"I think" — I closed my eyes to see it better — "you
lived in a white house. With green shutters. And a dog. A
little dog, and there were trees. Your mother wore an apron
with blue stripes, and your father . . . your father. It was a
farm, in the country. There were hills." I opened my eyes
to see if I was right.

She pulled a strand of her hair across her face, rubbing it
against her cheek.

"Yes," she said. A whisper.

"You had Cream of Wheat for breakfast every morning

96

with real cream. From the cows. And horses. You could ride the horses."

"How do you know so much?" she said.

"Am I right?" I couldn't help grinning.

"It sounds . . . lovely."

"Am I?"

Her eyes were pale. Dreamy. She twisted her hair around her finger, held it beneath her nose. Sniffing, like a rabbit. "I had a wonderful childhood," she said. She reached out. She touched me. For the first time.

The Common Room is crowded, kids and teachers drinking tea. A sea of blue blazers interspersed with tweed. The visiting team huddles in the corner, wolfing sandwiches, tiny triangles with crusts cut off. They don't look happy. Spencer, pipe in mouth, stands talking to their coach. I see his mouth moving. The sound in here is deafening. His wife, a small woman with bright beady eyes, darts like a hummingbird through the crowd.

I make my way toward the windows where Mrs. MacQuire stands behind the table pouring tea. The urn is silver. Steam rises from white cups when she turns the spigot. She doesn't see me. I look around. I don't see Manning. Hands reach out, clap my back. "Good race, Spaulding. Good race." The crowd is thick. It's hard to breathe.

She wears a white sweater. Her hands move from cup to spigot and back to cup. She passes the cup across the table. Her hair is swept back from her face. Her face is pale, but she looks better than the night before. I slip behind the table to stand beside her. She glances at me, but keeps on working. People press against the table. "You've never run like that before," she says. I slide a cup toward her. She takes it, fills it. Hands reach out. I pass another. "You're feeling better?" I say. She doesn't answer. The noise is all around us, voices rising like a wall. She frowns.

"Something's come up."

She doesn't say what, and I don't ask. We work together. I think of telling her about the journal. Maybe I should, I think. I don't. Cate gave it, to me. It's mine.

"You heard," she says, "about the autopsy?"

We keep on working. I nod.

"And what do you think?" she says, more quietly than before. There's something in the way she says it. I look at her. Her face is polished, hard as stone.

I shrug. "It's what you thought."

"Maybe I've changed my mind," she says.

My heart starts pounding. I feel things shifting, inside and out. Kids push against the table. I feel trapped. I think of Cate, of Willie Joe, a farm with Cream of Wheat and horses.

"What did she tell you about her childhood?"

She looks at me. "Why do you ask?"

I know I'm blushing, but I can't help it. I shrug. "Just wondering."

I don't know if she believes me, but she nods. "It was worse than yours," she says. She says it gently.

I can't stop blushing. "Mine was OK."

She smiles. Gently.

A hand settles on my shoulder, squeezing. "Fraternizing with the help again!" Spencer laughs, a juicy chuckle.

"I don't know as I find that too amusing, Chauncy," says Mrs. MacQuire.

"Nor should you, my dear," says Spencer, chuckling. "A private joke, between Spaulding and myself."

"I see," says Mrs. MacQuire. She hands a cup of tea to Spencer. Bending, he blows.

"Thank you, my dear."

The tea in his cup shivers. "A formidable woman, Spaulding," he says. Smiling. He looks at me.

"Sure," I say.

"Chauncy," says Mrs. MacQuire. "Please."

"Modest as well," says Spencer. "I've known her since

she was a child. Her father was a dear friend. A dear friend. Yes."

"Peter is not interested in my childhood," says Mrs. MacQuire.

"Quite right," says Spencer, "but I have only good to say. She has set an example, Spaulding, that other wives would do well to follow. They do not, I fear, the younger ones have the same commitment. Not anymore. Do you know young Polly Breen came to say I had a moral obligation to pay wives for services performed? Paid for pouring tea!" He shakes his head.

"Chauncy," says Mrs. MacQuire. "You have a great deal to learn."

"I only want what's right," says Spencer.

"I know that," says Mrs. MacQuire.

"If only there were more like you."

"Who?" Manning comes from nowhere, taking us by surprise.

Mrs. MacQuire freezes. I freeze too. Only Spencer smiles.

"My dear man. How good to see you! Spaulding, some tea for Mr. Manning!"

I don't look at him. I pass a cup to Mrs. MacQuire. She doesn't take it. She stares at Manning. He stares back, smiling. His eyes are dark.

"I hope I'm not interrupting."

"By no means," says Spencer. "No. We were discussing the present status of the faculty wife."

"Ah," says Manning. Spencer coughs. His tea spills into the saucer.

"How thoughtless," he says. "Forgive me, please."

"Of course," says Manning. He looks at Mrs. MacQuire, who looks at him. "Melissa," he says, "I would appreciate some tea." He smiles.

She stands so still she might be carved from wood. "You," she says. Without another word, she leaves. We watch her go.

"Did I say something to offend?" says Manning. When he looks at me, I look away.

"Naturally not," says Spencer.

"Did I?" says Manning, to me, as if Spencer hadn't spoken.

"How would I know?"

"Spaulding!" Spencer says.

"Never mind," says Manning. "He looks exhausted. Have you been sleeping?"

"He ran the best race of his life this afternoon."

"If I could be excused, sir."

"The best," says Spencer. "Thanks to him the title's won."

Manning doesn't move. He stands there, blocking.

"Ran as if the fiends of hell were after him," says Spencer, chuckling.

"I hope they weren't," says Manning.

I look at Spencer.

"I really have to go, sir."

"Naturally not," says Spencer. "He was running for the school. Weren't you, Spaulding?"

He looks at me and so does Manning, and suddenly I feel everything closing in. When I close my eyes, I see the river, a sheet of foil under sky. I see Cate running down the hill toward me.

I open my eyes. Manning leans toward me. Close.

"Are you all right?" So close I feel his breath against my cheek. I look at him.

"You did it." Whispering.

There is something in his eyes.

"Would that make it easier?" His voice is quiet. His hand is on my arm.

"I don't mind telling you, Oliver. Spaulding and I had a good talk this morning. We are both behind you."

I close my eyes again. Eyes closed, I see her. Running. She can't see me, crouched by the river in the reeds.

"And when the dust settles . . ."

"Peter," says Manning.

"Peter?" she said. Calling. I heard what she was feeling in her voice. I heard. But I stayed hidden. I knew what she was going to ask. It was too late. I knew what I was going to do.

"I trust, Oliver, you will not let us down. Let down the school."

"Peter," says Manning. "You must sit down. Please!"

"Please," said Cate, and birds rose, flapping, from the trees. Flapping on their dusty wings.

"Perhaps some tea," says Spencer. "A good hot cup."

"Hold on," says Manning.

But to what? So many birds. The sky moved, and when it did the earth moved too. Under my feet I felt it spinning.

I feel it now.

"Don't try to talk," says Manning.

He is so close. His eyes are gleaming. In slow motion I pull away. The room tips.

"I didn't . . ."

"Don't talk," says Spencer, as if afraid of what I know. What I might say.

I shake my head. "I . . ."

"Don't!"

His hand is on my arm again. I try to shake it off. I can't. My stomach heaves.

"Sick," I say.

And then I am.

ELEVEN

 "LET GO!"

He doesn't let go. His hand is pressed against my forehead. My head hurts and bright lights flash before my eyes.

He won't let go. He leads me across the room and down the hall. The smell of vomit follows up the stairs. Even breathing through my nose, I smell it. My stomach rises. "I'm not . . ."

"Don't," says Manning. "Don't try to talk."

Oh God. Does he remember?

"Don't talk," he said. Lifting me onto the infirmary bed. The bed was hard. The sheets were cold. The walls were green.

Now they are white. He doesn't lift me. I lie down, carefully. Through the far window I see the sun roll like an orange along the chapel roof. Flaming. It hurts.

"It hurts," I said. My voice trembled, but I didn't cry. I was twelve, too old for crying. He laid his hand against my cheek. "I know," he said.

He did know. I felt it in his fingers, heard it in his voice. "I'll be right back. I'm going to call." He left. I lay there, trembling. Snow brushed against the window. I watched it fall.

"Hold on," he says. "I'll go find Mary."

Does he remember?

102

"Hold on," he said. He held the phone. "Your mother. I called to let her know."

"Darling," she said. "I'd come, you know that, but Robert says . . ."

"It's OK." I closed my eyes, drawing my knees up to my chest to ease the hurt.

"He says it's such a simple operation. He had his appendix out when he was nine. There's nothing to it."

"OK."

"Darling, if you were closer . . ."

"OK, OK."

"Oh darling, I knew you'd understand."

Behind her, I heard Robert talking, heard her listening.

"Darling, Robert says you're old enough to manage on your own."

With my eyes closed I could see her, in Robert's apartment on Lake Shore Drive. I'd been there once, walked through the rooms with Bets, who held my hand. She was four. Our footsteps echoed. "Where's your room, Peter?" she said. "There's a room for everyone but you."

"Darling," said my mother, whispering. "He needs me here."

"I know that," I said. I did. He needed her. I knew my father never had.

"Your father," she said.

"In Europe, skiing."

"That's right," she said, and from the way she said it, I could tell it didn't matter anymore.

"Here's Bets," my mother said. "She wants to talk to you."

Waiting, I heard the phone being passed from hand to hand.

"Peter," said Bets. Her voice was small and hoarse. It filled the phone. "Where are you? When are you coming home?"

"Where's home?" I tried to laugh. I couldn't. It hurt. My stomach hurt.

"You know. With me."

"I'm going to the hospital."

I heard her breathing. "Shots?"

"Maybe."

"Are you going to die?"

"That's enough," said Robert. He took the phone. I heard Bets crying.

"Let's not make too much of this," said Robert. "There's no need to upset her."

"No, sir."

"There's no need to be sarcastic either. You'll be in good hands with Dr. Davis. I've told him to call in case of trouble."

"Wait," said my mother. "I haven't said . . ."

The line went dead. I held the phone against my ear. I heard a ringing, like the sea. My fingers ached but I held tight. My stomach hurt. My eyes were closed. I felt the tears. I tried to stop them. I felt them sliding down my cheeks. "I'm sorry," I said.

"It's all right," Manning said. "I'm here."

"Well, look who's here!" says Mary. "Long time no see."

I try to smile. I can't.

"He needs rest," says Manning. "If necessary, strap him to the bed."

Mary laughs. "It won't be. We're old friends."

She leans above me, and I smell starch and alcohol. Clean, sharp smells.

"Don't you look like death warmed over! Lift up."

When I lift, the room starts spinning. One hand holds my head, the other slaps the pillow. Hard. "Holy mother, soaked through already!" She flips the pillow.

"He's been under some pressure lately." Manning stands at the foot of the bed. Hands in his pockets, he's spinning too.

"Pressure!" Mary snorts. "Lie down."

Her hand holding, I lie back slowly. I close my eyes. The spinning stops. "Pressure, pressure. What else is new?" One hand is on my forehead. "Hold still." The other hand slips a thermometer under my tongue. Cool and slippery, it tastes of alcohol. "Pressure," she says. "Pressure cooker's more like it. I told the Reverend more than once, all this pressure; it's the healthy juices get squeezed out, not the others."

"I couldn't agree more," says Manning.

"You!" Mary binds her fingers to my wrist. I feel the rapid ticking of my pulse. "You're a fine one to talk. And as for you . . ." She taps a finger against my head. "If that pulse of yours runs any faster, you won't live to see tomorrow."

She slides the thermometer from my mouth, and glares at it. "What did I tell you!" She glares at me. "Look!" I open my eyes. She waves it back and forth. All I feel is the swish of air. "Nothing," she says. "Less than nothing." Glaring. "Minute I looked at you, I knew. Pressure!" She snorts. I glance at Manning. He winks. For a moment I almost forget, and smile.

"Not your appendix anyway," she says.

"Rest," says Manning. "He needs rest."

"And I don't need anyone to tell me that, thank you very much," says Mary. She looks down. Her face goes soft. "If you didn't give us a scare that time!" She shakes her head. From under her white cap, bobby pins spring loose. "Why you didn't come in sooner . . ."

But of course she knows. And Manning knows. And I know too.

All of us knowing that I'd called my father at his office. "My stomach hurts," I said. To him.

"I see," he said. Behind him, I heard typewriters pounding. "What have you eaten?"

I looked outside, saw the snow begin to fall. "It's not that," I said. "It's something else. I think it might be my appendix. I was reading in my Biology book."

"No," my father said. "I doubt it."

I heard the hurry in his voice. I knew the next day he was going skiing.

"Why?" I said.

Waiting, I watched my breath make circles on the glass.

"You'd be in *real* pain," my father said.

I held the phone, and pressed my fingers to my stomach. It hurt, but I was just thirteen; I didn't know how to measure pain. Outside the snow was falling fast. "OK," I said, and I hung up.

"Some people!" Mary says. She snorts.

Manning smiles. "Mary, Rock of Ages," he says.

"Speak for yourself," says Mary. But she smiles too, her face breaking into wrinkles when she does. "You're no spring chicken either." She steps toward him. "From the look of you, you could do with some rest yourself."

I look at him. He looks the same. What does she see? "Off you go," she says. "I have to clean him up."

He doesn't move. "Shoo!" She waves her hands, large hands, the fingers rough. She is almost as tall as he is, a large strong woman. Most people seem to shrink when they get old. Not Mary. In some ways she seems larger than before. She takes him by the shoulders, turns him around. "Git!" Treating him just like a kid. "Just make sure that someone brings his things."

He doesn't seem to mind. He takes her hand, and bending, kisses it. "I appear to have no choice," he says.

"You!" says Mary, but she laughs.

"Take good care of him," says Manning. He leaves. She scowls at me.

"As if I wouldn't!"

I rise up on my elbow. "Really, there's nothing wrong . . ."

She claps her hands. Her hands are hard, but the sound is soft.

"There's enough trouble without more from you. Strip!"

106

I strip. She helps me. I suppose I should mind it, but I don't. Her hands peel clothes. Her eyes appraise me.

"You've gone and grown up." She nods, pleased, as if the growing was her doing. "Sponge bath," she says.

"I can take a shower."

I try to stand. She pushes me back down. There's no arguing with Mary. Once set in motion, she can't be stopped. "Mary is a force of nature," Manning says.

She thumps my chest. "Up here you follow orders." She disappears into the bathroom. I hear the sound of running water, the ringing of the bells for chapel. There's nothing I can do but wait. She returns with a metal bowl and a large green sponge. "Doctor's orders," she says. The sponge moves in circles across my back. Her hands are gentle. "Speaking of doctors, how's Mr. Hotshot?"

The water's warm against my skin. Hugging my knees, I close my eyes. "How would I know?"

Mary snorts. "Stepfathers! Mine used to whip me every chance he got."

"Robert never whipped me."

She snorts again. "It's your mother needs the whipping. Where was she when you needed her, I'd like to know. You tell me that!"

"She came."

"Came! Roll over." I roll over on my stomach. The sponge moves down my legs. "Came once, and after it was over." She drops the sponge into the water. "If I'd seen her I would have told her a thing or two."

"I'm glad you didn't."

"Not that it would have helped," says Mary. "That kind never listen."

"You don't know. You never met her."

"Don't have to either."

The sponging over, she rubs me dry. The towel is warm. It feels good. I feel sleepy.

"Look at me," she says.

Raising my head, I look at her. I see that, somehow, in the past six years, she's gone to bone. Her cheeks are hollow, her jaw sharp. Something twists inside me. She shakes her head.

"Death warmed over," she says.

"Thanks."

"But you'll survive." She smiles. "Sleep." She leaves the room. The sun slips off the chapel roof. I hear my breathing rise and fall.

She did come. My mother. She came, and I was waiting, had been waiting for an hour, maybe more. She was coming, but she hadn't said the time. I stood there, shivering, in fading winter light, stamping my feet against the snow.

I wore my parka but my hat and gloves were in my room. My ears burned. I held my hands against them. It didn't help. The snow squeaked underfoot. From chapel came the sound of singing. "Now the Day Is Over."

Light shone through the stained glass windows. The snow was pink. When I stamped my feet, my legs hurt, weak from lying in bed so long. "Grant to little children, visions bright . . ." I was thirteen. I sang softly, sang along. My breath was clouds. My eyes watered from the cold, but I was afraid to go inside, afraid that I would miss her, afraid that if she didn't see me, she would leave.

When she did come she took me by surprise. I don't know why when I'd been waiting. Waiting so long that maybe I'd forgotten what I was waiting for.

The cab snaked up the driveway, its yellow light shining. She took my hands. Her fingers felt like glass. "Darling, I'd hardly know you. How you've grown!"

She was so small. I didn't know her either. Fumbling in her purse to pay the driver, the coins fell spinning. "Oh, dear." I didn't bother to pick them up. "Robert thought I might get lost. That's why he had me take a cab." Her face was pink in chapel light. There was a small suitcase in her hand. "Can we go in," she said.

"Where's Bets?"

"Darling. It's so cold."

Inside the school she clutched her suitcase like a shield.

"Where's Bets?"

"Don't I get a kiss?"

I kissed her cheek. Her fur coat glistened. I smelled dead animals and roses.

"That's better," she said. "Goodness." She looked around. "It's hard to believe I'm really here."

I shifted from one foot to the other. The school was warm. From cold to hot. I started to sweat. She looked like a doll, bright-eyed, circles of color on her cheeks. A paper cutout doll that blinked.

"Can I take my coat off, darling?"

She waited until I nodded. Her dress was pink, the color of roses. A silly dress. She saw me looking. I saw her blush. "Robert thought I should make some changes." She turned around so I could see. "He picked it out. He loves to shop for me. Can you imagine?"

I didn't want to, but I could. I could see him, his doctor's hands, picking, dressing, turning her. In circles.

"Where's Bets?"

"Isn't it quiet in here, though," my mother said, smiling. I didn't smile. She cleared her throat. "It just seemed, darling, a trip at this time, just when she's beginning to adjust . . ." Smiling. Waiting for me to smile too. "Robert said you'd understand."

"You told me she was coming!" My voice cracked. I bit my lip. "I wanted to see her."

"Darling. You're still weak, aren't you, from the operation. Isn't there some place we could sit. Your room? And I do want to meet your roommate."

"You don't."

"Darling!"

"You wouldn't like him."

"Of course I will. And Mr. Manning. Hasn't he been good to you? I'd like to thank him."

"Later." She looked at me. "They're all in chapel."

"Oh." She stood there. "That's why it's so quiet." She smiled. I could feel her wishing she hadn't come. "What would you like to do?" she said.

I shrugged. "I signed out. We can go have dinner if you want."

My mother smiled. "The two of us," she said. She took my arm. "Just like old times."

The two of us had dinner down in the village at the inn where she was staying. The inn is old with low ceilings and braided onions hung on strings. "What fun," my mother said. "New England charm." I waited while she went upstairs to change her clothes. I waited, wishing I could run away.

"A table for two," my mother said. The waiter bowed. We sat at a table near the fire. My hands were cold. I held my hands toward the flames. The table was small; under it our knees were touching. I watched the fire. "You're so quiet," she said. We ordered sherry and tomato juice. "The girls send love," she said. "And Robert too."

"That's a laugh." I didn't laugh.

She pretended not to hear me. She sipped her sherry. "Isn't it quaint," she said. The fire spit. She ordered crab-meat. I ordered chicken. I wasn't hungry. The waiter left.

"He hates me. Robert hates me," I said.

"Of course he doesn't, darling." She looked away, around the room. "Such a sense of history. Perhaps if Chicago hadn't had the fire . . ." Ice tinkled in her glass. "What do you think?"

Bright-eyed, she looked at me. I didn't answer. I waited. "It's simply that he feels you're something of a disturbing influence on the girls." She smiled. "Divided loyalties, you know."

The tomato juice was thick and warm. I drank slowly, trying not to gag.

"Is that what you think too?" Inside, I felt the juice congeal.

"Of course not, darling. No." Her hands fluttered. Flames danced like feathers across her face. "It's just that, well, imagine how difficult it is for him. A bachelor all these years, and now . . . He takes it very seriously, you know, being a father."

"They have a father."

Her hands played with the silverware. I watched them, watched the silver catching light.

"I know that, darling, but, where is he? In New York City with that woman."

"There's nothing wrong with Judith."

"She doesn't like children. She told Celia. Imagine telling a child that!"

"At least she admits it."

"Peter," said my mother. "Please."

"There's not even room for me. In his apartment."

"Darling, it's my apartment too."

I laughed then. "Is that supposed to make me feel better?"

"Darling! You've always been so understanding. Even as a little boy. 'My little man.' Remember how I used to call you that?"

I couldn't look at her. I put my hands across my face. Through my fingers I saw her fork pricking at the tablecloth. The tablecloth was thick and white. The fork left tiny indentations.

"I told him, you know. I told Robert what a help you were to me, especially after your father left. I told him I didn't know what I would have done without you. I mean that, darling. Really, I sometimes think that if it hadn't been for you . . . So it's not that he doesn't understand, doesn't acknowledge all that you've done, for me, for the girls. It's

111

not that at all. It's simply, darling, that he feels it's time for you to abnegate responsibility. You have your own life to lead, he says. He says it's not healthy for so young a boy to feel such familial burden. What he wants, darling, is for you to be free."

My mother. Listening to her, I heard Robert. I saw him too, standing by her, dressed in white, a scalpel in his hand. I took my hands away, and leaned toward her.

"What do *you* want?"

"Me? Oh, darling." The waiter came toward us. She smiled, relieved. "Dinner," she said. "Lovely! You must be starving."

"I'm not hungry."

She looked down at her plate. "Fresh crabmeat. What a treat!"

My mother. I looked at her. Looking, I saw Robert, saw the soundless slicing of his scalpel as he cut into my mother's skin. Painless. There was no blood. He knew what he was doing. He sliced her open, stepped inside.

"Eat," said my mother, smiling. I ate. My knife was sharp. Pink juice oozed through crusty skin. The meat was white.

"What I want, darling, is what's best for you."

The meat was rubbery, hard to swallow. I chewed and chewed.

"But you mustn't feel unwanted. Of couse there's room. Bets has bunk beds, you know, and there's the daybed in Robert's study. Bets misses you. They all do. And your father. Why, you've got two places instead of one."

"Lucky me."

"Are you pouting, darling?"

I didn't look at her. I jabbed my fork into the crust, and pulled. Skin peeled off.

"Don't pout, darling. Please. I'm happy. I want you happy too."

Leaning forward, she caught me by surprise.

"He *loves* me!" she said. Before I had time to pull away,

112

she'd wrapped her fingers around my wrist. "He loves *me!*"

"Sure," I said. "Great."

She smiled. My mother smiled. "I knew you'd understand," she said. In candlelight her face was soft, shaped like a heart. "There's a surprise," she said. "A secret. The girls don't know yet. Robert said I ought to wait, but I want to share it with you." Smiling, she held my wrist. I felt my knuckles press her skin. "Guess," she said.

All I could do was shake my head.

"When you were little," she said, "you were so good with the girls, with all of them, but especially with Bets. I used to watch you, when you thought you were alone, the way you held her, up to your face and talked to her. She was just a baby. The way you talked to her, you were just the sweetest little thing. I loved watching you." She smiled. "I loved having babies."

"Let go."

She did. I couldn't eat. I cracked my knuckles. "Just like your father," she said. I didn't stop. She kept on smiling. Smiling, her eyes were full of tears.

"Darling," she said. "Be happy for me. I'm going to have a baby."

"A baby?" My knuckles cracked. My voice cracked too.

My mother smiled. "I knew you'd be pleased," she said. "I knew!"

TWELVE

IT'S DARK when I open my eyes. Maybe I've been sleeping. It takes a moment to remember where I am, to see that it's not really dark.

It's twilight. The sky is purple, turning black. I hear starlings chattering in the eaves. I see a shape beside the bed.

"You're awake," says Mrs. MacQuire.

She sits on a chair beside the bed, sits very straight and very still. Her hands are folded in her lap.

"How long have you been here?"

"I brought your things up." She gestures toward the bedside table. I see a neat pile of books, of clothes. Did she see the journal? I don't dare ask. I look toward the door to Mary's office. The door is open, but the room is dark.

"She's gone to get a bite to eat. I told her I'd stand guard."

"I'm not a prisoner."

"You know Mary," she says. "Are you hungry? Would you like something to eat?"

I shake my head. It's quiet. Even the starlings are settling down. Up here, on the third floor, it's almost always quiet. Not like the dorms. Quiet and dark. As a kid I used to hate the dark. In a way I'm glad she's here.

"It's funny, you know. I was thinking about my mother. I hardly ever think about her."

"Peter."

I laugh. A croak. "If I can help it." I turn to look at Mrs. MacQuire. "It's being up here again, I guess."

114

"Peter. Cate left a note."

Everything goes still. Which is funny when you think about it because everything was still before.

"It was in the box of clothes she brought me, down at the bottom, tucked inside a sweater."

I am suddenly so tired.

"You were right, Peter."

So very tired. I close my eyes.

"You were right. She didn't kill herself."

I don't say anything.

"I never thought," says Mrs. MacQuire. "It never occurred to me that . . ."

Her voice trails off. The chapel bells chime. I listen, counting. They reach eight.

"She was planning to run away. She wrote to tell me, and to say good-bye, and . . ."

"I don't want to hear!"

She leans forward. "We have to do something." Her breath is hot. I turn my face away.

"It's too late."

"Peter, we can't let him get away with this!"

"Listen, you said yourself. It's over. The report's in. You don't have any proof. There's nothing anyone can do."

"You," she says. "You can, Peter."

Her voice is low and soft, right in my ear. I don't say anything. I shake my head.

She sighs. I hear her. I hear her rise, and walk away, across the room. I don't say anything. I hear the window sliding open, feel the air.

"I remember," she says, "when I was just about your age, thinking life was unfair but at least there was something I could do about it. Before that . . ." I hear her walk toward the bathroom, hear her flicking on a light. I open my eyes. The room is half lit now, light coming from the bathroom. "There," she says. "That's better." She comes back, and sits beside the bed. She looks at me.

"My mother did not like herself very much," she says. "She did not like women. She did not like me." She smiles when she says it. "She loved my brother."

"Dana?"

"Dana." Her eyes flicker. She glances at her lap. "My father drank. He wasn't much use for anything."

"Spencer liked him."

"Oh, he was a nice man. They were friends. He had a lot of friends. But not at home."

She looks at me. It makes me nervous. I don't know why she's telling me this. I wish she'd go away.

"Dana wasn't nice though. Not as a little boy. He collected insects, bugs, you know. My mother thought it was wonderful. She was sure he'd be a scientist, or a doctor. She gave him a tiny set of instruments." She measures with her fingers. "He collected these bugs, and then he'd cut off their wings or legs and watch them struggle. When I told my mother he was torturing them, she said I couldn't possibly understand. He was a boy, perhaps a genius, and those were scientific experiments." She stops smiling. She blinks. "It was always like that. He used to perform experiments on me. He said that Mother had given him permission. So you see . . ." She blinks again, and shakes her head. "The nice thing about growing up is that you can put all that behind you. I was your age when I realized that. I was smart enough, and I could go to college, could get away, so they couldn't hurt me anymore. And that's what I did."

"I know."

"And so can you."

"I'm going to college."

"I'm not talking about college. I'm talking about now. I'm talking about taking charge."

I swallow. "What do you want me to do?"

"Not what I want, Peter. You."

I don't say anything.

"Peter, he's still planning to be headmaster, isn't he?"

"I don't know."

I don't know, but she doesn't seem to care.

"When you think about it," she says, "really think, it doesn't seem quite fair that he should end up getting everything he wants, and you know how he gets it too. He gets it by stepping on whoever's in his way. Whoever, Peter. Cate."

"You don't know that."

"I know him. I've known him for a long time, Peter. Longer than you. Fifteen years. We've been here fifteen years!" And she laughs, a breathy gasp. Her eyes aren't laughing though. And suddenly I'm scared.

"There's nothing I can do about it."

"Oh, but there is."

"There isn't. She's dead."

"Yes," says Mrs. MacQuire, "and he thinks he's won. But, Peter, you can go to Spencer. For Cate's sake, Peter." She pauses. "Go to Spencer and tell him what Manning did to you."

My face turns red. I feel blood pounding in my ears.

"I don't know what you're talking about."

She smiles. "Shhh. I'm not blaming you. Don't look so guilty." She touches her finger to my cheek. I turn away. "If you tell Spencer . . ."

"There's nothing to tell."

"I know you loved him, Peter." Her voice is soft. I shake my head. It doesn't stop her. "It's hard, isn't it, when the person you love turns out not to be worth loving after all."

Is she talking about Manning? Is she talking about Cate?

She stands up slowly. "Think about it," she says. "There's not much time. You're the only person Spencer will believe." She kisses my cheek. Her lips are cool. "I'll be back to see you in the morning."

Before I can say a word, she's gone.

117

* * *

Mary smells of apple crisp. Her cap is crooked. White wings tilted, it looks like a bird about to fly. Hands on her hips, she stands there, frowning.

"And where is she, I'd like to know?"

"She just left. I told her she could."

Mary snorts. "You! She should have known better than to listen to you." But she stops frowning, stomps over to the window, and bangs it down. The glass rattles. She crosses back to me. Her fingers circle my wrist. She clicks her tongue against her teeth. "I never!" she says. She disappears into her office, returns with a paper cup, and two white pills. She hands them to me.

"What's this?"

"Ours not to reason why. Down the hatch."

She watches me swallow. Then she sits. From a bag by her side, she pulls out knitting, a large striped band that runs off of her lap and onto the floor. I look at it.

"What's that?"

"Won't know until I'm finished," says Mary.

"Listen, you don't have to stay with me."

She doesn't answer. She doesn't move. Only her hands move, the needles clicking. A friendly sound. The way she sits, legs apart, broad feet planted, reminds me of a mountain.

"How long have you been here?"

"Too long." She snorts. "What a question."

"I need to know."

"You need to sleep."

"Have things changed a lot?"

"You know better! Things always change." She frowns. "And if they don't, they should." The needles click.

"Were you here when Manning started?"

"Maybe," says Mary. "Maybe not."

"Mrs. MacQuire?"

"Mr. Nosy Parker."

118

"Mary, I need help."

Her needles stop. "Now that's the truth," she says. She says it kindly. "Never mind." Her needles start to move again. "There's others need it more than you."

I wait for her to tell me. She doesn't. The needles click faster than before.

"Mrs. MacQuire?"

"It takes all kinds." She sniffs.

"You like her."

"What's liking have to do with it? She's got her troubles, just like the rest of us."

"When she first came . . ."

"Young enough to spread on toast, and eat for breakfast. Pretty too. Logan, now, he was a charmer. I've known him since he was twelve."

"He went to school here, didn't he?"

The needles stop. "If I were you, I'd concentrate on the now of things. Not then."

"I'm trying to understand."

"Sometimes," says Mary, "it's better not to."

"Lying up here. There's nothing else to do."

"You ought to sleep."

"I remember before, when I was up here, with my appendix. All those days. There was nothing to do but think and think."

"One thing to think," says Mary, "no matter what. They saved your life back then. Between them. She came here to see you every single day."

"They hate each other."

"Naturally I deserve some credit too."

When I look at her, she smiles. A crusty smile. What she reminds me of is bread. French bread with a hard crust, and a soft inside. I smile too.

"You know more about this place than anyone."

Mary shrugs, pleased, trying not to show it. "The truth is up here I got a bird's-eye view. Inside and out. Eyes and ears and a mouth that closes. That's all you need. That, and to have been here since Creation."

I close my eyes. "Six years is long enough."

"More than enough," she says. She sighs. "You've found yourself some trouble, haven't you?"

I don't say anything. I lie still, listen to the needles clicking.

"I could use a glass of water," I say. My mouth is dry; it hurts to swallow.

"Mary," said Manning once, "will not go gently into that good night." He said it smiling. The way he smiled, I knew he liked her. I like her too. I always have.

"You!" says Mary. She brings me a pitcherful, with ice.

"Thanks."

"Don't mention it," she says. She smiles.

The water tastes good. My throat is dry, and my head feels full of cotton wool. Maybe those pills. She stands until I've finished drinking, then settles back.

"I don't suppose there's any harm in telling you, that Logan, oh he was a charmer. Cute as a button. A smile this wide." She flicks her needle up to show me. "And an athlete! You never saw the like. Why, he'd take that ball, and tear down the field, laughing! You never saw anyone having so much fun."

"That's what he says."

"What's that?"

"The best years of his life. Here, and Harvard."

"That's right. I've seen it happen. Time and again. They come back visiting, those men, wearing their school ties, talking about the good old days." She snorts. "The *only* days, if you want my opinion. So busy looking back, they forget life moves ahead."

"But he's happy. They're happy."

"If you say so."

"I know. I've spent a lot of time over there, don't forget."

120

"I'm not forgetting anything. Don't you forget how long I've been here. I've seen it all. I saw the promise. I thought, well, if anyone can bring the best out, she's the one. Feet on the ground, that one, I thought." She shakes her head. "That's what I thought." She looks at me. "But mind you, I'm not saying it's all her fault."

My head is spinning. Is it the pills? "What?"

She shrugs. "These things happen. It's never just one. Two, or three. Or sometimes four. Oh, I could tell a thing or two. Her, now she needs to mother. Always has."

"She's a good mother. I know her children."

"Children. I'm not talking about children. I could, though, if I wanted." She looks at me, sly, laughs. "If she could she'd mother the world. It makes her feel better, there's no harm done. That's what I used to think; I'll bet she did too. Bet she was thinking what people don't know won't hurt. Maybe she's right, except she chose the wrong person to try and mother. I could have told her."

"Who?"

She blinks. "None of your business," she says.

"Mrs. Manning?"

Mary frowns. "That one. Poor thing. She needed more than mothering. Oh no, not her. It's him. It's him. Not that he isn't a charmer too, but she should have known better than to trust him. If she'd asked I could have told her. He's a rogue, that man. A rascal!" She smiles.

"Manning?"

She stops smiling. "That's for me to know."

"Not mothering. They were friends."

"Friends." She snorts. "Mothering's not the right word either." She frowns. "Stop talking now, and try and get to sleep."

"I'm not the one who's talking."

"Don't be rude." She taps her needle against my head. "And stay away from business that doesn't belong to you."

"Are you trying to tell me that they were . . . Mrs. MacQuire, and Manning . . . you know — that they were lovers!"

"You said it," Mary says. "I didn't."

"I don't believe it."

"Don't then."

"How do you know?"

"I have eyes, don't I? There's evidence. If you know where to look."

I look at her.

"It's not your fault that you got caught right in the middle. These things happen." She looks at me. "I'd say," she says, "the sooner you get out of here the better."

THIRTEEN

 IN THE DREAM Robert jabs his finger at my chest. His gray hair bristles. "The sooner you get out of here the better," he says. His voice is gravel. I hear someone crying. He takes a step toward me. I try to move. I can't. I know I'm dreaming, but it's real.

And then, just before he reaches me, I'm standing on the edge of the clearing, an ax in my hand. Now it's not a dream at all. I smell cut pine, and wild strawberries. I hear bees humming in the grass. The grass is early summer green. I feel the weight of the ax in my hand, the smooth curve of well-worn wood. I know the ax. My grandfather's, and now it's mine. This land is, too. He left it to me when he died.

The wickiup faces south, its back to the trees. Bare poles rise from its center. The thatching is green, a tight lacing of pine boughs, moss, and meadow grass. I'm afraid the wickiup is empty, afraid it's just a dream. I stand there, waiting, not daring to go closer.

A flash of blue moves across the inner entrance. I hold my breath as Cate steps into sunlight. She stands, smiling, a basket of berries in her hands. She isn't dead! Her dress is the color of the sky. The berries glitter. She's alive. The rest was the dream. I remember the baby. I'm not quite sure about the baby. Was that the dream too? The basket hides her stomach. I don't dare ask. "Stillborn," she says, her voice clear, as if she is standing beside me, not up the hill, and I think, that's all right then, that can mean still-to-be-born.

And then Cate tips the basket so the berries spill into the grass. The basket's empty. She holds it out to show me. It's like a black hole. The eye of night.

"Rise and shine," says Mary. The shade slaps up. From the way her feet hit the floor I can tell her mood is bad. In the early morning light her skin looks gray. She takes my wrist between her fingers. "I don't mind telling you," she says. But she tells me nothing. Frowning, she listens to my pulse. Under her chin, the skin hangs loose. She nods. Her fingers release me. "You'll survive."

"We can survive," I said to Cate.

"Can we?" said Cate.

"Sure." I ticked them on my fingers. "Shelter, fire, food, and water. We'll have it all."

"Peter," said Cate.

"And love," I said. I put my arms around her. "I love you." She looked at me.

I look at Mary. "Maybe I shouldn't," I say.

"What kind of talk is that? I told you once there's enough trouble without your adding to it. Sit up." I sit up slowly. I feel empty, a body filled with air. Mary bends to the bed, tugs grunting, at the sheets. "Me and my big mouth," she says. She slaps the pillows. "Lie back." She stands above me, scowling.

"She came back," she says.

Cate, I think. Cate. I swallow. "Who?"

"You know who. And if you don't you should. She cares, more than she should, and I said more than I should last night."

"Mrs. MacQuire?"

"I get lonely sometimes. That's the truth of it, but with one foot in the grave I ought to know better."

"You didn't do anything wrong."

"Not me. You. It's what you do with it that worries me."

124

She wags her finger.

"Now I'm not saying she doesn't have her problems. She wouldn't be human if she didn't. But she's been good to me. He has too but he's one who knows which side the bread is buttered. What she does she does because she thinks it's right."

"I know that."

"You might, you might not. She didn't look herself this morning. I told her to hightail it into bed. She didn't like that. Never has liked people telling her what to do. Likes to do the telling herself. Didn't like it, but she left."

"Can I leave? I feel better."

"You're staying where I can keep an eye on you. I'll bring your breakfast. If you know what's good for you you'll eat."

She starts toward the door. "Mary?" She turns, scowling. "Do you think Manning killed her?" She draws herself up straight. Her eyes snap.

"What a question!" she says. "That man saved your life!"

"I love you," I said to Cate.

"You shouldn't," she said. A week ago. A whisper. The wind riffled the water. The air was cold.

"I can. I love you."

Her hair was down, wind blowing it across her face. I couldn't see her eyes.

"Who am I?" she said.

I couldn't see her; I thought that she was joking.

"Mine," I said, joking too.

"I'm a hole in the wind," she said.

The wind blew. I held her. The sky turned pink. My hands held her, made her mine.

That's what I thought. That she was mine.

It has been three months, and maybe three is a magic number like Aunt Effie said.

This morning I had coffee with Melissa at her house. I love her house, especially the kitchen. We sat where we always sit, at the kitchen table. Logan made the table without using any nails or bolts. Dove-tailed, that's what it's called, the way the pieces slide together. Melissa told me, and I said, isn't he clever, and she said he's very good with his hands. She smiled, and I was glad to have said the right thing.

She was holding Rufus who is four years old, and home with a cold. He lay against her. His eyes were bright, like plums, but they are always like that. He sucked his thumb. He has long eyelashes, and a cowlick of dark hair that sticks up in front. A beautiful child in every way. The top of his head was under her chin. It made me think of those Russian dolls, who fit inside of each other. It made me ache inside.

The kitchen has green plants on the window sills, and a wood stove in the corner. They put it in themselves even though the house belongs to the school and the school pays for the heat. A house needs a heart, Melissa said, and in winter she always keeps it lit.

The kitchen used to be the diningroom so there is molding on the ceiling, and the windows are very large but with tiny leaded panes. Very hard to clean Melissa says, but she does clean them and I can't see anything being hard for Melissa. I really can't. I wanted to say something nice, to let her know, so I said this to her, and she said, you don't know me very well then, and I was afraid I had said the wrong thing, but she smiled, and said, never mind, it's just as well, and she took Rufus upstairs for his nap.

I sat there, thinking about her house. It's an old house really, but what she says about a heart is true. Houses are like people I think. They are meant to hold you. And then I am ashamed because I think of Oliver's house. It isn't mine because it was all there before I came. And I go from room to room, the hall, the kitchen, the study, the livingroom with the big fireplace and the ceiling from Italy, and they are all pretty, filled with pretty things, his things and his mother's,

126

but there is nothing that feels like a heart. I know it's my fault because I am so afraid of breaking things that it's hard to breathe, and I think how I would like something of my own, something to hold, and then I am ashamed because I am so lucky.

Melissa comes down, and pours more coffee, and asks how things are going. And I say how lucky I am. And I smile to show I mean it. Only she doesn't smile. She says, it's been six months now hasn't it?, and I say yes. She just looks at me.

I can never tell what she's thinking, and I am always afraid she is thinking bad things about me, which dear diary, turns out to be true! Because after she looked at me, she sighed. She was fiddling with a gold chain she wears all the time, one Oliver gave her which I know because she told me. She sighed, and she said, I have a confession to make, and I thought she was going to say the only reason she was being nice to me was because Oliver asked her to, and she really didn't want to see me anymore. I remembered his asking, and maybe I have ESP like Aunt Effie said because I was almost right. When I first met you I was very cross, she said. I thought you might have married him for his money.

I said, I didn't know he had money, and she said, and I didn't know you. So I had to say it, I had to ask. Do you like me better now? And she said, what am I going to do with you, but she smiled. So I smiled too. Is he making you happy? she said, and I said, I'm very happy. I couldn't tell from her eyes if she believed me but I was telling her the truth. I am happy. She makes me happy. And then she asked why I married him, and I said because he asked me, and she laughed, and said, does anyone ever get married for the right reasons?, and I said, you. She didn't answer. She said, if he treats you badly, and I said, oh no, he's very good to me, and she said, if he does, and I said, if he does then I deserve it.

She was quiet then. Cate, she said, where did you come from? I wasn't sure what she meant. I thought about Aunt

127

Effie, her boy's galoshes, her singing, and the traveling roads.
But I couldn't tell her what I didn't know. I was ashamed
of not having any place to belong to. So I said, orphanage,
and may God forgive me, because she sucked in her breath,
slowly, and said, so! and then she stood up, and came around
the table and she put her arms around me, and she held me.
She held me, dear diary, and she said, it's the lion and the
lamb, isn't it. She stroked my hair. She said, never mind,
never mind, the way a mother would. We'll think of something,
she said. Maybe God will forgive me because it wasn't a whole
lie. I never did have a mother, a real mother. I only had
Aunt Effie. But I said, you won't tell Oliver, will you. She
said, about what?, and I said the orphanage. Not if you don't
want me to, she said.
   So you see, dear diary, she really is my friend!

Mary brings me breakfast, coffee, a fried egg, burnt toast,
juice on a metal tray. She lays the tray on my legs.
   "You look worse than before," she says.
   She looks the same, crusty and old. I shake my head. "I
don't know what anything means anymore."
   She snorts. "I'd like to know who does," she says. "Eat
up. Stay put. I'm off to get prescriptions."
   I do eat. Slowly. The toast is bitter. I hold it on my tongue
to soften. The question is: if he didn't kill her, then who
did? It's not the only question, of course. To be or not to
be. That is the question. The question is, be what? It's very
quiet, and I am all alone. I eat, not because I'm hungry, but
because I know I should. The coffee is cold, but I drink it
anyway. I think of it as substance, something to fill me.
   My plate is empty. I slide the tray off my legs. When I
get up, the floor rocks, the way it does when I've been sick.
I am careful to walk slowly so I don't fall. I walk to Mary's
office, and I close the door. The telephone is on the desk,
the desk cluttered with paper, letters, pens. A Harlequin
romance lies by the phone next to a battery of syringes resting

in a glass jar filled with alcohol. I smell the alcohol. Within the clutter is a sense of order.

I sit, glad to sit, and holding the phone on my lap, I dial, collect. Surprised I remember the number, but Judith doesn't seem surprised. "Hey kiddo, what's up?" she says before she even accepts the call. Her voice is gravelly, the way it always is in the early morning. Just hearing it, I feel better, and worse. She's alive and well, but she's down there, in New York. I want her here.

"Not much," I say.

Her laugh is a short explosion of exhaled breath. She coughs. "You shouldn't smoke so much."

"You and your father." She sounds amused. "So." I hear her swallowing. Coffee. Every day, all morning, she drinks coffee. "You call me collect at work to tell me that?"

"Why not?" I swing my legs up onto the desk. My feet are bare. "Maybe I just wanted to hear your cheery voice."

"I'm never cheery. Why the hell aren't you in class?"

"I'm cutting."

She laughs. "Tell me something I believe."

"Actually, I'm in the infirmary." I twist the cord around my finger.

"Sick?" says Judith. "Is that why we haven't heard from you? We've tried to call, you know."

"I've been busy."

"Busy being sick?"

"Just busy."

"We left messages. You might have called us back."

"I'm fine. Really."

"There are times when I could strangle you," says Judith.

"I thought I'd better check, make sure you were still there."

"I'm here, kiddo, in the flesh."

"Good."

She laughs. "I love you too, kiddo, but I haven't got all day."

"I know."

"So you better tell me. What's going on?"

I tip back in my chair, and stare up at the ceiling.

"Sometimes it's hard to believe there's a real world out there."

"There is," says Judith. "Here I am, in the flesh, and smoking like a chimney. I've also got an author breathing down my neck."

"Do you remember meeting Mrs. Manning?"

"Are you kidding? You think that's something I'd forget?"

My finger with the cord around it is throbbing. I hold it up. The cord is tight.

"Pouring tea at Parents' Weekend, right?"

"I guess."

The tip of my finger is white. In the center is a small pink scar. The fishhook.

"Pouring tea," says Judith. "I swear to God. Someone should write a novel about that place. Except nobody'd believe it. Really, sometimes I think it's a miracle you managed to survive."

"She didn't."

But Judith doesn't hear me.

"I swear to God," she says. "That place is a gold mine for some budding anthropologist. A hundred years of civilization under glass. A bell jar. That Spencer! Wonderful Spencer!" She laughs. "I told your father Dunster reminds me of the Tasaday, remember that tribe? In the Philippines, I think. Completely isolated for hundreds of years. He didn't find me very funny. The point is, I said, is that what you've got in Dunster is the world in microcosm. Every human foible known to man served up under glass. A magnifying glass."

"Actually they've discovered the Tasadays were frauds."

"Even better," says Judith. She laughs. "Anyway, sorry. Where were we?"

"Mrs. Manning."

130

"Speaking of glass," says Judith. "My God. Poor thing. She was pathetic. Is she still pathetic?"

"She's dead." I hear her take a breath. A deep breath.

"I'm sorry," she says. "You were trying to tell me, and there I was being flip. Your father hates it when I do that."

"It's OK."

"It isn't, but anyway, go on, tell me."

And so I tell her, tell her what Spencer told me, the fall from the bridge, the blow to the head, the autopsy. My finger starts to throb. I stare at it.

"Autopsy?" says Judith.

"They always do."

"And?"

"They said it was suicide."

"Suicide," says Judith. I hear her lighter snap as she lights a cigarette, hear her inhale. "Poor thing," she says.

"Not 'thing.' "

"Sweetheart, I'm sorry. A figure of speech. How is Manning taking it?"

"How do you think?"

"You sound angry, kiddo."

I don't say anything. I sit, listening to the silence. She does too. I hear her, listening.

"Peter?" she says. Her voice is careful now. "Why did she do it? Do you know? Did she leave a note?"

"Did I tell you she was pregnant?"

"No," says Judith. She says it slowly. "No, you didn't." From the way she says it, I can tell she knows; it doesn't matter; I was going to tell her anyway. I close my eyes.

"It was my fault."

"Come again."

"It was all my fault! Everything."

"Oh, baby."

"I mean it, Judith."

"Kiddo, how many times do I have to tell you. You didn't make the world."

131

"You know the land Grandpa left me in his will. Up in Vermont?"

"I know he left it to you."

"We were going up there, in June. We were going to live up there, the two of us."

I hear her listening, thinking.

"Peter," she says, "do you want us to come up?"

"No! I want to tell you! It would have worked out too. You know the stuff I learned at Outward Bound. I could have taken care of her. We would have been OK."

"Is this what you were trying to tell me in March?"

"It wouldn't have made any difference if I had. It had already happened by then anyway."

"It?"

"She was already pregnant. Only . . . only I didn't know. She didn't tell me."

"Is that why she killed herself? Because she was pregnant?"

"She wanted a baby more than anything in the world, only . . ." I try a laugh; it comes out choking. "I didn't know that either, I guess."

"So why did she kill herself? Does anybody know?"

I am careful to keep my eyes closed.

"How do you know she killed herself?"

"Sweetheart, because you told me she did."

"I didn't. I told you the autopsy results. That's all." She's quiet. "You know this school," I say. "Do you really think they'd like a murder on their hands?"

"Peter, I can imagine Manning as capable of many things, but . . ."

"Who's talking about Manning?"

"But," she says, as if I hadn't spoken, "for him to kill his wife because he discovered she was planning to run . . ."

"She wasn't."

That stops her. "What?"

"She wasn't. She told me she'd changed her mind."

132

"I see," says Judith. "In that case she deserves more credit than I've been giving her."

"Is that supposed to be funny?"

"Not at all. I'm just trying to figure out what really's been going on."

I don't say anything.

"Peter, I can't help if you don't tell me. You're not telling me everything, are you?"

What gets me is the gentleness in her voice. She's hardly ever gentle. My throat tightens. I know that if I try to talk, my voice will crack. Anyway there's nothing left to say. I hang up, quietly, and sit, holding. After a moment the phone starts ringing. I knew it would. But I'm not ready to answer. Yet.

FOURTEEN

 PARENTS' WEEKEND is always in the fall, always in October. For two days the place is swarming with tweed sportscoats, and sweaters in pink and green. For two days Dunster smells of perfume. Most parents come back year after year. Don't ask me why. How can they stand the endless speeches, sports, the awful food? My parents couldn't. Who could blame them, and anyway, it was fine with me.

So when my father called last fall, and said that he and Judith were coming, thinking of coming is what he said, he took me by surprise.

"It's our last chance," he said. "Your Sixth Form year."

"It's stupid," I said. "You'd have a lousy time."

"Well, in that case, if that's the way you feel . . ."

Only he didn't get to finish. "My turn," said Judith. She took the phone. "Sorry," she said. "Like it or not, we're coming."

They came.

They came on Saturday, after the game, in time for tea.

"I *am* glad," said Mrs. MacQuire, smiling, shaking hands, first with my father, then with Judith. Judith grinned. "Me too," said Judith.

"I'm sorry you missed the game. He played so well. We won, you know?"

"So I gather," my father said.

He stood, pressed up against the Common Room wall. The room was crowded, his face was tight. His smile was more a grimace. He licked his lips. I closed my eyes, hoping that when I opened them he'd be gone.

"My father doesn't like football," I said.

He licked his lips again. "It's contact sports," he said.

"That's what I mean."

He looked at me. He's got this thin face, my father, and this haunted look. Fatter, at least softer since he married Judith, but he's still thin. Even with all the noise around us I could hear his knuckles cracking. He looked so miserable that I almost could feel sorry for him. Almost. Not quite. It wasn't my fault he was here.

"I understand," he said to Mrs. MacQuire, "you've been very good to Peter." As if I were some charity case.

"I don't know about that," said Mrs. MacQuire. "He's been good to me. To us. The children love him."

I shoved my hands into my pockets. My face turned red. "Can we please talk about something else?"

"What *are* you talking about?" said Manning, slipping in beside me.

"Children," said Mrs. MacQuire. He glanced at her. She turned to Judith. "Oliver doesn't have much use for children, I'm afraid."

"I'm afraid I never have either," said Judith, laughing. "Not babies anyway."

Manning laughed too. He shook hands, first with my father, then with Judith. "Perhaps we should have started younger," he said.

"Perhaps," said Judith. Her eyes were bright. Her hair, sparked by static, sprang from her head like coiled wire. "I understand that since we saw you last you've acquired a wife."

Manning nodded. "I have a wife." He looked at Mrs. MacQuire. "Where is she?"

She looked at him. "Pouring tea," she said.

"Ah," said Manning. "Yes." He smiled at Judith. "You'd like to meet her?"

Judith grinned. "You guessed it."

"Judith," said my father. Warning.

Manning laughed. "It's quite all right. I understand. She's lovely, if I do say so myself."

"Perhaps," he said to Judith, "Peter's told you something."

"Nothing except that you were married."

"I imagine it came as something of a surprise," said Manning, "but he's been very kind. He helped her plant a garden last spring."

"I am not kind," I said.

"Peter," said my father.

"I was asked."

Mrs. MacQuire took my arm. "Shh," she said. I felt her fingers press my skin. "Never mind, never mind," she said. She said it softly. I saw Judith watching. I pulled my arm away. I saw Manning watching too.

"You've been kind," my father said. To Manning. He cleared his throat. "I want to thank you for all you've done." He jerked his head in my direction, not looking at me, as if I wasn't there.

"My pleasure," said Manning.

"For all you've done," my father said. "Above and beyond the call of duty."

"Not duty," said Manning. He smiled at my father, he smiled at me. I looked away, looked at my father. Judith took my father's arm, and leaned against him. "Davey," she said, rubbing her cheek against his sleeve. My father smiled, a real smile.

"Whatever," he said to Manning. "We're grateful."

"But so am I," said Manning. He turned, catching me by surprise. Before I could move, he reached out, touched my cheek.

136

"I love him." He said it quietly. He didn't smile.

"I see," said my father. "Of course."

But of course he didn't. What had he ever seen? His face flushed, and he coughed. I knew exactly what he thought.

Judith held his arm. "Let's get some tea," she said. She said it to him, but she looked at me, a silent look, as if asking me to understand.

"An excellent idea," said Manning. "Perhaps afterward you'll come up to the house for something stronger."

"I'm afraid you're too late, Oliver," said Mrs. MacQuire.

"Melissa asked us first," said Judith.

"A pity," said Manning. He looked at Mrs. MacQuire, and I got the feeling he was waiting for an invitation.

"Judith would like to meet Cate," she said.

"Ah yes," said Manning. And turning, he led the way.

She stood behind the table, all alone. As soon as she filled one cup, she'd take another. I heard the cups rattling on their saucers as she passed them to the waiting hands. Her hands were trembling. Head bent, she moved from cup to cup. I saw her chewing on her lip.

"Darling," Manning said. He said it softly, but her head jerked up, eyes filled with something that looked like fear. Something in my stomach turned over. She tried to smile.

"Oh," she said. A gasp. She held a cup in both hands, straight in front of her.

"Pass it, darling," said Manning in a voice I knew from class, a voice he used when he was bored, or mad, each word spoken slow and clear with no inflection.

Smiling, she bit her lip. "Oh yes," she said. "Yes." She did, and then she stood there, twisting her fingers. It's funny. I didn't know her then at all, but I remember hoping that Judith wouldn't notice she bit her nails.

"We'd like some tea," said Manning, smiling. "If you can manage."

"Of course she can," said Mrs. MacQuire, stepping in.

"Melissa!" said Cate. "I didn't see you." Her hair was

up, but a strand had fallen. She smiled. Her eyes went bright. Her hand brushed the strand back from her face. It drifted down. "Polly was supposed to be here too," she said. "Helping, but . . ."

"Never mind," said Mrs. MacQuire. "I'm here."

"Peter's here," said Manning. "He'll lend a hand."

"Oh," said Cate. Laughing, a short nervous giggle. Her hand pushed at the strand of hair. Hold still, for God's sake, I wanted to say. Hold still.

She glanced at me. "That would be nice," she said. She glanced at Mrs. MacQuire. Her eyes saying something. What?

"I'll help, Oliver," said Mrs. MacQuire. "I said I would." She started to move past him, behind the table. He stopped her with his hand.

"Peter would be delighted," he said.

What could I say? They were all watching. So was Cate.

"You don't have to," she said, whispering.

"I want to," I said.

She smiled. Her hand kept moving to her hair.

What I wanted was to hold her hand, and keep it still, to stop them staring.

"Judith, and David, darling. Peter's stepmother, and father."

"I'm very glad to meet you," she said.

"Me too," said Judith, grinning. I hated her then, hated the way she looked at Cate, the way people look at animals in a zoo. "What a hideous job," she said. She touched a teacup with her finger.

"Yes," said Cate. She blushed. "No, really, it isn't. Except when it's crowded. Like this. And then . . ." She looked at Mrs. MacQuire.

"You're doing fine," said Mrs. MacQuire. "Here." She handed her a cup. "Why don't you start with this."

She did. We poured the tea. Behind us, coming through the windows, I felt the sun. The air was warm, and in the study it was hot. I thought about the river, remember wishing I was there. I was one month into my Sixth Form year, and every day I went down to the river. Every day, mostly at dawn, I went, to get away, to be alone. At least that's what I'd always thought.

She stood beside me. When she reached across me for a teacup, her arm brushed mine.

"I'm sorry," she said, whispering, as if she thought that she'd done something wrong.

I looked at her. I really looked. I saw a green dress and a necklace of blue stones. I saw a pale face and frightened eyes. And suddenly being at the river didn't seem to matter anymore.

"It's OK," I said. Because it was.

The others got their tea, and moved away. We stood alone. I saw Spencer working through the crowds, working his way toward my parents. I saw Judith, smiling, lean toward Mrs. MacQuire. Her voice is low but forceful, and even when she doesn't mean it to, it carries. "I thought he only collected antiques," she said. She said it quietly enough but even through the rising voices, I heard. I hoped that Mrs. Manning hadn't. I glanced at her. Her eyes were on me, pleading. I couldn't stand it.

"I like your necklace," I said.

"Do you," she said. "Do you really?"

I nodded. I really did. She smiled then. She looked so pleased. "I picked it out myself," she said. "But Oliver says I have no taste."

Her voice was soft. My stomach tightened.

"What does he know," I said.

Her eyes flickered past me, to see if he was listening. He wasn't.

"A lot," she said with her nervous smile.

"He doesn't," I said. He didn't. He didn't know what I had just discovered, just discovered that all month I'd been going to the river, not to be alone at all. I went to the river to wait, for her.

"We better keep pouring," said Cate. Whispering. I looked

139

at her. "Spencer," she said. "He's coming over." Whispering. As if we shared some secret.

"Well, well," said Spencer, beaming. "What have we here!"

"Well, well," says Spencer. "What have we here!" He stands, squinting, in the doorway. "Not sleeping, are you?"

If I was I wouldn't be now. But I don't say it. I've pulled the shades. The room is dark, and he can't see my face.

"No, sir."

"Splendid!" He walks toward me. "There you are." He bends, stooping, to see if it's really me, then lowers himself onto the chair. His knees creak. "I confess to feeling older than I would like."

"Yes, sir."

"Do you mind if we have some light?" He doesn't wait for an answer. He turns it on. He blinks at me. "Better than yesterday," he says. "At any rate, not so green around the gills."

He frowns, his eyebrows bristling. Since yesterday his hair's been cut. Before, it was a crew cut; now he's almost bald. Through gray bristles his scalp gleams pink.

"I confess you gave us quite a fright. Your stepmother called, you know. Asked me to check in on you. I told her I was coming anyway." He frowns. "Apparently, Spaulding, you did not tell her about the race."

"Race, sir?"

"Yes, she was quite concerned, that is, until I explained to her that you had won the meet for us yesterday, at some cost to yourself. Even so, I am not sure she was entirely convinced."

"No, sir."

"She asked that you not be left alone for the time being. I could only comply."

"I'm OK, sir."

"Naturally, Spaulding, yes. Of course you are."

But he doesn't sound convinced. He peers at me.

"We need to have a talk," he says. "Yes." He clears his throat. But he doesn't talk. He clears his throat again. I've seen him, when he thinks no one is looking, spit, aiming out his study window at a flower, and smile when he hit his mark. "Yes," says Spencer. "Well." He laces his fingers together, and stares at them. "A slight digression perhaps, but it was left unclear, the exact nature of the information you relayed to your stepmother that was causing her undue concern?"

"I didn't tell her much, sir."

"I am glad to hear it, Spaulding. Very glad. It would distress me considerably to discover any of the information discussed yesterday, in confidence, Spaulding, bandied about, especially beyond the confines of the school."

"Yes, sir."

"I received, unfortunately, the distinct impression, Spaulding, that your stepmother does not think too highly of this school, this institution. Or, I'm afraid, of me."

"The institution, sir."

Spencer lifts his head, slowly, and looks at me. There is something in the slow uncertain lifting that makes me think of Bets. Bets as a baby. There is something that makes me want to cup my hand to the back of his head, and hold it steady.

"I would hate to think," says Spencer, "that I had, however unwittingly, done something to offend."

"She likes you," I say.

Spencer blinks. "Does she. Does she indeed?" His voice quavers, wanting to believe, not quite daring. The question is why does he care?

I nod. "She does," I say. "She told me."

She did tell me, told me that day of Parents' Weekend when she first met him. "Spencer," she said, "is priceless. A perfect treasure."

I thought at first that she was kidding.

"He's a fool," I said.

141

"What's wrong with that?" said Judith.

I laughed. "Come off it!"

She shook her head. "There are fools, and there are fools, kiddo. Read *The Idiot*, read *Lear*."

"She told you, did she?" Spencer clears his throat. "Well, well. Imagine that." His eyes are shy.

The funny thing is I like him too. Funny because I can't think of one good reason why I should.

"Well now," he says. "Down to business, I'm afraid. It is not my intention to tire you, but certain disclosures have come to light. Spaulding, I need your help."

He straightens so I straighten too, lifting up against the pillows. Easier to take whatever's coming if I'm not lying down. He pulls a letter from his inside pocket. "Edwards," he says, "has, most unfortunately, brought me the promised proof." He taps his nail against the envelope. The nail is yellow, thick, ridged like a beetle's back. I remember the beetle, trapped in my room, the day I heard that Cate was dead.

I look down at the floor.

"A letter," says Spencer, "written by Manning, and sent to you."

I look at him. "Where did he get it?"

"I did not ask, Spaulding, though I am afraid, yes, it was acquired by devious means. However, I'm sure you understand that, under the circumstances, I had no choice but to accept it."

I look at the envelope, the familiar cream-colored paper, the same sure, slanting hand. *"Peter,"* it says.

"I also hope you understand that I had no choice but to read it." He sighs. "Yes. But I am sure there is a perfectly acceptable explanation, and the whole matter may be laid to rest, once and for all."

He holds his hand toward me. "Edwards informs me he has made a Xerox in case he feels it necessary to take matters

142

into his own hands. You understand what I'm saying, Spaulding?"

"Edwards is a bastard, sir."

"We must remember, Spaulding, not to judge harshly." But his voice trails off. I hear him sigh. "Take it," he says. I take the letter. He leans back, waiting.

"I have to tell you something, sir."

"Good heavens, boy. Not yet. Prepare yourself."

"I've never seen this letter in my life."

"Spaulding, Spaulding." His face sags. "That will not help."

"It's the truth, sir."

It is the truth. I wish it wasn't. Holding it, I know, know it is the letter I was waiting for. To think that Edwards had it, all these years. . . .

"He must have stolen it from my mailbox, sir."

"Come, come, Spaulding. A man's reputation is at stake."

"I know that, sir."

I do know. Have I been blaming him all these years? For nothing?

"I'm glad to hear it. Read first, then be the judge. I am depending on you, Spaulding, to clarify the ambiguities. I have chosen to come to you first, to spare him, if I can, any additional stress."

"Yes, sir. But sir, if I never got the letter . . ."

"Spaulding, Spaulding. Please. Surely in six years you have received more than one letter from the man."

"Yes, sir." He waits. "I burned them all."

"Ah." His eyes widen. "Under the circumstances I suppose it's for the best." He looks relieved.

"That's not why I did it, sir."

"Never mind. The less said now the better. Read the letter, Spaulding. Then we'll talk. I'm sure there's a perfectly logical explanation." He stands up, slowly. "I should warn you, Spaulding, that what he writes about . . . is . . .

delicate, yes." He looks down, glowering. "Love, Spaulding, he writes of love."

I swallow. "Yes, sir."

"A delicate subject. In a school like this especially so. I am not a fool, Spaulding. I am aware what misconceptions can arise, yes, when a master befriends a student. Don't think I'm not."

"Yes, sir. No, sir."

"Tell me something, Spaulding. Do you know what love is?"

"Love, sir?"

"You heard me."

"I'm not sure, sir, what kind you mean."

"Nonsense. There's only one kind. You ought to know that. Love is forgiveness, Spaulding. As God forgives us, so we . . ." He doesn't finish. He bows his head, as if in prayer; and then he leaves.

FIFTEEN

I WAS THIRTEEN when I saw the shrink. I saw him twice. "What frightens you the most?" he said. I said the dark. It wasn't true. Silence frightened me even more.

In silence I hold the letter in my hand.

My dear Peter,

This is a difficult letter to write for several reasons, but I will give you only one: I love you.

I love you, Peter, and because I do, I must let you go. Can you understand that? For my sake I hope you understand that I am doing this for you. It will not be easy, for either of us.

Now I know what you are thinking, Peter. You are thinking that this letter is a direct result of what happened between us last night. You are probably thinking that what happened should never have happened. You are thinking it is all your fault.

Do you see how well I know you? It is because I know you that I love you, and because I love you that I let you go.

What happened last night, Peter, is nothing to be ashamed of. You should not be ashamed of anything that has happened between us.

We have known each other for four years now, and I trust there is no harm in telling you that you have meant more to

*me, Peter, than any student, any person I have ever encoun-
tered. You have a purity of vision that I envy.*

*You must not suppose that in the two years left to us I will
cease to care. I will cherish the memory of last night, of the
last four years as I will continue to cherish you. As I hope,
Peter, you will continue to cherish me, but from a distance
that is safe for both of us.*
Yours, always,
O. A. M.

It's funny, you know. What I remember most is silence.
Silence is louder than any sound. I remember, when my
father left, my mother didn't say a word. For three days she
lay in bed, staring at the ceiling. She didn't talk. She didn't
eat. I fed my sisters, sent them off to school. I waited for my
father to call. I waited for her to speak, tell me what had happened, and why. She didn't though. My father didn't either.

Silence speaks. I heard it then. I hear it now. Carefully I
fold the letter, slide it back into the envelope, get out of
bed. I figure it's important to keep on moving. I'm not sure
why. I walk, with the letter, over to the window. My legs
are shaking. I pull up the shade. Pressing my forehead against
the glass, I look down at the quad. There's not much to see.
Green grass, and roses. Nothing moves except the flash of
water coming from the dolphin's mouth. Listening, I hear
silence.

What I remember is the waiting, waiting for someone,
anyone, for Manning to tell me, what? That everything would
be all right?

There was that night; and then there was the morning. It
was in the morning that I waited. And waited, but he didn't
come. I went to him. It was June, and school was almost
over. I looked through the glass partition in his office door,
and saw him sitting behind his desk. Head bent, correcting
papers. I couldn't believe he looked the same. He didn't
see me. But I saw him slip his hand inside his jacket pocket,

146

take out a comb. He combed his hair, smoothing it flat with his hand, slipping the comb back into the pocket when he was done. I couldn't believe that nothing showed. I turned to leave and then he saw me.

"Peter," he said. He wasn't smiling. He looked at me. "You got it," he said. He said it softly. It wasn't a question. Got what? I couldn't ask because I thought I knew, knew that he was talking about the night before, that looking at me he saw it, like some infection, some disease. Maybe I nodded. I don't know. I can't remember. But I remember that it hurt to swallow, remember thinking that I was there, on trial. I think I nodded, and he said, softly, "And I hope you understand."

He didn't ask; he said he hoped. I hoped too, for something more, anything, explanation, conviction, pardon. I stood there, waiting. "I'll see you in the fall then," he said. And he smiled. It was when he smiled that I knew, knew that whatever had been was over.

Classes are over. From the floor below I hear the ringing of the bells, the rush of feet. Midmorning break.

The question is: if I had gotten this letter would things have turned out differently? That was the fall he came back married. Would it have made a difference if I'd known why?

Below, in the quad, I hear the voices, see kids sitting, cross-legged on the grass. Up here it's quiet, and I'm alone.

I walk back to the bed, and sit, turning the letter in my hands. Over and over. I love you, he said. Love. To think of Edwards reading the letter makes me sick.

There was a time I was sick; lying here, in this room, I watched the snow fall, wondering how to measure pain. Wondering what was real, and what was not.

"What were they thinking of, sending him back in this condition?"

I heard them, but I watched the snow. I liked the way it hid the world. The room was hot, but I was cold.

"It's too late."

147

"If the ambulance can't get through . . ."

"If it had ruptured on the plane, whose fault would that be, I'd like to know."

I knew. I tried to tell them, but I couldn't. I was cold but there was fire in my stomach. I knew that I was going to die.

The funny thing was it didn't matter. I wished I could have told them. There are worse things than dying is what I would have said. The words were swallowed by the pain.

"They say it's hopeless if the school drive isn't plowed."

"Well then, we'll get to them."

The snow fell, and I watched it falling. "Peter. Hold on, Peter," said Manning, his fingers on my cheek. "We're going to get help."

I was beyond help. I tried to tell him. "It's all my fault," I said. I think I said it. I don't know if he heard me. "Don't you give up," he said.

He lifted me, wrapped in blankets, held me, legs dangling, running down the stairs.

My head was tucked against his chest, the rough wool scratching. With each step, my head wobbled like a baby's. I was a baby. I was thirteen.

He bent to shield me from the snow. His breath was warm. He held me tight. "You'll be fine," he said. His breath was diamonds. "Believe me," he said. He made it sound so easy.

And so I did.

And here I am, six years later, holding a letter I never got.

I sit on the bed, and listen to silence, waiting for it to speak. And when it does, I hear it.

Everything I am I owe to him. Everything he did, he did for me.

The question is: what do I do about it. Now?

I think of Judith. I think of onions. Of all those layers. The layers in me.

And then I know.

I dress quickly. I feel so light, as if I'm floating. I hear kids lining up for medication. I take Cate's journal, the letter, and slide them in my inner pocket. The kids are laughing in the hall. "Pipe down," says Mary.

I slip out easily. No one sees me. The warning bell goes as I hit the stairs. Below me the floor shakes to the drumming of three hundred feet.

I am almost through when a hand takes me by the sleeve. I'd know those fingers anywhere. "Why, Spaulding, I had heard you were indisposed." The air is close, smelling of bad breath, chalk, and corned beef hash. "Another of those nasty rumors, I suppose." I don't have to look at Edwards to know he's smiling. But I do.

Smiling, he moves his tongue across his lips. His lips are pink. His skin is white. His face reminds me of the bloated underbelly of a fish.

There is just time for a flicker of fear to show in his eyes before my fist slams into his nose. My knuckles sink in as if his face was dough. He falls backward with a solid thump. His nose streams blood. Kids pass by, in silence, grinning.

Edwards stares up at me as if he can't believe I hit him. I can't either. But if he stands, I'll hit him again. It's a moment before he notices the blood dribbling down his chin. He wipes at it. "I'm telling," he says. Wiping only makes it worse.

It's all I can do not to laugh out loud. "You do that, Edwards."

Leaving him there, I walk down the hall to Spencer's office. I knock, waiting. After a moment he opens the door. He does not look happy when he sees me. "So soon, Spaulding?"

"I have something to tell you, sir."

"Do you, Spaulding, do you? If you could wait . . ."

I push past him, into the room, and Mrs. MacQuire looks up, smiles at me, from the chair beside his desk. "Peter," she says, "you must be better."

"Much," I say.

I turn back to Spencer, who's still standing by the door, sending signals with his eyes. "If you don't mind, Spaulding." His eyes move to Mrs. MacQuire, then back to me. I could tell him that what he thinks I've come to say, she already knows. He looks like an idiot, his eyes moving back and forth. "Later," he says. "If you don't mind."

I do mind, but the truth is I'm not ready to say it in front of Mrs. MacQuire. Yet. I glance at her. Her mouth moves in a flicker of a smile. Mary's right. She doesn't look well. I wonder if I've done this too?

"I'll come by later."

"You do that, Spaulding. There's my boy!"

He doesn't bother to hide his relief. As I pass him, he pats my back.

The hall is empty. Where Edwards fell, there is a small dark stain. I feel so light. I feel like laughing.

"I did it!"

At one end of the hall is the main desk. Next to it the door. The desk is empty too. I take a slip of paper, and a pencil, and I write.

DEAR SIR,
  I KILLED HER.

I write it in block letters, the way a child would. I don't bother to sign my name. He'll know. Everyone will know, soon enough. I fold the paper, and slip the note in Spencer's box.

SIXTEEN

THE SUN RESTS on the river. In the cattails a blackbird sings. The air is spicy with the smell of pine. There is no wind, and nothing moves. I remember my dream. Behind the thicket, the shelter is still standing. But this shelter is small, a lean-to, and the pine needles that were green last winter have turned brown. When I brush my hand across them, the needles fall like drops of rain. The roof is full of holes. I crawl inside. Looking up, I see green leaves, and above the leaves, the sky. I am no longer hidden, but then there is nothing left to hide.

Last fall, when I was building this, Cate came again. I didn't see her coming. It was Sunday, late afternoon and the way the light came through the trees reminded me of church. "What are you doing?" she said, sounding, somehow, so like Bets that when I turned that's who I thought I'd see. But I saw Cate, saw sunlight dancing in her hair.

"Getting ready for winter, I guess." My hands were sticky with the sap. I felt like a fool, a grown kid caught playing house. "Outward Bound." I said. "The stuff I learned. It helps to stay in practice."

She wasn't listening. Nervous, I rubbed my hands against my jeans. Back and forth. I couldn't stop. She stood there, twisting a strand of hair between her fingers, wearing a long skirt, a baggy sweater, boots, and a green scarf around her neck. The scarf was fringed with silver coins that jingled when she moved. "I hope you don't mind," she said.

I slid my hands into my pockets. It was cool under the trees, almost cold, but I was sweating. "Mind what?"

"My coming." She smiled, blushing. "I get lonely sometimes," she said. She bit her lip. "And everyone seems to want us to be friends."

I turned away, got back to work.

"I know you don't like me," she said. "And I don't blame you, I really don't."

"That's not true." But I couldn't look at her.

"Really," she said. "If I were you, I wouldn't like me either." And she laughed, a small sad sound. "Oliver told me. He just told me that the reason you helped me with the garden last year was because Melissa, Mrs. MacQuire, asked you to."

"I would have done it anyway," I said. My face turned red.

"I guess he thought you did it because you wanted to. And he was so pleased because he thought it meant we could be friends. I mean, all of us, be friends. He doesn't think I'm very good at making friends." That small sad laugh again. "He doesn't think I'm good at much of anything, I guess."

"That's stupid. That's not true."

"It doesn't matter. I mean, I know he's right. But I am trying. It's just that . . ."

"He's a bastard!"

Her eyes widened, pale eyes, blue, almost lavender. "Oh no, you shouldn't say that."

"He is."

"You shouldn't." She shook her head. "And you shouldn't feel that you have to help either, help me, I mean. The way you did with the garden, or yesterday, pouring tea. Not" — she blushed — "that I didn't appreciate your help, but, if you don't want to . . ." She flung her hands out, a flutter of wings.

"I did," I said. "I do."

She looked at me. "Really?"

I nodded. "Really. I could use some help too," I said. And she laughed, embarrassed, shy. She seemed so young, she made me feel old. "With this," I said. I touched the shelter.

"Oh," she said, "but I don't know how to . . ."

"I'll teach you." I felt so old. I felt so big.

"If you're sure," she said.

"I'm sure," I said. Because I was.

I was sure. Then. There are times when everything seems to come together, times when everything falls apart. One shove is enough to knock the shelter over. Needles hissing, it collapses in upon itself.

I come out from under the trees to stand by the river. With the sun overhead, the water is black, an opaque mirror absorbing light. Coming here is coming home. I stand, in sunlight, staring at the river. The water is a sheet of unbroken glass. I think of points converging, drops of water, freezing, joining, forming ice. My life converging. I think of home.

Standing, that last day, on the bluff above the Lake. Standing with my sisters. The next day I was leaving. I hadn't told them, but they knew. Except for Bets. That's what I thought. She was four, and I was twelve, and Polly and Celia were in between. "It's not as if I won't be back," I said.

They stood, backs stiff, eyes straight ahead, looking out across the water. "So what," said Polly. She wouldn't turn to look at me. "As if we care," said Celia. Celia was eight, and Polly ten. At ten she looked just like my father, his thin fierce face, accusing eyes. Neither of them would look at me. I wanted to touch them, but I couldn't. I picked Bets up, held her, squirming, in my arms. My arms were aching. I was tall for twelve, but skinny. She smelled of summer, sun and sand. "I remember when you were born," I said. I held her tight. "You're hurting me," she said. I put her

153

down. For a moment they stood, frozen. Then, they took off, running single file down the steep steps leading to the beach, their heads bobbing like small beads from a broken necklace, and there was nothing I could do but watch them go.

Cate asked me once. "What's the saddest thing that ever happened to you?" She was always asking things like that. Maybe she thought that's how you get to know a person. Maybe she was just making conversation. Maybe she asked so she wouldn't have to talk about herself. She really seemed to hate to talk about herself. But anyway, she asked, and I didn't even have to think. "The day I left for boarding school," I said.

"Why?" said Cate which, now that I think of it seems a stupid question. It didn't then. I knew why, but I couldn't answer. It hurt too much. I couldn't tell her that when I closed my eyes, I saw Robert at the wheel of the car, my mother there beside him. I sat in back, dressed in a new suit, wedged between my luggage. It was when I turned to look out the rear window at the house. I saw the house, windows winking as we pulled away. We pulled away, and I saw Bets, four years old, and running fast. As fast as she could anyway. "Stop the car!" I said. Robert, looking, saw her in the rearview mirror. She was still in her pajamas, and her feet were bare. Her hair was wild. "Come back. Wait for me." I heard her, heard her crying. Robert heard her too. He didn't stop. He just kept going. My mother sat like she was dead. "Do something!" I said, biting my lip to keep from crying. Which is why I couldn't tell Cate. Because when I tried I felt tears prick behind my eyes. "Never mind, darling," my mother said. My mother turned to me. She smiled. "It's for the best." Her voice as empty as her eyes.

"Really," said Cate. "It's for the best. That's what I want you to understand."

Five days ago she said it, here, down by the river.

154

"I don't get it. Is it me? Did I do something wrong?"

"It's not you."

"What, then? You better tell me."

She shook her head. "Really, it's better if you don't know."

She said it softly. The sun was setting, water turning red to gold.

"What do you mean, better?"

"Better," she said. "Trust me. Please."

I looked at her. Her skin was pale. Her hair was up.

"I did."

She bent her head. Her neck was long and thin, the color of cream.

My fingers ached. I heard them cracking. I saw a small vein ticking in her neck. I crouched down by the river's edge. The watercress was thick in flower, small white blossoms against the green. I saw the current tugging at the roots.

"It's all just been a game for you, hasn't it. Like maybe you didn't have enough to do?"

"Don't hate me, Peter. I couldn't stand to have you hate me."

I had to laugh. Hate is hot, but what I felt was cold. I couldn't look at her. I felt her, standing there above me. "I could kill you," I said.

"Peter." I heard the pleading.

I didn't look. "Fuck off," I said.

I could have killed her. But I didn't. Not then. I dipped both hands into the water, and caught the roots. They felt like worms. I pulled. It came out easily.

"Peter. Please, Peter."

"I mean it. Fuck off."

I pulled it up in fistfuls, great clumps of dark green leaves. I kept on pulling, tossing the plants onto the river, plants floating, spinning slowly as the current carried them downstream. I kept on pulling until every plant was gone, until four years of watercress was floating free.

155

Then I looked up, but by then she'd taken off. It was all over. All over, and I was all alone.

I'm all alone. The sun rises, and the sun sets. Nothing moves except a dragonfly, darting above the surface of the water. Not a trace of watercress remains. She could have told me. If she had, I wouldn't be here now. Alone.

Standing on the bank, I strip. Sunlight glitters on the water, but beneath the surface nothing shows. Arms back, I crouch, and spring. Springing forward, lifting, my body slaps against the water and the surface shatters, like glass, like tears.

SEVENTEEN

It is April first, and I have been married exactly nine months. When I write it down like that it makes it real.

Today is April Fools Day but I didn't know that until Melissa came up to the house. Oliver was at school and I was in the kitchen and when she came in I said I had just broken all six of Oliver's best wine glasses, the ones with the long green stems. His mother's. April Fools said Melissa, and she smiled until I showed her the pieces in the sink. She stopped smiling then. I told her I had put them on the window sill above the sink to dry because the sun is shining and the window was open just a little bit and they are so fragile that I am always afraid to dry them by hand. But a puff of wind came, and blew them over. What am I going to do, I said, and I started to cry. Never mind, said Melissa, and she scraped up all the broken glass and put it in the bottom of a trash bag and carried it outside and put the bag at the very bottom of the trash can. But he's going to notice they're missing, I said. I was shaking because I was so frightened but she said, no he won't, and she took me down into the basement where all Oliver's extra things are stored and she found a box that had twelve glasses just like the ones I broke. We carried six upstairs and put them on the pantry shelf. What he doesn't know won't hurt him, said Melissa. But what if he looks, I said, and she said, don't worry he's too busy thinking about other things. I didn't know what she was talking about, and she said, hasn't he told you that Spencer wants him to be the next headmaster. I said, oh yes, but she said, you don't have to lie to me, Cate. She said it gently. Never mind, she said, maybe he's saving it for a big surprise. I don't even know how to be a wife yet, I said. How can I be a headmaster's wife? You should be a headmaster's wife. I didn't mean to be funny, but she laughed. Can you see Logan as headmaster? she said.

I said, oh yes again, even though it isn't true. I like Logan. He's nice to me. Whenever he sees me, he smiles, and says, how's it going? and I always say, fine. He never can think of anything else to say and I can't either so we just smile and then he clears his throat and says, take it easy, and shuffles away.

But I said yes anyway. Cate, she said, you are too transparent for your own good. And I blushed. I just can't see him <u>wanting</u> to be headmaster, I said. She stopped smiling. You're right about that anyway, she said. Let's have some coffee, she said.

So we did. I made it, all by myself, grinding the beans and everything. Delicious, said Melissa. I could tell she meant it. We sat down at the kitchen table.

You haven't been down to see me lately, she said.

I've been busy, I said. I tried not to blush. I couldn't help it.

Cate. She said it softly, and I knew. She knew I was lying. I couldn't look at her.

It's Oliver, I said.

Oliver, she said. I could feel her waiting. I started to bite my nails. She reached out and took my hand and held it so I couldn't.

He thinks . . . he thinks I've been seeing too much of you, I said.

For a minute she didn't say a thing. I couldn't even hear her breathing. He does, does he, she said.

It's not your fault, I said.

What's not my fault? she said.

It's me, I said. It's mine.

Maybe you'd better tell me exactly what he said.

He said . . . he said that you were a bad influence on me.

Really, she said. Her voice was flat.

Please, I said. Don't be angry. It has nothing to do with you. He's not mad at you. It's me. How I feel.

How you feel, she said. How do you feel?

And I had to say it. I just had to.

I love you, I said. I whispered. And I couldn't look at her. I can't help it, I said. I just do.

Well, she said, she said it slowly, and I can't explain, but her voice was soft. And is there something wrong with loving, she said.

I can't help it, I said. I think about you all the time.

Would he rather you think about him? she said.

I don't know what he wants. I don't. He asked me how I felt about you, and I told him. I told him I loved you. I thought he would be pleased because he loves you too.

Does he? she said.

Oh yes, I said, he says he would have done better to marry you.

Cate, she said, Cate. She stopped holding my hand. She rubbed her forehead. Don't let him say these things to you, she said.

But he's right, I said. Only you're already married.

She looked at me then. I don't know, she said. I really don't.

You don't mind that I love you? I said.

She touched my cheek with the tip of her finger. I'm flattered, she said. He doesn't deserve you. He doesn't know what love is.

Yes he does, I said. He loves Peter Spaulding, I said.

Peter, she said. Yes, she said. Tell me, she said, what do you think of Peter?

He doesn't like me, I said.

Why do you think that, she said.

It's true, I said. Oliver says it's my fault Peter never comes to the house.

He's coming now, she said. Isn't he helping you with the garden?

Because of Oliver. Not me. Oliver asked him.

He said no to Oliver, she said.

I think maybe I looked surprised because she smiled. How do you know? I said.

We're friends, she said. He told me. Do you know what else he told me?

She was still smiling. I shook my head. I think maybe I was blushing.

He likes you, she said.

Oh no, I said.

Oh yes, she said. Laughing. And you know what I think? I think you could be friends. Good friends. You'd just have to make a little effort, to show that you like him too.

I do like him, I said.

It would make Oliver happy, wouldn't it? I said.

I'm not thinking of Oliver, she said. I'm thinking of you.

Dear diary. That's what she said! I think of her. She thinks of me!

The clouds take me by surprise. It's a while before I realize I'm shivering. Without the sun the air is cold. Only my hair is still wet. Where drops have fallen on the journal the ink has smeared. I get dressed quickly. It doesn't help. I'm cold, inside and out. The clouds have come from nowhere. Really, I shouldn't be surprised. After six years here I've learned it doesn't pay to trust the weather. Or people either.

I pull back, under the trees, and I build a fire. If there's one thing I know how to do it's build a fire. First clear a space, and circle it with stones. Stones I've got, rocks borrowed from old walls snaking through the woods. I chose them carefully, flat on top with rounded edges. Inside the circle is a bed of ashes. When I blow on them they rise like mist. For tinder I use cattail down from last year's heads. I make a nest, a small white nest, and with a broken knife blade and a piece of flint, I start striking. I keep my wrists loose, striking hard. Sparks fly, falling, and finally a thin wisp rises.

Around the burning nest I place the kindling, and then the logs. Most of the wood is soft and rotten. It doesn't matter. It burns more quickly. Poplar, pine, a piece of birch.

The fire crackles. I hold my hands out, trying to warm them. Crackling, the fire sounds warmer than it is. I can't get warm. My hands are stinging. I feel them burning. They feel so cold; they feel frozen.

They were, once. Long ago. December, before Christmas, and it was cold. I was fourteen, and Manning asked me up to dinner. My Second Form year. Thanksgiving was over, and I had just been home. I called it home. Of course it wasn't. When people asked, I didn't know what else to say so I just said, "I'm going home." I didn't even have a room. Not that it mattered. Because of what happened, I wouldn't be going back. As if I cared. After vacation I called my father, and said that from then on he'd be stuck with me. I didn't say why; he didn't ask. When anyone asked, I just said, yeah, sure, it was a great vacation.

It was dark when I signed out for Manning's, dark, and I was late. I started running. The moon was out. The snow looked blue. I felt cold burning when I breathed. I ran, snow squeaking underfoot. I ran until I was halfway up the hill, and then I stopped. I had to stop. The cold was like a wall, impossible to push against. I heard, later, that that night it broke all records.

I stood there, thinking stupid thoughts like, if I should die, would anybody care. Of course they wouldn't. It was my fault anyway. Did I have a coat, gloves, a hat? Of course I didn't.

Manning was waiting. "I called," he said, "to tell you not

to come." Standing in yellow light, he seemed to shimmer. "Come in," he said. "Come in." And when I did, he said, "My God, look at you!"

I couldn't look at him. At anything. My breath had frozen, coating face and eyes. My hands felt dead. "Quickly. In by the fire."

I sat there, by the fire. He sat beside me.

"Give me your hands." I held them out. I couldn't feel them at all.

He held my hand between his palms. "This might hurt a bit," he said. One finger at a time, he rubbed. His hands were hard and smooth, and smelled like lemon. He rubbed my fingers the way I rubbed two sticks together to start a fire. He rubbed, and slowly the ice melted from my lashes, trickling down my face like water. "Am I hurting you?" His voice was kind. His hands were too. I shook my head. "I'm not crying." I saw him smile. "I know," he said.

I couldn't feel anything except his hands. He rubbed and rubbed. The room was warm. The rubbing made me sleepy. When I yawned, he laughed.

"We're getting there."

He was so close. I heard him breathing. I felt his breath, but only on my wrist. I couldn't feel my fingers, but I felt his. It felt so strange. I closed my eyes. It was as if his hands were mine.

"You know," he said, "you haven't told me anything about Thanksgiving."

I kept my eyes closed. I felt my fingers start to prickle.

"Why don't you tell me now," he said.

I didn't answer. I felt the prickling, skin waking up. Tiny needles, sharp, like ice. My God, it hurt. I kept my eyes closed, trying not to cry. He kept on rubbing. "Tell me," he said, and so I did.

Eyes closed, I told him. I told him fast so that I wouldn't have to think. I heard him listening, felt him rubbing. I told

162

him about Bets. My mother. Robert. Robert's baby. I told him everything.

"Don't tell anyone," I said.

"Peter, it was not your fault."

"Don't."

"I won't." He took my other hand, and started rubbing. "It must have hurt," he said. I kept my eyes closed. He kept on rubbing. I didn't answer. It hurt.

It hurt.

It still hurts. Holding my hands toward the fire, I rub them. Hard.

Remembering once, watching Manning take Mrs. MacQuire's hand. Or was it the other way around? Six years ago or maybe five. Before Cate anyway. At the MacQuires', and I was there. He pinched a fold of tablecloth between his fingers, thick cloth, smooth, the color of ivory. "Lovely," he said, smiling, smiling at Mrs. MacQuire when he said it, but all the while his fingers stroking, and Mrs. MacQuire smiled too. She sat beside him. She was at one end of the table, and Coach at the other. "You!" she said. "You gave it to us." Rising, to clear, she laid a finger on his wrist. One finger, touching. Like a secret, I thought. Or a kiss.

Mrs. MacQuire kissed me. Her lips were cool, like peppermint. She kissed me first on one cheek, then the other. "Have a good summer," she said. She smiled. "Yeah," I said. "You too."

I'd come down, in the early morning, to say good-bye. The others were asleep, but she was up, standing on the back porch, waiting. Her hair was down, and all around us birds were singing. "Are you going to see Sukie?" she said. With her hair down, she looked different. Younger somehow, and her eyes still soft from sleep.

I shrugged. "I don't know. Maybe. Yeah, I guess."

"I liked her, you know. You tell her to come back, and stay with us."

"OK," I said. "She liked you too." I grinned.

"And, Peter, thank you for helping Cate . . . Mrs. Manning with that garden."

"I did it for you. Because you asked."

"I know that. I'm grateful. And she is too. She likes you, Peter. She'd like to be your friend."

"Listen, I've got to go. The bus leaves in fifteen minutes."

"I know that. Peter, she's not a happy person."

"Listen," I said. "I don't mean to be rude or anything, but I can't see what it has to do with me. She's *his* wife! He's the one who married her."

"Shh. It's all right. Don't get upset." Her finger touched my cheek. "A little kindness. That's all I'm asking." She looked at me. "He isn't very kind to her." She said it quietly. "He isn't kind at all."

"So what am I supposed to do?"

"Just be yourself. Your own sweet self." She smiled.

"Is that a joke or something?"

She stopped smiling. Her eyes went hard. "The fact is you're the only person he cares enough about to answer to."

I had to laugh. "You're wrong about that," I said.

"Am I? Well . . ." And then she smiled. "Go on," she said. "You'll miss your bus. Have a good summer. I'll see you in the fall."

I have been married for a year. One whole year. August 15. All day yesterday, I waited to see if Oliver would remember. If he did, he didn't say.

So I said to him, last night, I said, why did you marry me. Here, on the barge, in France, it was easy to ask. All day we float down the canal. The canal is narrow with trees on either side. Their branches touch, but no one touches me.

All day we drift. All day I think about Aunt Effie. There is an old woman kneeling on stone, washing her clothes in the

164

dirty water. She is dressed in black. She does not look up when we pass which makes me think that maybe we are not here at all. That maybe the hole inside me has become the world all around. Oliver sits beside me on the deck, reading. He does not look up either. Before he turns each page, he feels the corner of the page with his fingers, rubbing his fingers against the paper. To make sure it's there.

It is hard to tell what's real. When I think about Melissa, I can't remember what she looks like. She is everywhere, but I can't see her. I think, if she were dead, right now, I would not know it. I think, I love her. But what does that mean? Sometimes, when I am with her, I feel her inside me. But here there is no inside to feel.

Which is why it was easy to ask Oliver last night, why did you marry me? We were in our cabin. The cabins are very small. The other passengers were asleep. He came in quietly. Maybe he thought I was asleep too. Because the cabin is so small I always get ready for bed first. You're awake, he said.

Why, I said. I sat up, but he was turned away from me so I couldn't see his face.

That's a good question, he said. But not worth answering. Now go to sleep.

I lay down. I didn't sleep. The cabin was hot, but the sheets were cool. Pretty sheets, sprinkled with flowers, pink and blue and yellow. Babies, I thought. Babies. But he doesn't touch me. He has never touched me. I think he knows.

It is the way he looks at me sometimes, seeing me but not seeing me. Seeing right through me, knowing no one is inside.

There is only Aunt Effie, here, on the canal. Yesterday we reached the summit. There were two locks there. Double locks. The locks are made of gray stone, the sides curved. For three days we have been climbing. "I've been good to you, child, you can't say I haven't." I didn't say anything. I sat, beside her, watching the road slip under the wheels. Not much of a life for a child, she said. I know that. But better than dead. Who would have thought. Throwing you out. Like trash. She shook her head. The things I've seen, she said. I closed my eyes. I chewed my hair. I tasted ashes.

Yesterday I watched the water slipping through the lock. I felt the barge sinking. And today. We are going down. And down.

And I say to Oliver, will we ever go back? Reading, he frowns. His finger holds his place. What, he says, what are you talking about?

How can I tell him. When people asked, Aunt Effie said, Effie's the name, traveling's the game. I remember the laughing, and the way oil made rainbows in the dust. The smell of oil. Home, I said to Oliver. If we could go home.

Home, said Oliver. Frowning.

Borrowed houses. Borrowed time.

If I could have a baby, I said.

A baby?

I'd be someone with a baby.

You are someone, he said. I waited. For better or worse, he said. My wife.

The river's dirty, though not as dirty as it used to be. That's what they say. I think it might be true. There are more fish now, mostly rock bass, but they're bigger and don't taste so muddy. It's possible of course to go for days without a strike. But the clouds help. In the late afternoon I catch two without any trouble. I can't clean them without a knife so I pack them in mud from the riverbank, and place them in the coals to bake. The fire sizzles. I feed wood to the flames. Rocking on my heels, I wait.

"I can't wait," said Judith. "Tell me. Why do you think he married her? She doesn't exactly seem his type."

Coach grinned. "Could have knocked us over with a feather when he showed up with her last year." Tipping his head, he drank his beer. "Isn't that right, honey?" he said to Mrs. MacQuire, who stood, her back to us, cooking dinner at the stove. We sat, around the table, Judith, my father, Coach, and me. Parents' Weekend just last fall. "Knocked us over, but we were pleased. When a fellow like Manning hits fifty-five, you begin to think . . . I'm a firm believer in the institution, all right. Everybody ought to get married. Even you, old fella." Coach winked at me.

I glanced at Judith, saw her trying hard not to smile. "Can I get another Coke, sir?" I said, hoping he wouldn't notice Judith.

"Sure can," said Coach. "Our house is yours. Besides we've got a game to celebrate." He shook his head. "It's the big game all right. Do you know, Dave . . ." Coach grinned. My father grimaced. No one ever called him Dave. "The last time we gave them a beating like that was in sixty-one. Right here." He reached up to the wall, tapped the glass frame with his finger. "Yours truly."

"Logan," said Mrs. MacQuire. "You promised."

Coach grinned. Sheepish. Shrugging. "She's right," he said. "I did."

"You were a student here?" my father said, and from the way he said it I could tell it was pretty much what he expected.

Coach raised his beer. "Six years. That's right. Everything I am I owe to Dunster." He chuckled. He drank his beer.

"And after Dunster?" Judith asked.

Coach tapped the Harvard photograph. "Harvard," he said. He saw Judith look surprised, and grinned as if he knew what she was thinking. "I was something of a jock," he said. "That didn't hurt."

"You did all right," said Mrs. MacQuire.

"With help," said Coach. He looked at Judith. "Melissa helped. I met her there." He smiled, proud. "She was Phi Beta Kappa, weren't you, hon?"

"Logan, why don't you see who wants another drink."

Coach laughed. "She hates it when I boast." He stood up, stretching. "Who's for another? Besides myself."

167

No one, but me, I got my Coke. He got his beer. My father nursed his bourbon. Judith sipped her wine.

"Radcliffe?" she said to Mrs. MacQuire.

Mrs. MacQuire nodded. Bending, she lifted the roast from the oven. "I met Logan sophomore year. He was a senior." She smiled at Judith. A small smile. "In the jargon," she said, "he was B.M.O.C."

Judith looked puzzled. "As I recall," my father said, "that stands for 'big man on campus.' " He looked at Logan. "Is that correct?"

Coach shrugged, pleased. "She said it," he said, laughing. "Not me."

I saw Judith glancing at the photographs on the wall. Looking at them, and then at Coach, trying to put the pieces together. Maybe Coach saw too. "The fact is I needed someone to take care of me. A born mother. Isn't that right?"

"Of grown men?" said Judith.

My father nudged Judith with his elbow. Coach didn't notice. He laughed.

"You name it. Adults. Kids. Babies. Ask Peter."

"My failing, I'm afraid," said Mrs. MacQuire. To Judith. She turned to Coach. "Will you tell the children dinner is almost ready? They can eat in the study."

"Failing," Coach said. "I don't get it."

"You're not supposed to." She smiled at him, the way you'd smile at a kid. "Go tell the children," she said. "Please."

"Take Cate," said Coach. "Where would she be without you, now?"

"Right where she is. Married to Oliver, I expect."

"Honey, don't make me out to be more stupid than I really am." He turned to Judith, to my father. "The fact is — I hate to say this about a friend — he could be nicer to her."

"Which leads us back to the beginning," Judith said. "Why he married in the first place."

168

"He's not a fag," Coach said. "You should see him on the tennis court."

"Logan, please," said Mrs. MacQuire. Her voice was strained. She turned to me. "You call the children, will you?"

"That's not exactly what I meant," said Judith, "but it does seem that perhaps he doesn't think much of women in general."

"He loves them!" said Coach. "His mother. My God, he worshipped her. And her." He grinned at Mrs. MacQuire. "Right, honey? There's nothing he wouldn't do for you."

"Peter!" said Mrs. MacQuire. "Please."

I called the children. They came, running.

"Here they are," said Coach. He stood there, smiling, proud. They stood beside him. Naming them, he touched them, one by one. "Dana. Daphne. Rufus. Rufus here has Mr. Manning for his godfather."

Rufus grinned. "He's rich," he said.

Coach laughed. He picked him up. "He's spoiled you, you little bugger."

"Shake hands," said Mrs. MacQuire. "Manners, please."

They shook hands. "How do you do," said Dana, shy behind his glasses.

"He spoils all of us," said Daphne.

"Money!" said Rufus.

"That's what godfathers are for," said Dana, standing as always to one side.

"That's right," said Coach. "Godfathers give you everything. Even looks." Laughing, he looked at Mrs. MacQuire. "You ever thought that, honey? That Rufus looks like . . ."

"No," she said. "I haven't. Put him down now. It's time to carve."

Coach put him down. Judith looked at Rufus. I did too. It's funny. Maybe it was just the light, the way it caught his cheek, but for a moment . . . even though I knew it couldn't be, I thought . . .

I glanced at Mrs. MacQuire. She was looking at Judith. Their eyes met, locked, just for an instant.

The look surprised me. But I was pleased. I wanted them to like each other.

Judith cleared her throat. "Actually," she said, "he looks like you, Melissa."

"Does he?" said Mrs. MacQuire, as if she'd never thought of it before. She looked at Rufus. So did I. To me he looked like Rufus. Nothing less and nothing more. Rufus grinned. There's nothing he likes better than attention. "How nice," said Mrs. MacQuire. She smiled.

EIGHTEEN

"I DON'T SUPPOSE," says Manning. "I don't suppose it occurred to you that your, shall we say, sudden disappearance, might cause concern?"

He stands above me. It's almost dark. I don't have to look at him to know he's angry. I can hear it in his voice. With a sharp stick I stab the fire. Sparks explode like fireflies.

"How did you find me?"

"Not to mention that you've broken any number of school rules." His voice is tight. Trembling. He's holding a flashlight in his hands. It's trembling too.

"Rules." I have to laugh. "It's a little late to worry about that." I hunker down, closer to the fire.

"It's not like you, Peter, to be so thoughtless. Spencer is beside himself."

I look up. The light shines in my face, which makes it hard to see.

"You talked to him?"

"You had been placed in the infirmary for good reason."

"He told you, didn't he?"

The light goes off. "Told me what?"

"You know what. I'm tired of playing games."

"And you know what I thought, don't you? Given your present state of mind?"

I rake the coals, nudging the hardened clay out from the fire with the stick.

171

"I thought . . ." But he can't say it. "Do you mind if I sit?"

Before I can answer, he lowers himself to the ground. I don't look at him.

"As long as you're here, you might as well eat."

The clay cracks easily. In the firelight the flesh looks pink. "You'll have to eat with your fingers."

"Food is the last . . ."

"Be careful. Rock bass are bony." The fish parts neatly along the spine. I put his half on a dock leaf, slide it toward him. He sits, cross-legged, hands resting on his knees.

"Peter," he says.

"I've had it," I say. "All my life. Good old Peter. The answer to everybody's prayer. Jesus."

"What are you talking about?"

"I'm tired of it. That's all. Tired of being used by everybody. Used! Maneuvered into position like some stupid little shit. Too stupid to see what was really going on. Thinking people cared . . ."

"My wife?"

"Everybody. You. Mrs. MacQuire. My parents."

"You're angry, Peter. That's why you think you killed her."

In the silence I hear the fire hiss.

I take a bite. The fish flakes easily. It tastes like river. A small bone presses against my cheek. I work it to the front, and spit it out.

"I don't *think*."

"I understand," he says, "you never got my letter."

I am careful to keep on chewing. I hear him waiting, hear the river. Beyond the fire, the night is black.

"I'd rather not talk about that."

"Peter." Gently. "I think it's important that we do."

"No."

"It's all connected."

172

I pull the other fish from the fire. The clay is black with ashes. Hard. I crack it open with a rock, tossing the broken bits toward the water. I hear the ripples when they hit. I hear them, and I think of Cate.

"It's too late now."

"For some of us," says Manning, "but not for you."

"Me! For Christ's sake, why don't you listen! I was the one who killed her."

"Did you?" He leans toward me. "How?"

"You treated her like shit. Shit!" I spit the word. He doesn't flinch.

"I'm well aware of my responsibility in the matter."

"Are you?" I look at him. His eyes are on me. "I could have killed you. I should have. Instead of her."

He nods, once, briefly. "Which is why we need to talk."

"There's nothing to talk about."

"Oh, but there is." His hands reach out.

"Don't touch me!"

He smiles. His smile is sad. "It was not my intention. My fingers. I'd like to clean them."

I hand him a piece of moss. He wipes them carefully, one by one. Fastidious. Like my father. I lick mine, tasting soot and grease.

"Will you listen?" he says.

He waits for me to answer. I take a breath, and feel it trembling.

"How did you find me?"

"I went to Melissa." I look at him. "Mrs. MacQuire. I thought you might be hiding there. I was able to persuade her to tell me about this spot of yours. Frankly" — he pauses — "I was rather surprised she knew about it."

"Just because you didn't?" He looks at me. His eyes are dark. He holds his secrets. I hold mine. "You don't know everything," I say. Thinking of Cate's journal, the one she gave to me.

173

"She's not to be trusted," he says.

"Who says I trust her?" I turn back to the fire. Flames flicker, and the coals spark red. "I don't trust anyone."

"Trust me," says Manning.

"I used to." Knees up, I hug them, rocking. "Not anymore."

"Because you never got that letter?"

"I told you . . ."

"I don't care what you told me!" His voice is sharp. I sit still, holding. "It's time you listened. For three years you've been holding it against me because you thought, after that night, I dropped you with no explanation. I wrote to you, Peter. I can't be blamed for the fact that you never got that letter. Nor should you blame yourself."

"Who says I am?"

"It was," says Manning, "as we both know, the end of your Fourth Form year, the summer you were to come to England. Until you changed your mind."

I don't say anything. I watch the fire.

"It was also," says Manning, "the summer I married."

"Who's blaming who?"

"What?" He sounds surprised.

"Fine. It's my fault you got married. If I'd come . . ."

"That's not what I'm saying."

"Bullshit. If I'd gotten the letter, I would have come, and if I'd come you never would have married. And we'd all live happily ever after. Right?"

"You're saying it, Peter. Not me."

He's right. I am. Now that it's said I feel better.

"Maybe we should go back, if Spencer's waiting."

Manning moves so quickly he catches me off guard. His fingers circle my wrist. The strength of his grip surprises me. We are the same height now, the same size, but when I try to pull away, I can't.

"We need to talk, Peter. About that night. What happened."

"No!" A shout, and with the shout the strength to pull away. The water echoes.

"Peter." His voice as soft as mine was loud. "What do you think happened that night?"

I cover my face with both hands to make the darkness more complete. "I don't think. I know."

"What do you know?" His voice is velvet, soft and dark.

"I know what you're doing. Trying to blame it all on me."

"There's no need," he says. "You're doing it for yourself."

"Just because I killed her . . ."

"You didn't kill her, Peter."

I turn, and look at him.

"I used to come here with your wife, you know."

He doesn't blink. His eyes are fixed on me. Fixed! The eye of night.

"All the time. Almost every day. We used to screw. Right here."

He blinks. Once. "I'm glad you were able to give her some pleasure."

I clench my fists. "Don't you care about anything?"

"Yes," says Manning. He looks at me across the fire. "You."

I drop down, so the fire hides me.

"Why can't you get it! I killed your wife!"

"Peter, she was not a happy person."

"She could have been. If it hadn't been for you."

"In fact," says Manning, as if I hadn't spoken, "she could hardly be called a person either."

"You shit. You married her."

"I did. Yes." He looks at me across the fire. "Only to discover that it is impossible to make something out of nothing. As you would have discovered yourself, in time."

"I loved her!"

He shook his head. "You can't love what isn't there."

"Mrs. MacQuire loved her too."

"Ah." His voice goes still. "Did she?"

175

"You know she did. She did everything she could to help her."

"Help. And why, do you think?"

"I told you. She loved her." But even as I say it, I begin to wonder, hear the word, *love*, hang, lifeless, in the still night air.

"Has it ever occurred to you, Peter, that rather than loving Cate, she was using her. Using you. Turning shields into swords."

"I know you blame her, but . . ."

"Not because she loved Cate, Peter. Because she hated me."

"She didn't. She loved you. But she hates you now."

"Love," says Manning. "Hate. Are sometimes like this." He raises two fingers, crossed. "So, she's been pouring poison in your ear?"

"She doesn't have to. I've got eyes."

"And what do you see?"

"You. Playing with people."

"Do you think I've been playing with you?"

I shrug. "It doesn't matter. It's over."

"Oh no," says Manning. "It is not over. For three years you've been avoiding me. It's time we talked."

"We've talked." I stand up. "Spencer's waiting." Manning stands up too.

"For nothing but your safe return."

When I look at him, he smiles.

"You've nothing to worry about," he says. "I've taken care of everything."

It's the way he says it, and that smile. Tender, and yet mocking at the same time.

"I fucking don't believe it!"

He's still smiling as he moves around the fire toward me.

"As you might imagine, the note upset him. He came to me, asking what I knew about it. I told you had been going through difficult times lately; that you were, as he

176

knew, a sensitive boy, and when under pressure, you tended to take too much upon yourself."

"You can't do this to me." My voice rising, cracking. I hear my knuckles cracking too. But I can't stop.

"I killed her!"

He looks at me, unblinking.

"He told me, Peter, about Edwards, and the letter. He blames himself. In attempting to shield me in my, ah, present state of bereavement, he gave you more responsibility than your young shoulders could bear. I agreed with him. I told him, in no uncertain terms, that from now on he should deal with me directly."

"He'll believe me. When I tell him about Cate, and me. He'll believe me then!"

His eyes glimmer when he shakes his head. A brief shake.

"I also told him that if by any chance you came to him with tales of personal involvement with my wife he should recognize them for what they were. Pure fiction." A brief smile. The bastard smiles. "I said I was sure he would, that his splendid record as Headmaster rested on his unerring ability to distinguish fact from fiction. And that as much as Dunster had done for you, there were still, unfortunately, some unresolved childhood conflicts that caused you to experience, from time to time, something as real when in fact it was not."

"He didn't believe you! He's not that dumb!"

"Dumb?" He cocks his head. "You should know, Peter, that Spencer will believe whatever I choose to tell him." He jiggles his hand, as though Spencer was riding his palm. He slides his hand into his pocket.

I am so angry that it's hard to breathe.

"Why don't you tell Spencer you couldn't get it up for her? Tell him that. Tell him you're just what Edwards says you are. A bloody faggot!"

Manning looks at me. He doesn't speak. The fire flickers across his face.

177

"As far as Edwards is concerned," says Manning, slowly, "I told Spencer the same rules applied. That in order to protect me, you might well take it all upon yourself. I told him the entire responsibility was mine, and if necessary I would make public testimony to that effect."

"Why are you doing this to me?" My voice catches in my throat.

"*For* you, Peter."

I close my eyes. It's like drowning. As if I'm underwater with no way to catch my breath.

I open my eyes. He's turned away, looking at the fire. The fire's dying.

"Do you really think you can stand up and say you did it with a student, and have everything stay the same?"

Bending, he scoops up a small handful of dirt, sprinkles it on the fire. The fire smokes. "Did what?" His voice is gentle. Detached.

"You know damn well what. Do you really think that's the kind of headmaster they want?"

"It hardly matters." He straightens. "You're leaving, Peter. I'm leaving too." I stare at him. He smiles. "Don't look so shocked."

"I don't get it! You wanted it more than anything!"

"Anything?"

"There's nothing to stop you from being Head."

"Nothing," he says. He smiles, teasing. "Except my conscience."

"You don't have one."

His smile deepens. "You know me well."

"It's me, isn't it? You're leaving because of me."

"I'm leaving, Peter, because it pleases me to do so. We'd better get back. Will you help me with this fire?"

But I don't move. I can't. The darkness settles. I feel its weight, the weight of all those years, of all he's done.

"I owe you everything. Don't I?"

"Not everything." He's moved away, toward the river.

I hear the river moving, see him coming, with water in his hands.

"If I'd gotten that letter . . ."

His hands unfold above the fire. The water drops. The fire sighs.

"If you'd received it," he says, "nothing would have changed. Except perhaps you would have hated me a little less."

He walks back, into the darkness, to the river. I know that now I have to say it.

"Before that, before I hated you, I loved you."

"I know that."

"More than I ever loved anyone in my life."

"I know that too."

His voice is as gentle as his hand on my cheek. The touch doesn't surprise me. The coolness does.

"That night," he says.

That night.

NINETEEN

WHAT I REMEMBER is the light. The way the door opens, and the light pours through, through the eye of a needle. A needle of light. He stands in the doorway, wearing a dark blue V-necked sweater, white pants, a white shirt, open at the neck. The light comes from behind him, through the west windows that face the field where Cate's garden will someday be. The sun has just set, leaving only the light. It shimmers around him. I see dust motes shifting in the air. He smiles. "You're just in time."

Time stops, holds, like a photograph. I am sixteen. I am still growing. The cuffs of my blazer ride above my wrists. When I clench my fists I feel the strain of cloth across my shoulders. I am almost as tall as he is. He tells me often that we look alike. I don't see it, but he does. My hair is brown except in sunlight, when it turns to copper. His hair is dark, so dark that in the sun the black looks blue. His is straight, mine is curly, but every morning I slick it down with water, press it flat, part it, as he does, on the left.

I would give anything to look like him. To be him. There is something in the way he walks. When he enters a room, you know it; everyone knows it. And when he touches me . . .

He touches me. Where his fingers brush my neck, my skin prickles, comes alive.

"Come in," he says. "I've brought out the maps. We can look at them after dinner."

He looks at me. There is something in the way he looks, as if the rest of the world were stripped away.

"Actually," I say, "my father just called."

The air is cool, but my face is hot. He doesn't notice.

"Good." He smiles. "Tell me later."

He tells me, as he cooks, about the trip. Where we will go. What we will do. I hear the words, but I'm not listening. I can't. The kitchen, like a bubble, is filled with light. I sit inside it. Clock faces ring the walls. I feel time floating.

He cooks. I watch him. He pinches a sprig of green between his fingers. "Rosemary," he says. Crumbling the silvered needles on the lamb. "Rosemary for remembrance."

Here is what I remember. I remember his hands, spooning mint jelly into a crystal bowl. The spoon is silver, the handle curved. When he holds the jelly to the light, the light turns green. He hands me the bowl. I hold it up.

The world is green. The table is green, the clocks are green. He is a green shadow above the stove. Dark bits of mint hang in the jelly. It is like looking at the world from under water.

We eat in the dining room. The plates are thin, and rimmed with gold. The silver is heavy. The table gleams.

I am afraid the silver will crack the plate. I am afraid he will ask me what my father said. When the room grows dark, he lights the candles. There are candles on the table, and candles on the sideboard. Tall white candles in silver candlesticks. Above the sideboard is a large painting in a gold frame. The gold dances. The colors glow.

Manning sees me looking. "Surely it's not the first time you've noticed that?"

I shake my head. "It's the light," I say.

It is the light, the way it catches, brings to life the painting of Manning's mother, Manning as a little boy. A kid, not more than ten or twelve, he stands beside her, dressed in green velvet, a lace collar around his neck. Wearing knickers, and black shoes with silver buckles. He chuckles. "Lord Fauntleroy. My mother's favorite costume when she was young. I must admit I liked it too."

His mother sits. She's wearing velvet too, a velvet dress that leaves her shoulders bare. His hand rests lightly on her shoulder.

"That could be you. Don't you agree?"

I look at him and shake my head. He smiles. "*She* would have thought so. I wish she could have met you." He smiles. "She would have loved you, Peter."

Love, he says.

And I remember. "My father," I say. I swallow. His mother watches. I can't see him with a mother, can't see him as a little boy.

"He says I can't go with you this summer." I say it fast, eyes on the painting, not on him. Mother and son. He sits beside me, waiting. I feel him waiting. I feel time stop.

"Perhaps you'd like to tell me why." His voice is quiet. Too quiet. The silence speaks.

Next to the sideboard is a Chinese screen, a black panther poised beneath a willow tree. The colors are faded. The leaves are green, the panther's eyes are yellow. He could be resting. He could be coiled, set to strike.

"He wants me to do Outward Bound instead."

"I see," says Manning.

But of course he doesn't see; he can't.

"I assume he has a reason?" He waits. I don't say anything. My knuckles crack. "Something to do with me perhaps? The way the trip's arranged?"

"Not you. Me. It's my fault. It's the way . . ." I make myself look at him. His eyes are on me. Dark. "The way I talk about you."

He nods, briefly, as if he knew. "He minds, does he." Not a question, but an answer.

"It's just that he doesn't think it's . . . it's . . . right . . . for us to be together. So much."

182

There, I've said it. But my father said it first. Over the phone, for the first time, he said, "I've been thinking," and right away, I knew. Knew what he thought. Before he said it. "You can visit England later. When you're older. On your own."

"And what did you say to him?" says Manning.

"I said I wanted to go, now, with you. It wasn't fair, for him to change his mind like that. It wasn't fair at all!"

"No. Anything specific you may have said in the past, the recent past, that caused him to reverse his decision?" I shake my head. "Does he feel, perhaps, I've had a negative influence on you?"

"I told you. It's me he worries about, not you."

"Peter, has it ever occurred to you that your father may be jealous, envious of the liking we have for one another?"

"That's not what he says."

Manning smiles. "He wouldn't."

I don't smile. "What he says is that he thinks I like you . . . too much."

"Too much," says Manning. "I see. And what do you think, Peter? It's what you think that matters most."

"What I think," I say. I stop. Because it's not thinking; it's feeling, but how can I put feeling into words? Even if I wanted to.

Maybe Manning knows this. He leans back in his chair. Away from me. It makes it easier to breathe.

"Tell me something," he says. "When you think about your father, what's the first thing that comes to mind?"

"He never touched me." The words surprise me. That I said them surprises too. I look down at the table. "Not that it matters."

"I expect it matters." His voice quiet in the quiet room.

"I remember, once." I place my hands, flat against the polished wood. "When I was just a little kid, I figured I'd surprise him so I hid behind the front door when he was coming home from work."

183

The wood's so smooth it feels wet. I move my fingers back and forth.

"It was stupid, but I guess I thought that maybe if I took him by surprise . . . Anyway, I was wearing those feet pajamas, you know, all one piece. With feet. Really slippery. To walk you had to shuffle. So anyway, there I am behind the door, and finally he comes, and I was all cramped up, nervous I guess, and my feet were freezing. So he comes, and I jump out, and yell surprise. Really loud." I laugh; it doesn't sound much like a laugh though. More like a croak. "I mean, I jumped. My arms were out, and everything because I thought, you know, he'd catch me. I figured he'd have to, but instead of catching me, he pulls his briefcase up, and I hit head first. Hard. It really hurt."

"You frightened him."

"You know what he said? I was lying there, on the floor, trying not to cry, because it hurt, and he looks down, and he says, 'Don't you ever do that again.' Really mad. Like there was something wrong with me."

I look at Manning. I look at him. I have to ask.

"What's wrong with me?"

"Nothing." He says it firmly, as if he knows. He doesn't. "Your father is afraid of many things. Including feelings."

"I feel." My heart pounding.

"I know that." He smiles. "I'm glad you do."

"No. I mean, my father's right. How I feel. About you." I swallow. My eyes sting. My face burns. I close my eyes.

"Peter, it's to your credit that you care."

"You don't understand." I keep my eyes closed, bite my lip to keep from crying.

"Oh, but I do." His voice is close enough to touch. He touches me. He takes my hand, lifts it from the table, holding it between his own. "You need to know there's nothing wrong with wanting what you never had." Taking my hand, he presses it to his cheek. His cheek cool, smooth, like sand. "Come here," he says.

184

I do. He holds me. I am sixteen. I let him hold me. I let him touch me. "There, there," he says. As if I am a baby. I am sixteen. I am a baby. The world is green.

He holds me. Only the river whispers in the dark.

"Don't you see," he says, "I only wanted to give you what you never had."

His arms around me, I feel it closing in. His weight against me. All things coming back again.

"I should have known," he says. "Should have known it was too late."

"I let you." I pull away. He looks at me.

"No one's going to punish you for that."

I have to laugh. "That's what you think. And anyway, it's not just that."

"What else?"

"You know! I told you. Cate!"

"No one will believe you, Peter."

I look at him. He stands still, staring. His eyes are dark. And I can't take it anymore.

"That letter you wrote. About letting go. Bullshit! You haven't let go at all!"

He doesn't move.

"No one, Peter." He says it firmly as if he knows. He doesn't, though.

There is one person who will.

TWENTY

 THE SCHOOL is quiet, so quiet you can hear the furnace humming in the basement. Our footsteps echo. No one is around. Manning's hand is on my shoulder. Spencer's door is closed, but through the crack I see light shining. I slow down. Manning's grip tightens.

"You can see him in the morning."

I stop. "I want to tell him."

"All he needs to hear is that you're back. I'll tell him that. You go to bed."

I could pull away, push past him, but what's the point? His word, and mine. I shrug. His hand releases me. I feel him watching as I climb the stairs. There's time, I tell myself. There's time.

Snickers is waiting, sitting on my bed. The door is closed. Frozen in position, nothing moves except his eyes, watching as I cross the room.

"Beat it, kid. It's bedtime." I lean across the desk to open the window. The air feels cold.

"Where were you?" I hear the whine.

"The infirmary."

"I know *that*. I mean, afterward. Now?"

"Nowhere."

"I was looking for you!" His voice rises to a squeak. I look at him. Embarrassed, he clears his throat, ducking his head between his knees. He's wearing pajama bottoms and a white

186

T-shirt so much too big that it looks more like a nightgown than a shirt.

"Well, you found me."

"Yeah." With his mouth pressed against his legs, his voice is muffled. He rocks on the bed. The bedsprings creak.

"So what's up?"

"Nothing." He keeps on rocking, face hidden behind his legs.

I glance at the clock. "It's ten-fifteen. Lights out."

"Edwards," he says. A strangled whisper.

I should have known.

"Listen, kid. Edwards is a fucking asshole. You know that."

He looks at me over his knees. His knees are bony. He hugs them. "If I get kicked out, my father's going to kill me."

"Your father's an ass too," I say. Without thinking. His eyes widen. But it's true. I only met him once; once was enough.

"Come off it, kid. Kicked out! For what?"

His head goes down again. "You know," he whispers.

I know his father all right. He lives in California now, and looks it. The gold chain, pants so tight he's got wedgies up his ass. When we shook hands, he smiled when he heard my fingers crack. "The paragon!" he said, and laughed. The kind of laugh that goes in instead of out. "So give it to me. Tell me straight. This place any good at turning losers into winners?" With Snickers standing there beside him. I could have killed him. Should have killed him. Instead I sounded just like Spencer. "We don't have losers here," I said. Sounding like a loser myself.

"Edwards," says Snickers, head down. "He called me faggot."

No losers, I should have said, except for Edwards.

"Sticks and stones, kid."

"In front of everyone. After dinner, he asked if I'd slept well. With you. He said your name, and all the kids were listening."

"Big deal, kid." I mean it. "*Faggot* is Edwards' favorite word in case you didn't know it."

If he knows, it doesn't seem to matter. Only his hair shows, soft silver spikes, like thistledown. His ears stick out. I see them flaming.

"I didn't mean to fall asleep."

I walk over to the bed, and sit beside him. The mattress sags, and he scoots sideways, away from me.

"So what? You fell asleep. I did too. Just let him talk. In a week he's gone forever."

He lifts his head. I see his eyes. "You will be too."

"We've got a date," I smile. "Big Apple, here we come."

He doesn't smile. "You hit him."

"Yeah. I guess maybe I should have hit him harder."

"Did you . . . did you hit him because of me?"

"He's had it coming to him for years."

"Everybody thinks you did." He swallows. "Everybody thinks it's true."

"What's true?" I say it soft. He doesn't answer. His head goes down. I didn't notice he'd stopped rocking until he starts again. The bed shakes. "Who's everybody?"

"Me." A whisper.

"I hate to disappoint you, kid, but it didn't have a thing to do with you."

He keeps on rocking. Who knows if he believes me? Who knows what he wants to hear?

"He's saying things."

He stops rocking, but he doesn't move. "He's saying things, about you, and Mr. Manning."

Even with my eyes closed, the light's too bright. I lay my arm across my face.

I hear him take a deep breath, hear it quiver. "He says he's got proof." I hear him waiting.

188

What is it about silence? How can you have a language without words? If you listen, you can hear it.

"Say something," says Snickers.

"Beat it," I say. "Scram!"

I say it loud enough to make him jump. I hear his feet hit the floor. He's off and running. I hear the door open and close.

I wait a minute, then I get up, go out into the hall. The phone's at the far end, under the one hall light left shining. Next to the phone, a thin phone book dangles from a string. I check the number, and dial. It rings once, and Mrs. MacQuire answers.

"It's me." I say it quietly.

"Oh God! Thank God! Where are you?"

"Right here. In the dorm. Listen, I'm sorry, I know it's late, but I need to talk to you."

"You're at school? You're all right?"

"Yeah, listen, I need . . ."

"So he found you. Did he find you?"

"Yeah. He found me."

"And you're fine?"

"Fine?"

"You're not hurt? You didn't hurt yourself?"

"What's going on? That's what he thought. You think I should have?"

"Peter! What a monstrous thing to say!"

"Listen. I need to talk to you. I need your help."

I hear her breathing, short gasps, uneven, as if she's climbed some hill.

"I could not have borne it," she says.

"All you have to do is tell Spencer that you know I did it. He'll believe you."

"You know what Oliver believes. The day Cate was found, what he said . . ."

"If you said . . ."

"He said" — her voice cracks — " 'I hope you are aware,

189

Melissa, that you killed her.' And then, last night, when he came to find you, thinking I had you hidden somewhere in the house. I told him I thought maybe you might be down by the river, and he stood there at the door, you know how he is, how he looks. He said it again, 'You realize, Melissa, that if I find him dead, you'll have two deaths on your hands.' "

I hear her breathing. My grip tightens on the phone.

"Don't listen to him."

She laughs, or chokes; I can't tell which.

"Peter?" A pause. "You don't think I killed her, do you?" she says in a small tight voice.

"Don't be stupid."

And she laughs, a small laugh, embarrassed. "I needed to hear you say that."

"You had a name for it, remember? For what he's doing. Blaming you."

"Displacement," Mrs. MacQuire says. "The question is, of course, what's being displaced and onto who."

"Listen," I say. "I know you think he did it, but he didn't."

But she's not listening.

"Thank God you're back. I can't take any more tonight. I'll see you in the morning."

I hear a click. She's gone. I hang up quietly. I wasn't lying to Manning. I don't trust her anymore. But she's all I've got, the only one who really knows.

It's snowing. It snowed yesterday too just in time for Oliver's Christmas party, the one that he gives every year. Everything looked so pretty, just like a picture in a book.

Yesterday, down by the river, Peter showed me how to make an angel in the snow. He lay on his back and moved his arms and legs. He looked so funny I had to laugh and when I laughed, he laughed too. You try, he said, and so I did. I lay down next to him and moved my arms and legs, and when I stood up, there were two angels with wings and robes. Their wings were touching. They looked so real. He said, what you do is wish on them. So we closed our eyes and made a wish. I had two wishes, but I only told him one. I wished I had a brother like you, I said. I do. But his face turned all red, and then I wished I hadn't said it. What did you wish, I said, but his face got even redder. If you tell, he said, they won't come true so I was glad I'd kept my other wish a secret. But then he said he had to get right back to school, and I was afraid that I'd done something wrong.

Until today when I told Melissa, and she said, oh dear, you know what I think. I think the poor boy has fallen for you. I didn't know what to think when she said that. I said, but we're practically the same age, and she said, dear Cate, that is the point. And anyway, I said, I'm married, and she shook her head in the same way Aunt Effie did when I'd made her cross, but then she smiled. You, she said in her soft voice. You.

Sometimes I think I'm going to tell her about Aunt Effie, but I never do. I can tell she likes to hear about the orphanage so I tell her that. When I tell her, it feels real so maybe I'm not really lying. It's Aunt Effie who doesn't feel real, and I think maybe she happened to someone else, to Cathy, not to Cate. It was Oliver who named me Cate. Before that I was Cathy. Cathy is common is what he said. Cathy, Aunt Effie said, I'm doing this for your own good so you keep quiet. She did things for me. She did things to me. I didn't know what. Sometimes it hurt. Keep quiet, she said. So I kept quiet because what could I say, and anyway who would I tell. There was only Aunt Effie, and she knew all there was to know.

Only now there is Melissa. When we came home last summer, I saw her and I started to cry. I thought you were dead, I said. And she said, silly, I've been right here all summer. When I can't see you, I said, and she said, shhh, it's all right now. Look, she said, and she showed me my garden, the one

Peter helped me plant. There were tomatoes and squash and orange flowers. I watered it all summer, she said, keeping it alive for you.

When I see Aunt Effie now, it's in my dreams. She's always driving, and her face is wrinkled, the way it was. I sit beside her reading, Alice in Wonderland, *her favorite book. I read slowly, the way she taught me. Before she found me in the trash, and took up traveling, she taught little children how to read. That's what she says. She says she always did like little children best, but just like Alice I've begun to grow, taller than Aunt Effie now. I scrunch down so she won't notice. How old am I, I say, and she says, too old. She says it, frowning. We're going to have to cut your hair. My hair is long, almost to my waist, and every morning she brushes it. Alice, she says, my little Alice, and brushing my hair, her hands don't hurt. We're going to cut it, she says, and I say, no, a whisper to myself at first. No, I say, louder than before and then I make myself wake up because I know what's going to happen next.*

But I don't want to write about Aunt Effie. I want to write about Melissa, how last night at the Christmas party, she took my hand. Haven't you done a lovely job, she said, and I said, Oliver told me what to do. She turned to Oliver. Hasn't she, she said, and Oliver smiled. She's good at following instructions, he said, and Melissa squeezed my hand. She said, don't listen to him, and so I didn't. I'm glad I didn't because when I heard him say, we appear to be missing six of Mother's green-stemmed glasses, I didn't hear him. I didn't answer. Melissa did. I was hoping you wouldn't notice, she said, and he said, you ought to know, I notice almost everything. In that case, said Melissa, let me confess I broke them when I was up here helping Cate last spring.

You didn't think I'd notice, he said, and she said, when you did, I planned to tell you. I didn't want you blaming Cate.

I wouldn't, said Oliver. Not for the deception anyway.

192

She's too transparent for that, and besides the only one who knew I had the extra glasses was you.

And then Melissa squeezed my hand. There, she said, you've been acquitted.

Today she squeezed my hand again. I walked down to her house through the snow, and she was in the kitchen, holding Rufus in her lap. He was asleep. I looked at them, the way she rubbed her chin against his hair, and I couldn't help it. I said, I wish you were my mother, and she reached out and squeezed my hand.

In a sense, she said, I am. But Cate, she said, you need to grow up, need to learn to mother yourself.

I looked at Rufus in her lap, and thought about my secret wish. If I could be a mother, I said, and she said quickly, Cate, that's not the answer. She got up, holding Rufus, and she laid him in my lap. He stayed asleep. Sleeping, he was very heavy. I put my arms around his waist and held on tight. I felt better holding him. Please, I said.

Cate, she said, I'm hardly the person you should ask, and from her voice I knew I'd made her cross.

I'm sorry, I said. It's just I don't know what to do.

Some things, she said, you'll have to work out for yourself.

While I held Rufus, she made tea. Holding him, I tried to pretend that he was mine. He was too big. I needed something small, inside.

Besides, she said, can you see Oliver as a father?

She poured the boiling water into mugs. I saw steam rising.

No, I said. She looked at me. You asked him, she said, and I said, yes, and I could tell she was surprised. She laughed. A hard laugh. Actually, she said, serve him right.

She stirred her tea, but didn't drink it.

What would, I said, and she said, never mind, pay no attention, and then she closed her eyes.

The way she looked then scared me. You're not sick, are you, I said, and she shook her head. He's a sickness, she said, and I said, I don't understand.

Dear Cate, she said, you're not supposed to.

There's a hole inside of me, I said.

Dear Cate, she said, Oliver is not the one to fill it.

Who is, I said, and she said, someone who loves you. Someone who cares.

I wasn't sure just who she meant. If she meant anyone. I couldn't think of anything to say. I looked outside. The snow was falling.

I thought of Peter and his angels. I thought, well, I can tell her about that.

And so I did, and she said. The poor boy's fallen for you. That's what she said.

TWENTY-ONE

IN THE DREAM, Bets is singing. "Poor babes in the woods." She sings, verse after verse. Her voice is high and clear. We lie under the trees, looking up, as the leaves drop, oak leaves, like polished pennies. Bets stops singing. "Are we dead yet?" she says. The leaves fall. "Of course not," I say. Leaves, smelling of dusty sunlight, cover us. They are so light. "There's nothing to be afraid of," I say, and she believes me. She sings again, but her voice is muffled now, and suddenly I feel the weight shift, leaves pressing down, falling so thick and fast that no sky shows. "Get out," I say, try to say, "Run!" but the leaves cover me, and when I open my mouth they slide inside, and I know it is too late to get away. The dark is all around. Trapped, I fight it, kicking out.

"Hey, Spaulding! For Christ's sake!"

There are hands on my shoulders, pulling at me. Breaking free, I sit up, blinking. The sun's up, and my room is pink.

Thurston stands by the bed, my blanket in his hand. I'm drenched with sweat. He shakes the blanket. "You were under this," he says, tossing it back onto the bed.

I shake my head to clear it. "Jesus. I used to do that as a kid. All the time. Wake up under the covers, and not know where I was."

"I was coming to see you when the phone rang, out in the hall."

"Did the bell go already?"

195

Thurston nods. "It's your father," he says. "On the phone."

I pull the blanket around my shoulders.

"Tell him I'm not here."

"Too late," says Thurston. "I told him you were."

"Shit." I stand up slowly. The blanket rubs like sand against my skin.

"Hey buddy," says Thurston. He rocks backward, sliding his hands into his pockets. "You OK?"

"Sure."

He rocks forward, stands, his feet planted, eyes inscrutable, behind his hair.

"Don't worry," I say.

I edge past him toward the door. He shrugs. "Who's worried," he says.

The hall is filled with kids. All quiet. At this hour no one talks. All First Formers, in the dim light they look like dwarves, shuffling to the john, and back again.

I pick up the phone, and hear my father breathing. I don't say anything. My father does.

"Peter?" he says. I clear my throat to let him know it's me. "I understand you've had some trouble lately." There's an edge to his voice; he doesn't like to be kept waiting.

"Not really."

I see Snickers scuttling, out of his room, toward the john. He stops when he sees me, freezes, then scuttles back. Too scared to even take a leak. My father sighs, an angry hiss like steam exploding through a sidewalk grate.

"Not really," he says, his voice an echo of my own. "Judith thinks otherwise. You talked to her yesterday."

"Maybe I should talk to Judith then." Thinking he'll pass the phone to her.

"We tried last night," he says, "but you were out."

He waits. I hear him waiting. Any minute I'll hear his knuckles start to crack.

"Yeah. Out to lunch." I even laugh. He's breathing louder. "That's a joke," I say.

"Out," he says, "and no one, including Spencer, knew where you were."

"Don't worry. I'm back."

"I told Spencer I found the lack of supervision distressing, and I do."

"What's wrong? Don't you think I'm old enough to look after myself?"

"Peter," says my father. "Will you please tell me what's going on?"

"Ask Judith."

"She knows only what you told her."

"I'll bet the only reason you're calling is because she told you to."

"Peter!"

"Well, you can tell her not to worry. I'm fine."

"Frankly," says my father, "it's the situation I find disturbing."

"You think it's my fault that nobody believes me?"

"Peter." He pauses. "Why don't you let someone else handle things for a change?"

"That's a great idea. Who? You got any good ideas?"

"You've got a right to be angry, Peter."

"I'm not angry."

"I do realize," says my father, "that it hasn't been easy. I feel badly that I wasn't paying closer attention, to what was going on. That I didn't know . . ."

"Oh, you knew. You knew. You guessed. And I might as well tell you you were right."

"Right?"

"About Manning and me. Remember when you said I couldn't go to England with him. Because you were worried? Well, you were right to worry. OK?"

"Peter!" His voice is sharp. I've done it now. One touch, and zap.

"Just don't sweat it, OK? You've always known what I was really like. I mean, I know why you left."

197

"Left? What are you talking about?"

"I know you left because of me. I don't blame you. I really don't. I'm a shit. Okay, I know I'm a shit. If Cate were here, she'd tell you. Not that she has to. You already know."

"Stop it, Peter!"

"Maybe you don't know I killed her."

The silence is incredible. Really incredible. He's not even breathing anymore. The line zings and fizzes. Maybe he's hung up. Given up. Who could blame him.

"Why didn't you tell Judith that?" It's him all right. Still there. His voice is harsh.

"Maybe I wasn't ready yet."

"You stay right where you are!" he says. "Don't leave that school!"

I have to laugh. I really do. "Where would I go?" I say.

I hang up before he answers me. Not that there is an answer. But I feel better because I told him. Now he knows. There's nothing he can do I don't deserve.

Thurston's still waiting in my room. Leaning against the wall, arms folded, humming. His head's down, but I'm not fooled. I know he's watching as I dress.

"I could kill him for you," he says, and for a moment I think he's talking about my father. "Edwards," he says.

I shrug. "Don't sweat it."

"Not that I'd give a shit." He slides slowly down the wall until he's sitting. "If you'd done it." His arms unfurl, his fingers play the air. "With anyone." Behind his hair, his eyes are closed. His voice is sleepy.

"Thanks."

I have to step across his legs to get my shoes.

He hums a few bars. "Bach," he says. "Great for depression."

I stand up. "Who's depressed?"

Thurston stands up too, a slow and easy shambling.

"If you want help," he says.

"I'm beyond help, buddy." I laugh, to let him know it doesn't matter.

"If you want help." His voice is stubborn.

"Thanks anyway."

He shrugs, eyes flickering behind his hair, and leaves. Silence. I listen to it. I smell syrup, sugar, eggs. When I hold my hands in front of me I see them shaking.

Spencer's in his study, behind his desk. In the dim light his face is putty-colored, wrinkled like old cloth. "Ah, Spaulding," he says. "Just the man I want to see. Come over here."

His study smells of stale smoke, and varnished wood. He holds a cup of coffee in his hands. Outside it's raining. A gentle mist.

"Now then! I have to say I am sorely disappointed, Spaulding. Sorely disappointed! It is most unlike you to be so thoughtless."

"Yes, sir."

"As I'm sure Manning told you, your precipitous departure caused considerable concern."

"Yes sir. I can explain, sir."

Spencer frowns. "I'm not asking for an explanation! I wish to point out that your behavior was not only thoughtless, but delinquent. As Senior Prefect, Spaulding, surely you are aware that to vacate the infirmary without official discharge constitutes an offense, however minor, against school rules."

"Yes, sir."

"More serious, of course, is the matter of leaving school grounds without permission. There is, as you well know, a sign-out book for precisely that purpose."

"Yes, sir."

"And finally, Spaulding, there is the physical assault. On Edwards."

"Yes, sir."

199

"Not," he looks down at his coffee, "I must add, entirely undeserved."

"No, sir."

"I hope you don't expect to be let off scot-free, Spaulding. I assume you know some punishment is called for."

"Yes, sir."

I think he is about to say something else, but instead he places his coffee on the desk.

"The quality of mercy, Spaulding," he says, and sighs. I don't say anything.

"You're a good boy, Spaulding." His chair creaks. "To understand." He rests his elbows on the desk. "And I hope you will forgive me."

"For what, sir?"

"For not setting a better example, Spaulding! As head-master, it is imperative that one's mind and heart remain open. Open and aware. Edwards, for all his intelligence, has not had an easy time."

"I know that, sir."

"He has not, as you have, Spaulding, been graced in such ways that will win the world's approval. My approval." He squeezes his fingers together. Veins rise like blue ridges on his hands. He grimaces. "I shall continue to hope. To pray. But I should tell you that I've sent him packing."

"It's not Edwards, sir. It's me."

His hands hit the desk with volcanic force. The cup rocks, coffee slopping onto papers. "I will not have it, Spaulding! I will not! I've already heard from Mr. Manning. I do not need to hear from you!"

"I know that, sir, but the truth is . . ."

"The truth, Spaulding, has already been explained to me."

"I killed her, sir."

"I will pray," says Spencer, "for patience." Eyes closed, he prays. Bells ring. His lips move. Outside the door I hear feet moving too, hundreds of them, marching down the hall, and out, down stone steps, across the cloisters. Closing my

200

eyes, I could be moving with them, their footsteps echoing inside. Down the hall, and out the door.

Standing there, I first saw Cate. When was it? Yesterday, or a hundred years ago.

"Now then," says Spencer. I open my eyes to see his open too, fixed on some point above my head. "Under the circumstances, grounding until graduation is most appropriate. That way we keep an eye on you. No more mischief, Spaulding. Good food, rest." He leans back.

"That note I sent you, sir."

"Say no more, Spaulding." Under his chin, the loose skin wobbles. "All is forgiven. And forgotten."

"No!"

He blinks.

"It's as if I count for nothing!"

"To the contrary." He sighs. "At least where Manning is concerned. You realize, that in order to protect you, he's perjured himself. You are in his debt, Spaulding."

"Can't you understand! I don't want to be."

"It appears you have no choice. You have heard, I assume, he's decided to leave."

"He doesn't have to!"

"He's made his choice, Spaulding. It's left to us to honor that decision." He clears his throat. "A good man, Spaulding. A noble man. As you well know."

I close my eyes. Is it just Spencer? Or is it everyone who listens only to what they want to hear?

"And as for you, Spaulding, you have the makings of a fine man. A fine man. I'm proud that Dunster had a hand in shaping you."

"You shouldn't be."

"Now, now. Humility becomes you, but it's not necessary to go so far. Surely you did not for a moment imagine I'd believe such a tale as you proposed to tell me."

"It's the truth, sir . . ."

"The truth, Spaulding, is that you were as willing to per-

201

jure yourself, for him, as he was for you. Noble, Spaulding, most noble, but most definitely misguided. However." His chair squeaks as he stands. "I hold myself to blame. Had I not come to you first, this never would have happened."

"She'd still be dead, sir."

"Beside the point, Spaulding. Quite, beside the point."

"Not if I killed her."

He walks across the room toward me.

"Enough of that." He pats my shoulder. "Manning tells me you went out of your way to befriend the poor girl. Most commendable, Spaulding. But you must not hold yourself responsible. No one, Spaulding, no one is going to blame you for what you did not do."

His hand drops from my shoulder. Rain rolls down the window like small glass beads.

"The fact is, Spaulding, had you not felt compelled to accept all responsibility, Manning would not, in his turn, have felt compelled to do the same. He has told me that rather than give Edwards the perverse pleasure of verbal denial, he prefers to abdicate. In silence. Let Edwards interpret the silence as he wishes. I did suggest, quite strongly, that if he must leave, it was not necessary to leave under such a cloud. He assured me it was of no concern to him. A man, Spaulding! An example to us all."

"Yes, sir." I stand up. "If I could leave now."

And Spencer lets me go.

TWENTY-TWO

THERE WAS A TIME, last winter, when Cate came to me. In January. The snow had thawed, then frozen solid so that the crust cracking sounded like breaking bones. So that I heard her coming as I was kneeling by the fire in the shelter. Hearing her, I held my breath.

It had been three weeks since I'd seen her, but she didn't say hello. She said, "It's all right." Smiling. I'd never seen her look so happy. At first it scared me.

"What is?"

"Oh, everything," she said. She laughed. Her laugh surprised me, a light laugh, rising. I'd hardly ever heard her laugh before, except once, when we were making angels in the snow.

"Peter, I've been thinking about what you said."

What I'd said? All I knew was what I hadn't said.

"It's all right," she said. "But maybe first, you'd better learn to call me Cate."

Cate. I called her Cate, but only to myself. To her face I didn't call her anything. When I shook my head, she reached out, and touched her finger to my cheek. A light touch. Teasing. "Go on, try."

I swallowed. "Cate," I said.

"Good," she said. She knelt beside me. "You can kiss me if you want." Smiling. As if she knew all fall I'd wanted to.

I edged backward. "That's OK." My face was burning.

203

"It's easy." She leaned toward me. Her lips were cool. She smelled of pine. "See?"

What I saw was the way she sat there, in the firelight, her skin glowing as slowly she peeled off her clothes. First her gloves, and then her coat. Slowly, eyes on me, smiling. Her fingers worked the buttons on her blouse, a white blouse sprinkled with blue flowers.

My throat was dry; it hurt to swallow. I wanted to ask what she was doing, but I couldn't. It sounded rude. And anyway, once her blouse was off, and then her skirt, I knew. Her arms lifted, and her hair fell, over her shoulders, across her breasts.

She knelt beside me, close enough so I could see small hairs glinting on her arms. All I could do was shake my head. She smiled.

"You do like me, don't you?"

"I love you," I said. Without thinking. But it was true.

She didn't move. She smiled. "It's all right then," she said.

I'd never heard her sound so sure.

As soon as Mrs. MacQuire shows up, I tell her.

"She thought you'd given her permission." I say it even before she's in the room. She's standing in the doorway, frowning.

"What?"

"To have a baby."

Moving quickly, she closes the door.

"Peter!"

"No one's out there. They're all studying for exams."

"That's not the point." Frowning, she bites her lip. "I didn't come to talk about that."

She crosses the room, sits on the bed. I sit watching from my desk. We sit the way we sat three days ago, only this time I'm prepared. Even my bed is made, and Cate's journal hidden, out of sight.

She doesn't seem to notice. Maybe it's the dull gray light, but she looks different, muted, like someone seen through cloudy glass.

"Do you know how glad I am to see you," she says. She doesn't look glad; but who can blame her.

"I'm ready to talk," I say. My voice sounds hoarse. I clear my throat. "You wanted to know. About me and Manning."

"Ah." She looks down at her folded hands. "It's Spencer you should talk to, Peter."

"I have."

She looks up fast. "And?" Her eyes are wary.

"He won't believe a thing I tell him. That's why I have to talk to you. But not because of Manning. Because of me."

"What about you?" Guarded.

"It was my fault."

"Peter." She sighs. "*What* was your fault?"

"Everything."

She says nothing. She waits. She waits in the same way I remember Manning waiting. Like a cup, an empty cup, just waiting to be filled. And so I fill it.

And so I tell her, about the night two years before. Tell her what happened. Before that summer. Before Cate.

She sits still, very still, when I'm talking and when I'm done. She sits so still I wonder if she's heard me. My knuckles crack.

"Say something."

She passes a hand across her eyes.

"One night, Peter." Sounding as if she can't believe it. Or doesn't want to.

I try a laugh. "It's not enough?"

She laughs too, a short sharp sound. "No." Her head shakes slowly, back and forth. "One night spent sitting in his lap."

"That's not all! You know it's not!"

She looks at me. "So he seduced you. Once. Oh, Peter." She gets up slowly, and walks over to the window.

"It wasn't *him!*"

She presses her hands against the glass. The rain is falling without sound. "And I was so sure I knew." Her voice a whisper. "All those years I thought . . ."

"It wasn't him! Listen! It was me. My fault. The way I felt. I loved him. He only gave me what I wanted."

"What *he* wanted," says Mrs. MacQuire. "The fact is, Peter, you're the only person he's ever loved, besides himself." She looks at me, and tries to smile. "I'm not blaming you," she says, "but it's a fact."

"Listen," I say. "I know you're mad at him. Because of Cate. You don't like him, and I don't either. He was a shit. But it doesn't matter anymore. I mean you don't have to work at getting rid of him because he's leaving."

"Of course he's not. He's taking over."

"Not anymore."

Her eyes widen. "What do you mean?"

"He's leaving. He told Spencer yesterday."

She stands still, rooted, like a tree. "I don't believe you," she says, her voice small and far away.

"It's true."

"I don't," she says, but I can see that she's beginning to.

She shudders, and I think of lightning, think for a moment that she's going to fall.

"Well," she says. Her breath catches in her throat. Her eyes stare. They frighten me.

"I thought that's what you wanted. For him to go."

"I want him to pay. For something." Her eyes are glass.

"He didn't kill Cate."

"At the moment," she says, "it's not Cate I'm thinking of."

"If I told you I killed her."

She looks at me.

"I wouldn't believe you."

"If it's the truth."

"Dear Peter. The truth is you're not capable of murder.

You may have felt like . . . but, no, I'm sorry to disappoint you. I really am. You didn't kill her." She looks down at her hands. "Leaving," she says. "I can't believe it." She says it softly, talking to herself.

"Maybe you don't know the whole story." I say it loud, to bring her back.

"Maybe you don't," she says. I watch her fingers pluck her skirt.

"Listen," I say. "Did you know she came back, to me, after saying that she was going to stay with Manning. She came back. She told me that she'd changed her mind."

Her hands go still.

"When?"

"The day she died."

"No," she says. A whisper. "I didn't know that." She walks back to the bed, and sits. "She didn't tell me she was going to do that." She looks down at her lap.

"She didn't tell you everything."

"She did. She was my baby." She starts to rock. "He killed my baby." A small rocking, back and forth.

"Listen," I say.

"My baby." Her voice a moan.

"She left a journal."

She stops rocking right away.

"She really loved you," I say. "She did."

"Journal? She kept a journal?"

I nod. "She left it. For me. There were things she never told you, told anyone. So I mean it's not your fault."

She blinks. "Fault? I never said it was my fault." Her voice is shrill. "It's his. She was too young to have a baby. She wasn't well. That's why I told him. Because I knew what would happen. If I didn't. And then." Her mouth twists. "It happened anyway."

"That's what I mean. It's not your fault."

"I did everything I could!"

"I know that."

207

She hugs herself. "She had so little. I wanted to give . . . to make her into something. Somebody. Was that wrong?"

"No. Of course not."

Hugging herself, she rocks. The bed squeaks. Her eyes are closed. "*He* thought so. He said . . . said, in that voice of his, you weren't helping her, Melissa, but hurting me." She says it in his voice, a cold voice with a cutting edge.

I don't say anything. She sighs.

"I suppose he said as much to you."

"I didn't believe him."

She rocks faster. "Maybe you should."

"No." I shake my head.

"Maybe I should." She goes still. "Maybe . . ." She looks down. "I hate him." Her voice is calm.

"I know."

"And did you know that we were having an affair?" Her voice still calm, and very flat. When I don't say anything, she looks up. Her face reminds me of a mask.

"Did he tell you?"

I shake my head.

"Who?"

"Mary. But I didn't know if it was true."

"Mary." She almost smiles. "Yes, Mary would know."

"Not that I cared," I say quickly. "I mean, it didn't matter to me."

"How kind." Her smile mocks.

My face gets hot. "You know what I mean."

"I assume you mean you didn't hate me when you heard." I look away to hide my face. "Why would I?"

"Because no one likes to have illusions shattered."

"They aren't," I say. "They haven't been." I say it fast. Too fast. I think she knows. "I know what he's like," I say. "How good he is at sucking people in."

She stares at me, not saying a thing.

"Anyway, whatever it was. Between you. It was a long time ago."

208

Her laugh is sharp. "That's true enough."

My face gets hotter. "So why would I care. I mean, it's over."

"Over." Testing the word, she nods, and eases back. She lies flat, arms folded across her chest, lies so still that if I didn't know I'd think her dead. "So why pretend . . ." Her voice trails off. "Sometimes I think I've spent my whole life pretending."

She's talking to herself again, so I don't answer. We're both quiet. Outside the rain makes a hushing noise. In the quiet I think of Cate. Of Mrs. MacQuire.

I look at Mrs. MacQuire on my bed.

I see her breathing rise and fall. Her dress is blue. Her arms are firm. A large woman, but not fat. Looking, I try to see her through Cate's eyes. She lies still, but there's weight to her, a density. Her wrists are thick, not fleshy but full-boned. Cate's wrist I could circle with my fingers. Her bones were brittle. Lifting her was lifting air. She was that light. A leaf with small veins, violet-colored, showing through transparent skin.

There's nothing transparent about Mrs. MacQuire. If Cate's a leaf, then she's a stone. Even her age has weight to it. Thirty-nine. Not twenty-two.

I watch her breathing. Her stomach's flat. Her hands are clasped. Watching, I see the shape of things. That's all. I don't see what's inside, what holds the pieces. What, if anything, connects us. What she knows.

Her eyelids flutter, and I think, maybe it doesn't really matter what she knows. It's what I know, and how I know it. When I close my eyes, the world goes dark. I think of stars, stars coming together, then apart. The space between them. What it holds.

"It's funny," said Mrs. MacQuire, "what I remember." Her voice is quiet, woven into falling rain. "It was winter," she says, "just after Christmas. A terrible day. One of those days when you wake up and feel life is over. Just like that.

But the fact was I was twenty-nine. It seemed important somehow. A watershed. I reminded Logan so he wouldn't forget. I was exhausted. It was still dark when he woke me up. He came in rattling. Wearing chains like Marley's ghost. Snow tire chains. My birthday present! And he was so pleased. I couldn't even look at him. He kept saying, but hon, you said you needed them. Needed them! And I remember thinking, what have I done?"

She's staring at the ceiling, staring, as if Coach was up there, dragging chains.

"He's a nice guy," I say.

I see her blink. "Do you think that makes it easier?"

I clear my throat. "He loves you."

"How can he," she says, "when he doesn't know me?" She shakes her head. "Some people never do grow up, you know."

"If you let them."

She turns her head and looks at me. "You think it's my fault?"

"I'm thinking of Cate. The way Manning treated her. Just like a baby."

"We all did," says Mrs. MacQuire. "She was a baby. Oh, God." She lays her arms across her eyes. "To think I'm saying all this to you."

"It's OK." That's what I say. Of course it isn't.

"The keeper of the journal," she says. She glances at me. "What does she say?"

I don't say anything.

"Does she . . ." Her voice goes shy. "Say anything about Oliver . . . about us? Did he tell her?"

I can tell from the way she asks that's what she really wants to know.

"She thinks you're everything."

In the light her face is gray. "No one should be everything," she says. She sighs. "No one can be."

210

I get up, my legs stiff from holding still. I walk over to the window and look out.

"You can forget about it now," I say. "I mean, he's leaving."

"That same winter," she says, as if I haven't spoken, "was when it started. At parties. We used to have a lot of parties then. Wonderful parties. His were the best. One night at his house, I sat next to him, wearing a lilac-colored dress I'd made myself, a lovely dress really, and we were talking about God. The Gnostic Gospels actually. The two of us. You know how he is, the way he has of making you feel that no one else exists, and I hadn't talked about those things since college. I used to love to talk ideas, but what with Logan and the babies . . . I don't know . . . and suddenly there it was again and all with flowers and candles and champagne. Oh, it was lovely! I'd forgotten almost everything but somehow he made me feel smart, made me feel as if I mattered. We talked for hours, in the dining room. Everyone else was in the study. Well, he talked, really, and I listened, and I remember watching the bubbles in my champagne, you know how they rise, watching them and thinking, that's me, that's me. And then he said, in that voice of his, 'Melissa, they believe God is inside,' and he touched my lips with his finger, and when he did I felt . . . there was something in that touch . . . I felt as if I'd been sleeping for twenty-nine years and had just woken up."

I hear her sigh. Turning, I see her eyes are closed. I see her smiling.

"The next day," she says, "he brought me flowers." Smiling, her face is young and soft. "Birds of Paradise." Her hands rise, shaping flowers in the air. "I was kneeling in front of the fireplace, trying to get it started. The fire, I mean, but I couldn't . . . everything was cold and damp, awful, and suddenly, there he was, standing in the doorway with these flowers. 'Birds of Paradise,' he said, and I said,

'They must have cost the earth.' It just came out. I was stunned. Absolutely. Logan had never given me flowers in my life. But he just smiled. 'I thought we should celebrate,' he said. I was so stunned I never asked what we were celebrating. I just stood there, holding those silly flowers, trying not to cry. Anyway, I suppose I knew. I suppose I must have, but it was safer to pretend . . . And . . ." She turns to me.

"And here we are," she says. She tries a smile. "And now you know. Are you terribly shocked?"

"Why should I be?" I turn back to the window again.

"I can think of lots of reasons."

"It's your business what you did with him."

"Yours too." I look at her. She looks at me. "Six years ago, when you arrived, is when it ended." And she smiles. Maybe to soften the words.

I swallow. "You're blaming me?"

"I'm not saying that. I'm telling you why I thought what I thought, about you and Oliver. Because the fact is when you came I went out." She's still smiling, but not her eyes. Her eyes, in this light, are brown and hard.

"But you were friends! I mean, you always were together, and it seemed like . . ."

"Nothing is what it seems," she says. "You ought to know that." Head in her hands, she rubs her forehead. "Something," she says, "was better than nothing. And I kept hoping, and he kept saying how marvelous I was to understand. Marvelous." Her laugh is harsh. "So I kept hoping. Until Cate came along."

"You must have hated me."

"Of course I didn't!" Her voice is sharp. "You were a baby. Like you said, he's very good at sucking people in. No." She stands up slowly. "If I hated anyone, it should have been myself. I was old enough. I should have known." She sighs. "I didn't, though." She walks toward me. "I didn't want to." The room is small. Two steps, and she's

212

standing by my side. "He's evil, Peter." She whispers it.

"No," I say. I'm whispering too.

"Evil," she says again. She's very close. I see a nest of wrinkles at each eye. "This time he's gone too far."

"You can't prove anything."

"Can't I?" She smiles. "I have the note, remember. I have Cate's letter." She touches my cheek. "I'm sorry if you got hurt." Her voice is soft. "I truly am." She starts toward the door.

"Wait!" I wait until she stops. "What are you going to do?"

"I'm going to Spencer." Her voice is calm. Her face is too.

"To tell him what?"

"Everything." She spreads her hands.

"What do you mean? Everything?"

"Don't worry," she says. "It isn't you."

"It is! That was my baby!"

She shakes her head. "You don't know that, Peter. And I don't either." She folds her hands. "There were some things I didn't want to know." Her voice is soft.

"You mean if they slept together? They wouldn't. He couldn't. He hated women!"

"You're right," she says. She smiles. "He did. But he used them, Peter. He used me." She looks at me. "He's using you, as his excuse to leave."

She opens the door, and looks out into the hall. The hall is quiet. I hear rain dripping from the eaves.

"If you're wondering," she says, "about us. If we slept together . . . if that would make a difference."

My face turns red. I shake my head.

"Ask Judith," she says.

I stare at her. "You talked to Judith?"

"Ask her," Mrs. MacQuire says. "She knows."

TWENTY-THREE

It was snowing the last time I wrote, and now it's spring. Spring! I am so happy.

In England spring went on forever, cold and wet. Dark. Brian said I'd like it there. Do you, he said, do you? Oh yes, I said, I do, and his mother looked at me. Where'd you find this one then, she said, and Brian said, isn't she lovely though, isn't she, to follow me all the way across the ocean like she did. She'd follow anyone, the mother said.

When Brian went out, she sat me down. It's not you, dear, she said. It's him. Just like his dad. Bring things home and drop them on the step and when he's had enough he's off, thinking I'll pick up the pieces.

I understand, I said. I did. He left in June. My mum will look after you, he said. She looked at me. Are you in the family way, she said. I shook my head. That's something then, she said. You're a good girl not to carry on.

She put me on the train to London. You're pretty, she said. Someone's sure to pick you up. Pretty, just like Aunt Effie used to say. Too pretty for your own good, Cathy, we're going to have to cut your hair. No, I said, no! I said it loud, and her mouth opened. Who do you think you are, she said. If I hadn't found you, you'd be dead. For your own good, she said. It's my hair, I said, and she said, nothing's yours, you know that, and her hand hurt me, and I said STOP. And

214

her hand stopped, but the car kept moving, and I said stop, we're going to die.

But I didn't die, and Oliver picked me, Cathy turning into Cate.

I am happy. It is May, and yesterday we had a picnic on the hill, Melissa and me. I am so happy, I said, and she touched my cheek. When Melissa touches me, it doesn't hurt. You look happy, she said.

Don't ever leave me, I said, you won't ever leave me, and she smiled. She said, where would I go. She touched my heart. I'm right here, she said. Inside.

And I put my head down in her lap. I felt her fingers in my hair. I've never been so happy, I said, and she said, you, what is it about you, and I said I love you.

And she kissed my cheek. She was so close. I had to say it. I have a secret, I said, but her face went still. I'd rather you didn't tell me, she said, and anyway . . . I heard her sigh . . . I'm afraid I know. No one knows, I said, and she said, it's easy to see it, in the eyes. But I was hoping it wasn't true. You're too young, Cate, to have a baby. Her voice was soft. Whose is it, she said, and I said, mine!

Cate, she said. Cate, try to understand. Oliver doesn't want a baby.

I do, I said. He doesn't have to know.

Cate, she said. Cate.

And when he does find out, if he doesn't want it, I can come and live with you.

Cate, she said, Cate. She closed her eyes, and I took her hand, and put it on my stomach. Feel it swimming, I said. Remember when you took me swimming. You taught me everything, I said. I smiled.

She didn't smile. I hope not, she said. She said, what have I done? And I said, you've made me happy. I want to make you happy too. She closed her eyes. My hands moved across her lap. I'll do anything to make you happy.

And Peter, she said. Poor Peter?

I made him happy too, I said. He doesn't want a baby. He wanted me.

Dear God in heaven, she said. What am I going to do, and I said, don't do anything. My hands moved up and down. It's our baby, yours and mine. No, Cate, she said, but my hands kept moving. Yes, I said. I want to make you happy. I know how to make you happy.

No! said Melissa. She grabbed my hands. She held them still. It's not right, Cate, that is not how to make me happy, and I said, are you angry, please don't be angry.

I'm not angry, she said. I'm worried. About you, and I said, but if I don't make you happy . . . She said, you've made me happy. Stop giving yourself away.

That's what she said. As if I have a self to give.

In the basement, Timothy sits rocking in his chair. He stops rocking when I come close. He stops and looks at me. I crouch beside him, and I start to talk. I talk.

I tell him everything.

"And that's the story," I say when I'm done. Timothy says nothing. I didn't think he would. Which is why I told him, could tell him. "Maybe I should have known," I say.

He says nothing. Whatever he knows is held inside.

"I counted for nothing. Nothing. Of everything, that hurts the most."

Over our heads a moth bumps against the bulb. In all the basement the only moving thing, the only sound.

"When you come right down to it, she never meant to run away with me at all. Until the end."

But in the end, I think . . . the end. . . .

In the end, when you come down to it, maybe I didn't either. Who knows. In the end is the beginning.

And in the beginning, there was Bets.

*   *   *

"You promised," said Bets. "You said!" Her face was pale, and oak leaves crackled in her hair.

"To take you camping," I said. "And I did."

My eyes were stinging, and the air was cold. My back ached from sleeping on the ground.

"Roll up your sleeping bag," I said.

"Forever. You said forever!"

"I said maybe. I didn't say forever. Nothing is forever."

"Dead is. Dead is forever!" Her nose was running, and her eyes too. Her fists beat against my legs. I caught her wrists, held them.

"You've got to understand, Bets. I'm only fourteen. There's no place to go. We can't stay here. Winter's . . ."

"I wish you were dead. You promised!" Her voice rising, she twisted, trying to get away. "You said!"

"Shut up, will you!" Holding her, I shook her. Her shoulders were thin as sticks. Her head jerked. "I don't have any money. I don't have anything. We can't. I can't . . ."

My voice broke, cracking. I heard it. I heard a squirrel chattering in a tree. I heard Bets crying. "I'm sorry," I said. I tried to hold her. She pulled away.

"I hate you," she said. "I do."

"Not only," said Robert, "have you lost your sister's affection, you've lost whatever trust I had in you."

"I told you I wanted to take her camping."

"And I told you no. Under no circumstances. Instead of complying, you deliberately disobeyed me. Deliberately!"

"I'd promised her. It was just one night."

"One night, and look at her!"

I looked at her. She stood by Robert, pressing against his leg. Her hair was dusty, and her eyes were dark. When she saw me looking, she hid her face behind her hands. "I hate you," she said.

217

And Robert smiled. "Whatever you hoped to accomplish," he said, "it appears you did not succeed."

His glasses glinted. He wore a gray suit, and black shiny shoes.

"Where's my mother?" I said.

"In bed," said Robert. "Too upset to see you."

I looked down the hall. The hall was dark. The doors were closed.

"Let me talk to her."

"I told her I would handle this myself. I'm afraid I have no choice but to ask you to leave." He looked at his hands. "And not come back." He looked at me. "I'm sure your father will be glad to take you in."

I looked at Bets but she was hiding, behind Robert, behind her hands.

"Bets?"

"Go away."

"It's better for all of us if you do," said Robert.

"OK," I said. "Great." I slid my hands into pockets to hide their shaking.

"Are you being sarcastic?"

"You think I'd want to stay where I'm not wanted?" I started down the hall.

"Where are you going?"

"To pack."

"I'm sorry it has to end like this," said Robert. "If it's any help, feel free to tell them it was your decision."

"What makes you think it isn't?" I said.

"I'm glad to hear it," said Robert. "I'm glad you understand."

I didn't, though. And I don't now. Why is it that the more I know the less I understand? I shake my head to clear it. The light bulb swings. Beside me Timothy starts to rock. The chair creaks. An old chair, the wood dull where the varnish has worn through.

218

"Timothy," I say. To hear a voice. But he doesn't answer. He rocks. "Who killed her?" I say. "Was it me?" He doesn't answer. "I swear to God, I think I'm going crazy. I can't keep things separate anymore."

The chair rocks. "Help me," I say. "Where do I end? Where does someone else begin?"

Rocking, he turns his head, and looks at me.

"Listen," I say. "Manning's leaving. I'm leaving too."

A shadow moves across his eyes so quickly that I think I'm dreaming.

"The same thing," I say. "Over and over. Leaving. Or being left. I mean it, what's real? Besides leaving?"

He stops rocking.

"Tell me!"

He looks at me. In his lap his hands unfold, as if releasing something. His palms are pink, his fingers curled like petals. He presses thumb and forefinger together. I think of fireflies. I think of Cate. He raises his hands, and places them, cupped on my head like a cap. He doesn't move. "Peter," he says. He smiles. He has never said my name before.

"So this is where you've got to," Manning says. His voice echoes off cement. I stand quickly as he walks toward us. I I hear his footsteps echo too. Timothy's hands fall to his lap. He looks at Manning but it's hard to tell exactly what he's seeing. Or who. He doesn't blink. Manning looks right through him. "I confess I find your predilection difficult to fathom." He shakes his head, and turns to me. He smiles. Something tightens in my stomach.

"He understands more than you think." I glance at Timothy, who's looking at Manning, who looks at me.

"Peter," he says. "Your parents are here."

He says it softly, so softly that for a moment I think I haven't heard him right. Then I think he's kidding. I look around. He sees me looking. He smiles.

"Not here," he says. "Upstairs, with Spencer. At least your father is. Judith's waiting in your room."

219

When I look at him, he smiles. His teeth gleam. So do his eyes. "Better late than never," he says, and I feel everything closing in.

"I didn't ask them to come."

His face smooths over. "There's nothing to worry about, you know."

"I'm not worried."

"Though I expect some fireworks." His eyes glitter. He leans toward me.

"Melissa, I gather, is out for blood. As I gather you know."

He waits. My face goes red. I turn away, to Timothy.

"Hey," I say, softly. He doesn't blink.

"She thought it only fair to warn me," says Manning, "that she had talked to you and planned to talk to Spencer. You are aware, I hope, Peter, that she'll say anything to discredit me."

"Peter," says Timothy. Naming me.

"I don't give a shit if you guys had an affair."

Manning glances at Timothy. "How much does this fellow understand?"

"He doesn't give a shit either. Besides, he doesn't talk."

"Not that it matters," Manning says, "with Melissa planning to talk enough for all of us. The new Melissa," he says. He chuckles. "When I suggested she might hurt herself more than she hurts me, she looked at me as if I was quite mad. Do you really think that matters anymore, she said. Melissa." He smiles. "Mistress of self-deception. Among other things."

He looks as if he's expecting me to smile too. I don't. The moth thumps against the bulb above our heads. The bulb swings. I watch it swinging.

"Peter," he says, "I can hardly be blamed for the fact that she fell in love with me. I never claimed to love her. Enjoy her company, yes, and I told her so. If she chose to conjure up emotions that on my part were never there, well then . . ." He shrugs, smiling. A charming smile.

220

And I think: she's right, he's evil. Even if I don't really know what evil really is, I feel it. An evil man.

I owe him everything. An evil man I have to help.

"Listen," I say. I swallow. "Maybe I should tell you, it's not the affair she's going to Spencer about. It's Cate. What happened to Cate."

He stops smiling. "Not your part in it, I hope?"

I shake my head. "Yours. She says . . . she thinks you killed her."

"Does she?" He rubs one hand against the other. "Does she indeed." And he laughs. "Really," he says, "it's amazing how far one goes when driven." He looks at me. "And what do you believe? Do you believe I killed her?"

"How could you? If I did."

"Of course. I keep forgetting. We are all driven, I suppose, only some, like you . . ." He smiles. "More selflessly than others."

"Just because I blame myself . . ."

"Precisely. And for everything, it would seem. While she's unwilling to blame herself for anything at all."

"She loved Cate."

"I'm sorry to disappoint you, Peter, but I'm afraid the only person she's ever cared for, besides herself, is me."

"That's not true."

He smiles. "Perhaps you're willing to concede my knowledge of Mrs. MacQuire is more intimate than yours?" He waits, smiling, and for a moment I'm tempted, tempted to tell him about Cate's journal. But only for a moment; his smile stops me.

I shrug. "I just thought I should warn you."

"I appreciate that." Still smiling, he brushes his hand along one sleeve, inspects his fingers. "I suppose she has proof?" he says lightly, as if it doesn't matter in the least.

"A note from Cate." He glances at me. "I haven't seen it yet," I say.

"I doubt you've missed much. Shall we go?" He smiles, and there is something in his smile that makes me clench my fists.

"You really think you've got the bases covered, don't you?"

He smiles. "Yes," he says, "I rather think I do."

I glance at Timothy. "I'll be back," I say.

He says nothing, and I see him, for a moment, through Manning's eyes, an old man with white hair and crumpled skin. I see his blue sneakers, the untied laces trailing on the floor, and for a moment I'm ashamed, of him, ashamed of being ashamed. He looks at me, as if he knows.

"Peter," he says. Gently. Forgiving all.

TWENTY-FOUR

FROM THE HALL outside my room I hear Judith pacing, back and forth, her heels tapping against linoleum. The door is closed. As soon as I open it, she stops.

She puts her hands on my shoulders, and she looks at me. Under her freckles her skin is tight, across her cheekbones, around her mouth. Her fingers dig into my back. She shakes me. "You!" she says, and for a second I'm afraid she's going to cry. Instead she kisses me, an angry, almost savage peck. Her mouth trembles when she tries to smile. "You look in one piece anyway." She coughs to hide the huskiness in her voice.

"Sure." I smile to show I mean it. "So do you." She does. She always does. Seeing her, it hits how much I've missed her. My throat goes tight.

I move away from her, walk over to the window. Nothing to see except wet grass, and dripping trees, but overhead the sky holds still.

I hear her walking to the bed, hear the bed creak as she sits. "Come here," she says. When I turn she pats the space beside her. In the damp air her hair's a frizz of copper-colored flames. She's dressed for work, a white blouse, a light gray suit. "It's OK if I smoke?" She pulls a pack of cigarettes from an inside pocket, and looks at me until I nod. Around her neck is a string of wooden beads, a necklace I gave her

223

two years ago. I'm glad she's wearing it. I wonder if she was before I called.

I sit beside her. We slide together as the mattress sags. She lights up, inhaling, exhaling, squinting at me through the smoke. Our shoulders touch. If she should die, I think. . . . If . . .

"Now tell me," she says. "What's going on?"

I push back so that my back rests against the wall. She has to turn to look at me. I pull my legs up so my chin rests on my knees.

"Onions."

"Kiddo?" she says, faltering. The first time I've ever known her at a loss for words. I have to smile.

"The layers," I say. "The fucking layers. In everyone."

It takes her a moment to remember. When she does, she shakes her head.

"That visit," she says. "You came down to tell me, didn't you?"

"It wouldn't have made any difference if I had. She was already pregnant, but I didn't know."

"So tell me now."

"From the beginning?"

"No, I can guess at that. The end. How you killed her."

"You think I did?"

"I want to hear you tell it."

I take a deep breath. "It's not easy."

"I know that, kiddo. Try."

She leans back against my legs. The wall supports us. I feel her weight.

"Try," she says. "I'm listening."

I clear my throat. "She changed her mind."

I hear her breathing, a quiet steady sound. "I'm listening," she says. Listening, with her head bowed slightly, I see her neck, freckles dusting pale skin.

"Twice. First she came and told me she was going to stay, with Manning, and then . . ."

224

She drops ash into a glass of water by the bed. I hear it hiss. "I'm listening," she says.

"The first time," I say, "when she changed her mind, I could have killed her. I felt like it. I wanted to."

"Yes," says Judith. There is only her voice, the back of her bowed head. It's easier to talk not seeing her face.

"But I didn't. Not then I didn't. Later. A couple of days later there was a note in my mailbox. Asking me to meet her at the river. She didn't sign it, but I knew her writing. I knew . . ." I close my eyes. My throat is tight. "I was so angry. But she said she needed me. And I still loved her."

"Yes," says Judith.

"So I went. I shouldn't have, but I did. I went down early, and I waited."

The chapel bell begins to ring. Listening, Judith lifts her head. It sounds so loud. It strikes twelve and stops.

"Go on," says Judith in her husky voice. "I'm listening."

"I waited. I waited a long time, but it didn't matter because I knew what I was going to do. I was going to kill her. If I killed her, then maybe I wouldn't love her anymore. If I killed her, well, at least I wouldn't have to think of her, with him. I'd just do it, and then I'd turn myself in. I didn't care what happened after that. In some states they still have the electric chair. I figured that would be as good a way to go as any, you know, one touch, and zap."

Judith drops her cigarette into the water. I hear the sizzle.

"Zap," says Judith. "Go on."

"It was one of those evenings, what they call a 'weather breeder.' You know, everything was still. There was no wind. The water was like glass. So was the sky. I just sat there, waiting, and I got this feeling that whatever was happening had already happened before. You know that feeling?"

"Déjà vu," says Judith.

"I guess. Anyway, maybe that's why I didn't mind the waiting. It was like whatever was coming had already come. So I didn't have to worry. Like it was written in the sky. I

225

mean, I didn't even have to think. I heard her coming really fast down through the trees, and these birds, crows I think, took off. Her running scared them. There were a lot of them. Their wings were flapping. I don't know. It was like some omen. Like they knew I planned to kill her. I can't explain, but somehow I'd been so sure. And suddenly I wasn't sure of anything. It happens to me running sometimes. It's like I lose track of who I am."

"And Cate?"

"It was awful. She was all out of breath when she reached me, but trying to pretend she wasn't. Trying to pretend she wasn't scared. She was terrified. I saw it in her eyes. She said, I thought maybe you wouldn't come. Trying to smile, you know, but she really couldn't. I just stood there. I couldn't think of anything to say. I didn't know what was going on. I thought maybe she was scared of me, that she somehow knew what I'd been planning to do. But that was crazy. It was all crazy. I stood there, looking at her, trying not to look up. At those birds, and she says, Peter, you've got to help me, and I just stood there, and all I could think about was my mother. My mother! I never think about my mother."

"What did she want?"

"I told you. She'd changed her mind, and wanted to run away with me again."

"And what did you do?" says Judith. Gently.

"She said she hoped I'd understand. But shit! How could I? How could I when she never told me what was going on?"

"What did you do?"

"What do you think? I said no! I said no way! And if you want to know what a shit I really am, I liked saying it. I mean, she was really hurting, I could see that, and there I was getting off on hurting her some more. I said, what do you take me for? Some God damn puppet? You think you can just tweak the strings, and I'll come running? Well, forget it, you can just forget it. Not anymore! And oh God, you should have seen her face. Her eyes. But do you think I

226

cared? Not me. I was having the time of my life. Killing her."

"How did you kill her, kiddo?"

"Don't play dumb. I'm telling you, what options did she have after I turned her down? She had Manning who hated her, and Mrs. MacQuire who'd told Manning Cate was pregnant. I didn't know that then, that she was pregnant or about Mrs. MacQuire, and I hadn't read her journal, but I knew about Manning, how he treated her. I could see that. Anyone could."

"What journal?"

"She kept one, but I didn't know that either. Until afterward. She left it for me. I didn't know, until I started reading it, what she was like, really like. She wasn't like anything. A cloud or something, something with no center. Do you know what I mean?"

"Your mother maybe," says Judith. Softly.

"Maybe. I don't know. It doesn't matter. I mean, sure, I knew she was kind of helpless, and I liked feeling needed, I guess, and then when all of a sudden she changes her mind, and then changed it again, I didn't feel needed. I felt used."

"Who wouldn't?"

"The thing is I hadn't read the journal yet so I didn't know where she was coming from, and let me tell you she came from nowhere. No wonder she was nothing. I mean, reading it, it's easy to see why everything happened the way it did. Like it couldn't have happened any other way. Now all I can do is feel for her. Now that it's too late."

"And then?"

"I told you! I could have killed her. I did. You should have seen me. I was worse than Manning, worse than my father. I mean, there I was enjoying myself. She said she hoped I'd understand, and I said, I hope you understand. You made your choice, and I've made mine."

"And then?"

"And then . . ." I take a deep breath, hear it shuddering. Judith doesn't move. I feel her weight. My legs are trembling. I hold on tight. "And then just like that, she changed. Her eyes changed. They went all glassy, like something in her turned to ice. That's when she knew it was all over. For her anyway. I said I hope you understand, and she changed, like that. She'd been fiddling with her hair, pulling it across her face the way she did when she was nervous. She stopped. She just stood there, and she said, I do, in this hollow voice. She was wearing this green dress with little pink hearts. It was too dark to see the hearts, but I knew the dress. A kid's dress really. Only she didn't look like a kid; she looked like, I don't know, some kind of ghost. Her skin was so white like wax somehow, and her eyes . . . her eyes . . . She even smiled, or tried to, and I remember thinking when she said, I do, of the times I'd imagined her saying it for real. I really figured we'd be getting married. I really did. And then she just turned, and walked away. She didn't make a sound. Even though it was almost dark, she seemed to know exactly where she was going. And of course she did. But I didn't. I didn't even watch her leave. I stayed down there for a long time, not doing anything, not even thinking, and when I left it was completely dark. The school was locked up, and I had to climb the vines to Thurston's window so he could let me in. Two stories up. I kept hoping that maybe the vines would break, and I'd fall, but no such luck. And then the next day Mrs. MacQuire came to tell me she was dead, and . . . that's the story."

Judith doesn't move. She doesn't speak. I lean forward, resting my forehead on my knees. My hands are sweaty; I'm having a hard time holding on. I feel Judith pull away, and turn toward me.

"Kiddo," she says. She touches my knee. "You didn't kill her."

I feel her fingers, but I don't look up.

"Oh yeah?" My voice is hoarse from talking. "If I didn't, then who did?"

"Sweetheart, she killed herself."

"Give me some credit, will you. I know that, and you know why!"

"I give you a great deal of credit." Her fingers touch my hair. She tugs. Gently. "Look at me." When I don't, she tugs again. I lift my head; she's looking at me. She touches my cheek. "When will you understand," she says, "the world doesn't balance on the head of a pin?"

And something gets to me. I'm not sure what. Not the words exactly, but the way she says them, in her husky voice, as if she cares. I hear the caring. She's here. And maybe that's enough.

"You calling me a pinhead then?"

It takes her a moment, and then she grins, a slow grin. Cautious.

"I'm glad you told me, Peter."

I shrug. "It's not over, you know."

"I didn't say it was."

"My father . . ."

"He's with Spencer. He'll be here soon."

"I wish he wasn't."

"It's going to be all right."

"I wish he hadn't come."

"Believe me, kiddo."

She touches my cheek again, then turns away to light another cigarette. I lean to light it for her. When I was just a kid it made me feel grownup. I hold the match. My hand is trembling. Hers is too.

When he arrives, we're still sitting on the bed. Just sitting, not talking. He comes in slowly, as if afraid of what he's going to find.

"Davey," says Judith. She drops her cigarette into the glass. "We've been waiting."

229

"Yes. Well." He clears his throat. "I was detained. By Manning." His voice is tight. He looks at Judith, not at me. "Do you know what he told me?" His voice rises. Under the words, I hear the anger.

Maybe Judith does too. She gets up, and takes his arm. "Tell us at lunch," she says. "I'm starving." She smiles at me, but I don't smile: my father doesn't either. He looks at me. "Peter," he says. "We need to talk."

TWENTY-FIVE

"SO TALK," I say at lunch. Let's get it over." He tries. He can't. He shakes his head. He orders a martini, and Judith looks at him, surprised. He doesn't believe in lunchtime drinking. She orders wine. I get a Coke. We sit in silence.

The inn is empty except for us. The floor buckles underfoot, and fake flames flicker in the fireplace. White-coated waiters cluster in the corner, waiting. I'm waiting too. The last time I was here was with my mother.

When the martini comes, he doesn't drink it. He looks at Judith. "Sweetheart," she says. "It's up to you." Her voice is tender. She lights up, and sips her wine. My father takes a breadstick from the basket, snaps it in two. Seeds scatter. I think of cracking fingers. He drops the bread, and clears his throat, and I can't stand the silence anymore.

"So how was Spencer?"

He looks up, startled, as if Spencer was the last thing on his mind.

"Extraordinary." He turns to Judith. "I find it difficult to fathom how a man like that could run a school." He turns to me. "On second thought maybe that's why."

"Why what?"

"Why this has happened."

"It's not his fault."

"He certainly thinks the world of you."

"He thinks the best of everyone."

231

My father's smile is strained. "So it would seem from what he said. From what I could follow, anyway. There was a great deal about the soccer field of life." He turns to Judith. "You might be interested to know that he sees Peter as the sweeper."

Judith looks at me. "What's a sweeper?"

I don't answer. My father does. "A sweeper, according to Spencer, is responsible for covering the field, for covering the other players' mistakes." He turns back to me. "Is that correct?"

I shrug.

"Maybe Spencer's not the fool you think," says Judith.

"Maybe not," says my father. "However." He coughs, sips his martini, and coughs again. His fingers tighten on the glass. "It's not Spencer who concerns me. It's you." He looks at me. "And Manning. What Manning had to tell me." His eyes burn. I see a muscle working in his jaw. So does Judith.

"It's OK, sweetheart." Her voice soothing, as if talking to a kid.

"It is *not!*" His voice cracks into splinters.

"It's OK," I say to Judith. "I mean, how'd you like to have a son like me."

"What I want to know," my father says, "is why you didn't tell me? Tell me yourself so I didn't have to learn it secondhand."

"I did. I told you on the phone this morning." He stares at me. Eyes burning. I feel my eyes burning too. "Or weren't you listening!"

"Oh God," he says. His eyes close. "I'm trying to help."

"Isn't it a little late?" He flinches, and I lean toward him. "Where were you when I needed you?" My voice rising, cracking.

"You listen to me!" His hand leaps toward me, and I pull back. His fingers grab my wrist, cold fingers holding. Sweat glistens on his forehead. "*You* listen," he says. "My leaving

232

your mother had *nothing* to do with you. Nothing. Do you understand?" His fingers tighten.

"Let go." I try to pull away. I can't.

"Do you hear me?"

"Is that supposed to make me feel better?"

His face is sharp, cut in angles by fake firelight. His other hand lifts. One touch, and zap. I flinch. He turns to Judith.

"What can I do?" His hand cupped, pleading.

"Talk," says Judith.

"Let go," I say.

He lets go. "Why didn't you tell me that Robert kicked you out?"

"What?" says Judith.

"Why didn't you tell me, when it happened?"

"When?" says Judith.

"Why should I?"

"I'm your father."

My father looks at me. I look at him.

"Would someone please tell me what's going on?" says Judith.

"All these years," my father says, "I've been thinking it was your choice that you stay with us."

"Big deal." I look around. "Can we please eat?"

"I gave Judith full credit," says my father, "but it mattered. To me. That given the choice . . ."

"It happened a hundred years ago. It's over. Anyway, I took her camping when I wasn't supposed to, so it was my fault."

"No," says my father. "Mine. I feel responsible."

"You didn't even know."

"That's what I mean."

I look at him. His fingers tap the table. The breadcrumbs bounce.

"I suppose you think if you'd known you could have stopped it all from happening."

"No," says my father. "Not necessarily, but . . ."

"I suppose you think that if you'd known about Cate, you could have stopped me from loving her, could have stopped all that from happening too."

"I think . . ."

"You don't have to tell me. I know what you think. You think I fucked it up, don't you?"

"No," says my father. "I did."

"You! For Christ's sake, I was the one who screwed her. I got her pregnant. And I was the one who left her in the end."

"Peter," he says, his face working, "it's not easy for me to say this."

"Then don't," I say, but he ignores me. His face working, and his hands working too, kneading breadcrumbs. "It has never been easy, which is why I'm grateful to . . ." He glances at Judith, then back to me. "I want you to know I'm not proud of what I did, the way I left you, left your mother. The girls. Left, leaving you in charge."

"Forget it, will you."

"You haven't."

I look at him, my father, sitting straight, rigid with the effort of holding still, putting feelings into words. "Nor am I proud of your part in the present situation. I wish to God you had never become involved. I wish I'd known. I wish . . ." He frowns, struggling. His hands rise to chop the air. I watch them, remembering how they frightened me when I was small. "I lost the girls," he says. "I do not want to lose you too." His face twists as he smiles. A terrible smile. A grimace. "If I haven't already lost you," he says. His eyes are filled with tears.

"I love you," my father says.

His face flushes. Embarrassed. We're both embarrassed. Judith grins. "Well put," she says, handing him a Kleenex. He blows his nose.

I finish my Coke, sucking loudly through my straw. My

234

face is hot. "If that's all." I push my chair back. "I'm really not hungry."

"Suit yourself," says Judith.

I stand up, shoving my hands into my pockets.

"Maybe I'll see you later."

"You'll see us," my father says, but I'm already at the door.

Today is June, and today it's over, and I don't know why.

Last week was the picnic, and I said to Melissa, do I make you happy. Do I?, and she said, shh. She put her finger on my lips. She said, Cate, it's not right what you were doing. Do you know that? And I said, isn't it right to make you happy?

She said, what am I going to do with you, and I said, love me, and she sighed. She said, I'm afraid loving's not enough. And something in the way she said it frightened me. Don't leave me, I said, and she said, how could I? Now?

And then. This morning, in the garden, and Melissa too. Both of us kneeling. Picking berries. Cate, she said, about the baby . . . and I said, I told him, and she looked at me. Peter, I said, I told him I couldn't go away. She looked at me. I saw the way the sun made shadows on her cheeks. Did you tell him about the baby? she said, and I said, oh no, the baby's mine. My secret. The only one who knows is you.

Cate, she said, and I saw the shadows in her eyes.

Don't worry, I said. It's going to be all right. The wind's not blowing through me anymore.

It's not that simple, Cate.

Oh yes, I said. If you don't leave me.

But I can't help you now, she said. There's Oliver . . .

And Oliver came. Like that. I saw his shadow on the grass, Melissa saw it too.

What brings you here? she said. Her voice was cold.

I might ask you the same, said Oliver, standing, arms folded, looking down.

Unlike you, she said. I care about her.

I gather, said Oliver, and there was something in the way he said it.

What do you mean? she said, hard and slow. Her eyes hard too. I didn't know her.

Edwards has just been to see me, he said.

Edwards? she said. She sounded lost.

Edwards, he said. You know Edwards. Iago. A part played to perfection. A part he still plays to perfection. I thought you might be interested in what he had to say.

I'm not, Melissa said, but that won't stop you.

How well you know me, Oliver said. Melissa stood. I knelt, holding the berries in my hand.

Apparently, said Oliver, he was up on the hill the other day, behind the house, and so, I gather, were you.

Was he? said Melissa. We didn't see him. Her voice was dark.

From what he tells me, I'm not surprised, said Oliver.

Really, Melissa said. What did he tell you?

Dear Melissa, he said, if you choose to make a public spectacle of yourself that is your business entirely but I would appreciate your not involving my wife.

I see, said Melissa, and did it ever occur to you to doubt his word?

Under the circumstances, said Oliver. No. Given that you'd lost the husband, it makes sense you'd try to take the wife.

Is that how you see things, said Melissa. Always in terms of yourself?

You ought to know, said Oliver. Yes, Melissa said, I should.

When I asked you to look after her, said Oliver, I'd no idea you'd carry things so far.

Is it my fault, said Melissa. If you'd treat her more kindly.

How I treat her, said Oliver, is no concern of yours.

Isn't it, she said. Isn't it. Her voice was shaking. She crouched beside me. Cate, she said. Come home with me.

I kept my eyes closed. If I couldn't see them, they weren't

236

there. But I heard the breathing. Eyes closed, I saw the car
stopped on the desert. I saw Aunt Effie's open mouth. I heard
the sand.

Aunt Effie, I said.

Go to the house, said Oliver.

For God's sake, said Melissa. She's not well.

I don't need you to tell me that.

Aunt Effie, I said. She didn't answer.

This minute, Oliver said. Right now.

Cate, please, said Melissa. Come with me.

And I was a wishbone pulled apart.

Aunt Effie, I said. Her eyes were open. She didn't speak.

This can't go on, Melissa said.

She couldn't speak. I left the car. I left her there. The sand
was soft and wind was blowing. Blowing the sand so nothing
showed. Where I'd been. Where I was going.

My eyes were closed. I'm here, I said. I held my stomach.
Does anybody know I'm here.

I'm warning you, said Oliver.

Cate, said Melissa. Open your eyes.

I opened them. I saw sun shining. Cate, she said, look at
me. I looked at her.

Cate, she said. Tell him. Tell him, and he'll let you go.

I shook my head. I shook, shivering. But she looked up.
At him.

In case you don't already know, Melissa said. She's preg-
nant.

She. As if I wasn't there. And he stood a tower against
sky.

I see, he said. I suppose this is your doing too.

Actually, she said, I thought it might be yours.

Did you, he said. Did you indeed?

It's mine, I said. Mine.

Why not, Melissa said. You are her husband. Surely you
don't think it's mine. As a woman my powers are somewhat
limited in that direction.

237

But not in others, Oliver said. You planned this, didn't you.

No, she said.

He laughed, the sound of falling rocks.

And you expect me to believe that?

I don't care, she said, what you believe. She turned to me. Are you coming, she said.

Does Peter know, he said.

Ask him, said Melissa. She touched my arm. Cate, she said. Cate.

No, I said. No.

I assume it's not too late for an abortion, said Oliver.

Oliver, she wants this baby.

Is it, he said.

No, I said. It's mine. You can't take it. Mine! It's me!

Can't I, he said. He turned, he started walking toward the house.

Melissa stood. Oliver, for God's sake! she said.

Think of her! Melissa said. Just once.

Were you? he said. When you set this scheme in motion?

I didn't, said Melissa.

Didn't you, said Oliver. Then why is it you feel so responsible for her now? Has it occurred to you it's guilt, Melissa? Guilt!

She took one step toward him. One step.

All you'd have to do, she said, is claim the baby as your own.

Aah, he said. Ah. There it is. Of course. You'd like that, wouldn't you? Your bit of flesh.

No one would know, she said.

No one, he said, except for you.

I wouldn't tell, she said.

That's right, he said. You wouldn't, because you know what I'd do if you did. One cuckold to another. Only I suspect Logan might mind it more than I. Considering the consequence.

You wouldn't, she said.

238

Wouldn't I, he said. Smiling.

You don't care who gets hurt, do you, she said. You never have.

With one exception, he said. No.

I hope it hurts, she said. He hates you. All this time he's hated you. You didn't know that, did you?

I would appreciate it, Melissa, he said, if you would pack up your emotional baggage, and depart.

You thought you knew it all, she said. Didn't you? All this time you thought he was hanging around because of you?

I'm warning you, he said.

How do you like it, she said, feeling like a fool?

He raised his hand.

No, I said. Don't hit her.

Melissa turned. She looked at me. Her face crumpled. Her eyes were red.

Oh God, she said. What have I done.

Her eyes were wet. I stood up. I put my arms around her. Don't, I said. Don't cry. I promise. I'll be good.

TWENTY-SIX

THAT'S IT. The last page. I close the book, and crouching, look through the reeds. The river's running fast. The reeds dip, swaying. I think of magic wands. Of whips. The light is gray, the color of pearls. Everything is damp and dripping.

The book tears easily. I take it page by page. Crumpled, the pages look like Ping-Pong balls. I toss them one by one above the reeds, and watch the river carry them downstream. I watch until the last one disappears around the bend.

That's it. I take a deep breath. I feel empty. I also feel light.

Looking down, I see my hands are stained with ink. I rub them back and forth against wet grass, and then I stand and look around. Except for the circle of fire rocks, there's nothing I can call my own.

Lifting the rocks, I heave them one by one, into the woods. They're heavy, and I can't throw far but I keep at it until they're gone. That leaves the ashes. I scoop them up and send them flying, and then I scatter leaves across the ground.

When I'm done I feel better. Now nothing's left. It looks just as it did six years ago.

I turn to leave when I hear someone coming. Whoever it is is coming fast, almost running down the hill. I hear twigs snapping, and for a moment I think, Cate!

But Mrs. MacQuire steps through the trees. She's breathing hard. Her arms are scratched. She stops and stares. "I hoped you might be here," she says. I see her trying to catch her breath.

Her face is pale. I watch her as she walks toward me, clutching a piece of paper in her hand. She holds it up. The paper flutters.

"Spencer's read this. I want you to read it too." Her voice is shaking. So is her hand.

I back away. I've had enough. Her eyes are wild.

"He says nothing can be proved. The fool!" She spits it out.

"Oliver," she says. She laughs. The way she laughs it sounds like choking. "He says he didn't care enough to kill her! In front of Spencer." She chokes again.

"At least he's honest." Trying to joke. Hoping I can calm her down.

It doesn't work.

"Are you on his side too?" Her voice is sharp.

I shake my head. "It's just . . ."

Her hand claws at my wrist. "Spencer is," she says. Her voice rises, cracking, and I think of glass. "He read this" — she shakes the paper — "and all he said was 'Poor girl, quite mad, quite mad,' and I said, 'Chauncy, that is NOT the point.' I said . . ." Her voice breaks. She looks at me as if she can't remember. Her eyes are crazy. "And when I looked at Oliver, he smiled. Smiled!" Her nails are sharp. "He knew he'd won."

"Why does he have to torture me?" Pleading, her fingers tugging at my arm. "Please!" Her voice goes high.

I look at her, and think of Bets.

I nod. "OK."

Her eyes are blank, uncomprehending as if she's forgotten what she's asking. Gently, I take the letter from her.

"You're the only one," she says. "You know the story. You'll know what's true." Her hands press against her face.

"It's going to be OK." I say it gently as if I'm talking to a kid.

241

I don't think she believes me but she nods before she turns away.

She turns away, and I look at the letter in my hand. The edge is jagged, ripped where it was torn away. I know the paper. Blue book paper. The missing page.

Oh, Melissa, I told Oliver we had to talk, and he said, there's nothing to talk about. When he looks at me, Melissa, his eyes burn but they don't see me. He never sees me. He sees the baby. He wants to kill the baby.

And he sees Peter. Did you think, he says. Did you ever think what you were doing, who you would hurt. His eyes when he says this, oh, his eyes. You don't know how to think, he says. You're nothing. Do you hear me. Nothing.

But I am, Melissa. I am something.

When Aunt Effie died, I thought, I will die too. I didn't though. I left the car, I left Aunt Effie, and walked across the sand. The wind blew but my feet kept moving and I followed them to the road. The road had no beginning and no end and I didn't know which way to go.

I stood and waited, but I didn't die. The wind blew and my eyes filled up with sand but after days or hours I saw a truck. It stopped. A big blue truck. It stopped for me, and I climbed in.

His name was Eddie and there was a green mermaid wriggling on his arm. His arms moved and his hands. He said, be a good girl, Cathy. You be good. And I was good, Melissa. It hurt but I was good. I'm always good.

I'll be good, I said to Oliver. Please let me stay. Let me stay here with my baby.

You're staying, he said. The baby isn't.

Melissa. There is no stopping him.

But I will stop him. The baby's mine, belongs to me. I will go to Peter and I will say, will you have me, will you, and if he won't I'll go to Oliver. And I will tell him. This is me,

*my baby. Mine. His eyes will burn but he will see me. He
will see me when I say I'm leaving.*

I'm leaving, Melissa. I'm going away. I am.

Will you remember? Remember me?

*I will remember. When I hold my baby, I'll remember. I
will name my baby after you. Melissa. And I will hold her.
I will never let her go.*

I listen to the silence. I hear the river, water running,
water dripping. Mrs. MacQuire stands, her head bowed,
waiting. I open my mouth, but no words come.

"See?" she says. Her voice is hoarse. "She made a choice.
To keep the baby. To run away."

I look down at the letter. I clear my throat.

"Going away. Maybe she means dying."

"You know she doesn't!"

"I don't know. We're never going to know."

"He killed her, Peter!" Her voice is shrill.

I look down. In the grass I see a small web, shimmering.
I shake my head.

"I think we all did."

I hear her catch her breath. When I look up, I see a muscle
twitching in her cheek.

"I think we're all responsible."

"No." Whispering, she backs away.

"All of us. We all played a part. Manning. You and me."

"No," says Mrs. MacQuire. "No."

"Spencer too. And Cate."

I stand up slowly. My pants are wet. I think of when I
used to wet my bed at night. She's looking at me, eyes wide,
as if waiting to see what's coming next.

"It's all connected. We're all connected. Whether we want
to be or not."

She turns away, toward the river. Her head is bowed. I
see tears sliding down her cheeks.

243

"No." A small sound like a drop of rain.

I stand beside her. Our shoulders touch.

"It's over now." I say it softly. She shakes her head.

She watches as I crumble the letter, and hold it for a moment, a small white ball that's almost weightless.

She watches as my hand lifts. She doesn't try to stop me. I toss the small ball onto the river, and we stand there watching as the current carries it away.

Moonlight. The mist is spun sugar in the trees. The rain has stopped. The air is cold. I stand, hands in my pockets beside the car. Judith and my father sit inside, my father behind the wheel. He turns on the headlights. Behind us the inn is dark.

"Give me a kiss," says Judith.

I bend down, lean in the open window. Her cheek is cool. She smells of smoke. Shaking her head, she smiles. "How you survived six years," she says.

I shrug. "It wasn't so bad."

"Now that it's over," she says.

"There's a week left."

"You know what I mean." She stops smiling. The engine idles. My father taps his fingers against the wheel. A rented car, a silver Honda.

"We'll miss the shuttle," he says.

He looks at me. His face is sharp-boned. His mouth is tight. "We'll see you in a week."

I nod. My back aches from leaning over. I start to pull away. Judith takes my hand.

"Do something for me," she says. "If you have time, keep an eye on Mrs. MacQuire."

"What makes you think I won't?"

Judith laughs. A tired croak. "Nothing. Knowing you."

"She said to ask you once . . ." I stop. I can't remember. What?

"What?" says Judith.

"Something. About her and Manning. About Coach. That you knew."

She glances at my father first. He nods. Then back to me.

"The youngest child. What's his name?"

"Rufus."

"Rufus. Yes. In a way I'm surprised you never guessed. Who his father is. Or isn't."

And as soon as she says it I know. Have I always known?

"Manning?"

"It seems likely, doesn't it?"

"Does Manning know?"

"Sweetheart, I expect they all know, in their own ways."

"Coach?"

"Maybe not in words. But feelings, yes, I suspect he might."

"On that note," says my father. He puts the car in gear, leaning, to look past Judith, at me.

"In a week?"

"OK."

"Is your mother coming?"

"I don't know. I haven't heard."

"If there's any trouble, will you call?"

"Yeah. Sure."

"And you're all right?"

I nod, and he nods too. Slowly the car begins to slide away.

"Dad!"

The car stops. I walk around it to his window. His window's closed. He rolls it down, and looks at me.

"Thanks for coming."

He nods. "Anytime," he says. He smiles.

He rolls the window up. I stand there, watching as they drive away, and when they're gone I walk slowly back to school.

The clock strikes nine. The air smells green and wet, of damp earth, and growing things.

Thurston is lying on my bed, hands behind his head, his

245

eyes closed. He might be sleeping. Except that when I close the door, his eyes open, and he grins.

"I was beginning to think you were never coming back."

"I'm back." I look around the room. "You're right, though. I feel like I've been gone forever."

I walk over to the window and push it up, feeling the cool air hit me through the screen. "It's nice out there."

"Yeah." Rolling over, he lifts up on an elbow. His hair hangs across his eyes. "You heard the news?' he says.

"Depends on what you mean."

I bend down, pulling off my shoes, my socks. I toss them in a corner.

"Edwards," he says, "is leaving. Early. Maybe he's already left."

"He's not the only one."

"You leaving too?"

My chair is covered with clothes. I push them off, before I sit.

"Some ways, I feel I'm already gone." I lean back. "I'm wiped."

"Yeah," says Thurston. "Yeah. Well." I hear him rolling back again, the mattress shifting, casters creaking. "I have to say, you had me worried."

"Don't sweat it, buddy. It's over."

"Yeah. I wish you could have seen him. Edwards. Was he pissed!" Thurston chuckles.

"I saw him."

"*All* over?" says Thurston.

"All but the shouting. And exams. Jesus! Exams!"

"That paper?"

"Nope. I haven't done it. Not going to either."

"Bad boy," says Thurston.

I shrug. "Call it what you like."

"Progress," says Thurston. He wings a pillow across the room. It hits my face.

"You shit!" Laughing, I heave it back. He grabs for it. I

246

get there first. The bed groans. I pound him with the pillow. "Turd," he says. Laughing. Doubled up laughing, head hidden in his arms.

The door opens.

"Excuse me," Snickers says, his voice high, and his face bright red.

"Hey kid." I sit, breathing hard, Thurston behind me, lying down. His eyes closed. "You know what *he* thinks, don't you?" Thurston says. A gentle teasing.

"Don't," I say. I nod to Snickers. "Come in, kid, close the door."

He shakes his head.

"If you're busy," he says. His ears redder than his face.

"Nope. I was coming to look for you. You found me first."

He comes in slowly, pushing against the door to close it. He takes a deep breath.

"I brought you this."

He holds it out. A bird's nest. A perfect circle tightly woven. His arms are straight, his legs locked in position.

"I found it, on the ground behind the gym. Eggs even. See." He tips the nest so I can see, two eggs, unbroken, pale blue. "Robins' eggs," he says. "So I thought maybe you could use it." He nods toward the window. "For that robin. You know."

"I'm sorry, kiddo. It won't work."

His mouth works. "I bet you hate me." His chest heaves, in and out.

"I don't hate you." I hold my hands out. "You better give me that before you drop it."

He scuttles sideways, to the desk. He puts the nest down. His feet are bare, his heels dirty. "You ought to," he says.

Behind me, Thurston starts to hum, a tuneless humming that somehow has a tune.

"I would," says Snickers.

"Listen, kiddo, no bird'll sit on another bird's nest. Except a cuckoo. They just don't do it."

247

"It was a dumb idea."

"A good one. It just won't work is all."

Face burning, he reaches for the nest.

"Leave it," I say. "If it's all right with you I'd like to take it home with me."

"I don't know why you'd want to," Snickers says. Mumbling. Not knowing where to look.

"You've got me, kid. What do you say?"

"Shit," says Snickers. "Shit." A quick grin sneaks across his face. He glances at me, then away.

"Now listen," I say. "I need your help." I walk over to the bureau, and from the top drawer take a jar, a clean glass jar with holes pricked in the lid. "You ever collected fireflies before?"

"Once."

"OK. Well, not tonight, but this week I need some more." I hold the jar toward him. "A lot," I say. "As many as you can get."

He stares at the jar. "What for?"

"You get them for me. Then you'll see."

He takes the jar.

"OK," he says.

He leaves, but Thurston's eyes stay closed. He stops humming.

"Buddy," he says, "you're something else."

One eye opens. Thurston grins.

TWENTY-SEVEN

SHE CALLS in the morning, three days before graduation. "Peter?" she says. "How are you?" Her voice like clouds, or cotton candy.

"Fine."

I squint up at the ceiling.

"I was afraid I wouldn't get you," says my mother. "I was afraid you'd be in class."

The ceiling is soundproof cardboard, white squares pricked with holes.

"Exams," I say. "But mine are over."

Behind her, I hear the baby playing. From the sound he's making he must be banging pots and pans.

"You must be so excited," my mother says.

"What?"

"Graduation, dear. You're so grown up."

"Yeah." I don't know how she stands the banging. I can hardly hear her voice. I close my eyes. "I'm working on my speech."

"Jeremy. Darling. Please! Mummy can't hear."

Jeremy keeps on banging. Even he's no baby anymore. Four or five.

"Actually," says my mother, "the reason, darling, I'm calling . . . Jeremy, please!" Slowly the banging moves away. "Robert," she says.

"Don't tell me," I say. "Let me guess. Robert doesn't think it's possible to come to Graduation."

Silence. The line crackles. The line hums.

"Oh dear," says my mother. "You're not angry, are you? I hope, darling, you're not angry."

I don't say anything.

"I did hope you might even be relieved. Robert thought it would be awkward, with your father, and that woman there."

"That woman is his wife."

"I know that, dear. Your father hasn't been very nice to Robert lately. Not nice at all."

I don't say anything.

"They are coming, aren't they, darling?"

"They're coming."

"Then you won't be all alone. I do feel better. Knowing you'll have someone there."

"Thanks."

"I'm terribly disappointed, dear. You know that, don't you? And the girls too. They did so want to see their big brother graduate. You meant so much to them, when they were little."

"I'd better go now."

"Say something, darling."

"I just did. I'd better go."

"Tell me you're not angry."

"I'm not angry."

"I'm so glad. I knew you'd understand. You know, Robert thought you might come for a visit this summer, a short visit, as a treat. For all of us. Instead of Graduation. Better than Graduation, he says, because we'd have the time to really catch up. It's been so long. I can hardly remember what you look like. Isn't that silly?"

"Very silly," I say out loud, and under my breath, "fucking asshole."

"What's that, dear?"

"Very silly."

"You're so understanding, darling. I feel so lucky. And

250

Robert's wonderful. Really. He knows how disappointed I am, we all are. So as a treat . . . he's taking us to Rome, on Sunday. Just for a week. He has a convention, and he thought Celia, and . . . the two oldest might enjoy it."

"What about Bets?"

"Bets is staying home, with the baby, dear. To keep him company."

"Doesn't she want to go?"

"Well yes, dear, of course, but Robert thinks . . ."

"Do you know something?"

"What, dear?"

"I don't give a shit what Robert thinks."

"Darling!"

"Robert is a fucking asshole."

"Darling!"

"A fucking asshole!"

I hang up. Smiling.

Spencer smiles. "Come in, come in!" Midmorning, and the study's filled with light. On bookshelves leather bindings gleam like jewels. "Two days left, Spaulding! I wanted to have a small chat, in private, before you go."

"Yes, sir."

"Sit, boy, sit."

I sit on the chair before his desk. He doesn't sit. Pipe in his teeth, he circles. Blue smoke drifts toward the ceiling.

"Your parents, Spaulding. I hope I was able to put their minds at ease. Concerning the situation here, you understand."

"They felt better when they left, sir." He stops, and, frowning, peers at me. "Once they understood, I mean. Once they'd talked to you."

"Ah," says Spencer. He can't help smiling. "I'm glad to hear it. Very glad." He looks at me. "I must confess to you, Spaulding." He moves behind his desk, and sits.

"Yes, sir."

251

"There are times when my faith in human nature is severely tried."

"Yes, sir."

"But we must never shirk from duty, Spaulding."

"No, sir."

"In the end, Spaulding, all that matters is the truth. Do you understand?"

"I don't think it's that easy, sir. I mean, how do you know, sir. Really?" I lean forward. "How do you know the truth?"

He looks at me. His pipe is out again. He doesn't notice. He might be thinking, but it's hard to tell.

"I'm not a fool, Spaulding."

"No, sir. I mean the real truth. You read her letter. How do you know he didn't kill her, really kill her."

He puts down his pipe, and clasps his hands together, his fingers laced. He stares at them. "In the end, Spaulding, what does it matter?" His voice is soft.

"Murder, sir!"

"Each of us, Spaulding. In our hearts we murder every day."

"I'm talking about real murder, sir."

"In the end, Spaulding, we all stand naked. It is not our duty, Spaulding, to bear final witness on our fellow man. The truth is we are all flawed. All. To believe in ourselves, in each other, is an act of faith. An act, Spaulding. A leap across a chasm."

"Yes sir, but murder . . ."

"Murder, Spaulding. You know by now that kindness can kill as well. The road to hell is paved with good intentions, as well as bad."

"But isn't there a difference?"

"In whose eyes, Spaulding? I am a man of God. I don't know either. I ought to. But I don't. All I can do, Spaulding, is keep on believing. As best I can."

"Yes, sir."

"You're a good boy, Spaulding. Let me tell you some-

252

thing." He sighs, and leans across his desk toward me. "Tell me, Spaulding. Do I look like a murderer to you?"

"No sir. Of course not."

He nods slowly. "Which is why, Spaulding, we should not presume to judge our fellow man. For in fact . . ." he leans back. "I have killed, Spaulding. Countless numbers."

"If you're talking about the war, sir, everybody did. It was their job."

"Not the war, Spaulding. After the war. Directly after."

He peers at me, but his eyes have a glazed, unfocused look. "With the best of intentions, you understand." He doesn't blink. "To restore life, Spaulding. Yes. The war was over." His eyes water. "A curious fact, Spaulding, that evil backward spells live. To live, Spaulding. Yes. To feed the hungry. To raise the dead. In the camps, you understand. You can't imagine, Spaulding, the desecration. Human beings left lying in their own filth, treated like . . . But we were saviors, Spaulding. One child, Spaulding, I held her. Her knees were larger than her head. All bone. Yes. But her eyes. Oh, her eyes. The fear. The hunger. And I thought, yes, to feed her is to save her life. To save a human life, Spaulding. Not one life, but many! We set up kitchens. The camp smelled of soup, and death. And we fed them, Spaulding. I fed the child. I had to pry her mouth open. But she ate. She drank. Soup and milk. Bread. They all ate, Spaulding, and I remember thanking God for the privilege, of being in such a place, at such a time. To be responsible, Spaulding, for saving lives." His mouth trembles.

"Yes sir. I understand."

He looks at me. His eyes are glazed. "I was very young, Spaulding."

"Yes sir. I can understand how you must have felt."

"Can you, Spaulding?"

"Yes, sir."

"They all died, Spaulding. Men and women. Children. The child in my arms died first."

He looks at me, waiting, but I can't think of anything to say.

"Their systems," he says, "could not tolerate the food."

I shake my head. I swallow. "It's not as if you did it on purpose, sir."

"The desire to do good does not always lead to . . . good." He clears his throat, rubs his sleeve across his eyes. "You would do well to remember that."

"Yes sir, but Manning . . ."

"To forgive others, Spaulding, we must first forgive ourselves. No easy task. A lifetime, Spaulding."

"Yes, sir."

"For some, yes, more than a lifetime. This school, Spaulding, has been my chance to build again. Not to destroy. A school of dreams, Spaulding. Yours. And mine. We all have dreams. Dreams, Spaulding, can blind one to the truth."

"What is the truth, sir?"

"Truth, Spaulding. The truth is we must continue to believe in man's innate goodness. Despite . . ." He sighs. "Some evidence to the contrary." He looks at me, and sighs again.

"I should tell you, Spaulding, that Manning came to me, and offered to stay. If it would help, he said. Most commendable. Yes. However . . ." Spencer clears his throat. "I turned him down."

"So you think . . . "

"Now, now, Spaulding. I make it a habit not to think. As I expect you know." A glimmer of a smile, and then he frowns. "Truth, Spaulding, lies in our hearts, not in our heads. And there are times when our hearts lead us astray. All of us, Spaulding. You and me."

"So we'll never know . . ."

He looks at me, a clear sharp look I've never seen before, a look that makes me think of fall. Late fall when the sky is bare, and all protection's swept away.

"I think perhaps it's better if we don't." His voice is soft. His eyes cloud over. Rising, he holds out his hand.

254

"Busy days, Spaulding. Let this be our good-bye."

His grip is firm. My fingers ache.

"I've got a few years left," he says, pumping fiercely up and down.

"Yes, sir. I guess you do."

He smiles, pleased.

"Six years, Spaulding. A long time to have known each other. I want to say again I'm proud."

"Yes sir. Thank you, sir."

I try to pull away. He won't let go. "And Spaulding," he says. He stops smiling. "I hope you understand." His hand grips mine. "That under the circumstances, I've done the best I could."

"I know that, sir."

He lets me go. I'm at the door when he calls my name.

"Peter," he says.

I turn. His hand lifts. A brief salute. A silent pleading.

"Remember me kindly, will you?" His voice is shy.

I nod. "Yes sir," I say. "I will."

TWENTY-EIGHT

 IT'S SUNDAY so everybody's home. Coach sits on the porch steps, a beer in one hand, Rufus on his knee.

"Look who's here," says Coach. He smiles.

Rufus grins. "We're watching grass grow," he says. His legs are dappled. He swings them, back and forth.

"Not anymore," says Coach.

He tips him off, and stands. He's wearing cutoffs, and a baseball cap. His legs are hairy. He tips his cap to look at me. A red ring runs across his forehead.

"How 'bout a beer?" he says. "Coke?"

I shake my head. "I've come to say good-bye."

"Flowers," says Rufus. "Gross!" Wrinkling his nose, he laughs.

"I'll gross you," says Coach. Hand raised. "Get!"

Laughing, Rufus runs around the house. Coach looks at the flowers too.

"I couldn't think what else to bring."

"She'll like them," Coach says. "Go on in."

She's in the kitchen. No lights are on. Because of the trees, the room is dark. She's baking cookies. I smell sugar and vanilla. Bending, she slides a tray into the oven. She doesn't see me until she straightens. Her face is flushed. I hold the flowers behind my back.

"I've come to say good-bye."

She looks at me. She doesn't speak. It's like she's carved of wax, of stone.

"I would have come sooner, but I had exams."

"I'm surprised you came at all."

She turns away. Her back to me, she flips cookies from tray to plate. Round cookies, brown around the edges. Perfect circles, like yellow moons. Their edges touch.

"Cookies," I say, sounding dumb.

Her hands lift, sliding the cookies from the tray. "Life must go on," she says. Turning. "Mustn't it?"

I hold the flowers out. "I brought you these," I say. Embarrassed. "They're not much." Actually, in this dark room they look like nothing.

She bites her lip. Her lips are chapped. She shakes her head.

"You didn't have to bring me anything."

"I wanted to."

She turns back to the cookies. "Don't feel sorry for me. I couldn't stand it."

"I don't," I say.

She glances at me. I hear her sigh.

I sit as she bends to the stove, lifting the tray out, and up, onto the counter.

"You talked to Judith, didn't you?"

"A little bit."

Outside I hear the lawnmower starting up, a droning whine.

"And she told you?"

Carefully, I lay the flowers on the table.

"Can I ask you something?"

"If I don't have to answer."

"How do you know it's his?"

She glances out the window. From where I sit, I can't see anything but blowing leaves and bits of sky. Late afternoon. The lawnmower goes back and forth. I feel things moving, standing still.

"Timing," she says. "If nothing else." She turns to smile. A sad smile. "But, as he'd be happy to tell you, there's no proof. There never was."

"Would you have married him?"

"I would have done anything for him," she says so softly I can hardly hear. She lifts the cookies one by one, onto the plate.

"After Rufus. Did you stop seeing him?"

"That depends," she says, "on what you mean by seeing. We saw each other. Certainly."

"I mean . . ."

"I know what you mean." She holds her hands above the plate of cookies to catch their warmth. "Yes, but it was different." She glances at me. "For one thing, there was you." I look away. "Before you I could pretend he wasn't capable of caring. For anyone. Which made it easier. . . . I used to think all I needed was the right kind of magic wand, and . . ." She brushes her hand across her face, leaving a smudge of flour on her cheek. "Maybe I thought Rufus would be. I don't know. I don't even know if Rufus is really his. But I hoped. I wished . . . Not to trap him. But to have a piece of. Him. No matter how small, because really, before you, before Rufus, I already knew it wouldn't work. To give him credit, he never lied about his feelings. I lied, though. To myself. I didn't know how angry I was. How much I cared. I thought, well, if that's how he wants it, we'll play it his way. We'll have fun, and no one will know, and no one will get hurt. So after Rufus, I pretended it was just a game for me, the way it was for him. So it would hurt less, I suppose. So I could keep on seeing him. Because without him . . . I felt as if I didn't exist." She laughs, a small laugh. "There you have it."

She turns the oven off. She turns to me.

"Do you hate me?"

"No."

258

She laughs again, a laugh that catches in her throat. "You're too nice to hate anyone," she says.

"That's not true. You know it's not."

"What I can't bear," she says, "is having been such a fool." She shakes her head. "Loving him."

"You're not the only one."

"I hate myself for that," she says, "more than I hate him."

I take the flowers from the table, and hold them up, dull petals drooping.

"You better get these into water."

She smiles, slowly. She takes them from me, holds them gently.

"They're pretty," she says to be polite.

"Not Birds of Paradise."

"If they were I wouldn't want them." She looks at them. "I don't know them all," she says.

"Celandine, and Coreopsis. I picked them on the hill."

"Forget-me-nots?"

I nod. "They grow along the river."

"They're lovely," she says. "I like wild flowers best."

"They looked better outside," I say. It's true. They do.

She doesn't answer. She fills a blue glass vase with water, testing the coolness with her finger.

"Do you remember," she says, "when you took me to the river?"

"With the kids. We had a picnic."

She nods. Carefully she separates the flowers. I watch her fingers working.

"Years ago," she says. "Rufus was a baby on my back."

"I carried him."

She glances at me, smiling. "You did. You were so proud of everything. The watercress. You'd even built some kind of shelter."

"Yeah, but it wasn't very good. I hadn't been to Outward Bound. I didn't know much about surviving."

"You knew enough," she says. "Do you remember telling me you were going to live there when you grew up? All by yourself, you said, and then you changed your mind. Well, maybe with your baby sister, you said."

"I remember the picnic. What we ate. Ham and cheese and brownies. I taught Dana and Daphne to skip stones. Tried to, anyway; they were too young."

She turns the vase, head tipped, inspecting, then slides it to the center of the table.

We stand in silence. In silence the sun slips slowly beneath the trees outside the windows, and slowly the kitchen fills with light. Incredible light. The color of cider, of champagne. After the dark, it's almost blinding. The whole room has been transformed.

The floor gleams and white walls dazzle and on the table, the flowers shimmer, blue and gold.

Mrs. MacQuire stares at them.

"Jewels," she whispers. Gently she touches them with her finger. The petals shiver, come alive. She shakes her head. "They're wonderful." She looks at me. Her eyes are green, the color of leaves.

"You did end up living there," she says. She says it softly. After a moment I nod my head.

"But not alone." I say it softly too.

She blinks. "The worst is, I think he's right." Her voice is low, and tight with pain. She swallows. "I set it up, to hurt him. To see him treating Cate the way he'd treated me . . ." She looks down at the flowers. "I can't bear him being right."

"Who says he is?"

"I do." She sighs. "Now that it's too late."

"It isn't that simple." I reach out to touch a petal. "I mean, maybe you did want to hurt him, but you cared about her, too. You tried to help." The petal feels like skin. Skin touching skin.

"Did I?"

260

"I think so. Yeah. I mean, maybe neither of us tried to help for the right reasons, but . . ."

"What's right?"

"You know. Doing it for her, not for ourselves."

"And is it possible to separate like that?"

I shrug. "I don't know. Maybe not. It's like I said, we're all connected, but maybe if we know where we're coming from, then we can see . . ." I squint up at the ceiling. "I mean, take stars."

"Stars!"

"Yeah. What do you know about the Big Bang theory?"

"Nothing," she says, and from the way she says it I can tell she doesn't want to know. "Tell me something," she says. She waits until I look at her. "Do you think it's too late to change?"

"Change?"

"I'm thirty-nine."

"That's not so old."

"Oh, Peter." Smiling, she reaches out to touch my cheek. "Some of us start learning late."

I grin. "Better than not at all," I say.

She laughs. "That sounds like Judith."

"Jiggers," says Coach. "What's going on?"

I turn fast, and she turns slow. Coach stands in the doorway, grinning.

"Judith," says Mrs. MacQuire. "His parents were just here."

"I heard," says Coach. He comes in, shuffling, and settles in a chair. "I heard that bastard Edwards put on quite a show."

"He's left."

"Good riddance," says Coach.

Mrs. MacQuire sets the carton on the table.

"What's this?" says Coach.

"Milk and cookie time." She brings the plate of cookies from the stove.

Coach takes a cookie. "So what's new?" he says to me. He pops the cookie in his mouth.

"Not much." I smell the lemon as he chews, a sharp sweet smell that makes me think of something lost.

"He's leaving," says Mrs. MacQuire.

Coach smiles at me. "I guess I knew that. He's not the only one, from what I hear."

I don't say anything. She doesn't either.

He looks at her. His look is sharp. "How about a cookie? They're awfully good."

"I'm not hungry actually."

She walks over to the sink.

"Not another headache, is it?"

"No." She turns the water on. "I'm all right."

"Well," says Coach. "That's a start, I guess." And then he turns to look at me. His eyes are soft, and sad.

He winks.

By the time I get down to the basement, it's almost dark. Snickers is one step behind me. I can tell from his breathing that he's scared. I haven't told him anything; I couldn't think of what to say, or how to say it. Timothy isn't easy to explain.

"Careful," I say. "Don't drop the jar."

My voice echoes off the stairs.

"It stinks down here," says Snickers. A breathless whisper.

Without the furnace running, it does. Its summer smell of mold and rot. Damp cement and sweating pipes.

Timothy sits upright in his chair. His eyes are closed.

"Is he dead?" says Snickers. Whispering, he stands behind me.

Timothy opens his eyes, and smiles. I smile too.

"I've brought a present."

I take a quick step sideways. Snickers stands, mouth open, staring.

"What do I do?" he says.

262

"You don't have to do a thing."

Timothy looks at him. He doesn't blink. He doesn't move.

"Timothy, this is Jamie." I look at Snickers, who stands, frozen. "You've seen Timothy in the kitchen."

"Does he talk?" says Snickers.

"Sometimes." I put my hand on Timothy's arm. "I've come to say good-bye."

His head turns, slowly. He looks at me.

"Peter," he says. His voice is rusty, warm water running through a pipe.

"I've brought two presents," I say, "but for the second we'll need it dark."

I reach up for the string. The light clicks off.

"Give it to him," I say to Snickers.

He doesn't move. He holds the jar cupped in his hands. Through his fingers I see the stars.

"Far out," says Snickers in a whisper.

"Give it to him."

Snickers leans toward him, and slowly Timothy reaches out.

"Fireflies," he says.

His face glows, and his hands, a green glow, spreading.

"Awesome," says Snickers. "It's like the universe in there."

We stand in silence. Listening, I think I hear the tick of wings against the glass. But maybe not. It could be it's just my heart.

After a while I turn on the light. We stand there, blinking.

"Remember," Timothy says.

He looks at me. He lifts his hands, both hands, slowly, the jar resting on his lap. Slowly he presses two fingers together, together and then apart. Blinking. Like Cate. I nod.

"You did that before."

He looks at me, and does it again, with both hands this time. His eyes are on me, holding, as if there's something he wants me to see.

I watch his hands. Two hands. One held straight and still

263

and quiet, the other curved, the fingers blinking, slowly moving, backing off. Two hands. Two people. One moving, one standing still. Watching as the other moves sideways, through the air, and suddenly, with no warning, falls. Falls fluttering like a leaf into his lap. The other hand holds, just for a moment, before it moves away. Not falling. Moving sideways. Out of sight.

I look at Timothy. His eyes are open, clear as water. I swallow hard.

"You saw, didn't you? You were watching from your window?"

He doesn't answer. He doesn't have to.

"Hey," says Snickers. Nervous. His fingers plucking at my sleeve. "What's going on?"

"Nothing," I say.

He leans close, whispering in my ear. "Is he crazy?"

"No." I shake my head. "It's just his way of saying good-bye."

TWENTY-NINE

"I CONFESS," says Manning, "I was beginning to think you wouldn't come."

He smiles. It's hard to look at him so I look down at the table, at my plate, a white plate rimmed with red and gold.

"I had some things to do."

He carves the lamb, deftly, into thin pink slices, and for a moment I think of Robert, his scalpel slicing. My mother's flesh.

"Even so."

He lifts the lamb onto my plate. The juices run. I smell the mint.

"You asked me."

"Ah." He helps himself, then both of us to peas and roast potatoes. "And do you always do what you're asked?" His voice is teasing.

"Do you?"

He laughs. "Hardly ever." He pours red wine into crystal glasses. The crystal sparkles. "The last supper," he says. He slides his napkin from the napkin ring. "I thought it only appropriate that we eat in here." He lays his napkin in his lap.

We sit at one end of the table, exactly where we sat two years before. At the other end the terrace doors are open. When the breeze blows, the candles ripple across the table, across the portrait on the wall.

The lamb cuts easily. Butter glistens on the peas. When the breeze blows, I smell the garden.

"I have to ask you something."

"By all means," says Manning. He sips his wine.

"Why did you marry her?"

"Haven't you asked me that before?"

"Was it because of me?"

He sets his glass down carefully. The wine glows red. One drop quivers on the rim. I think of tears.

"So you can blame yourself?"

"No. I'm trying to understand."

"Well then, there were several reasons."

"You wanted to be Head."

"Quite right," he says. "I did." He smiles. "Shall we eat? It's getting cold."

He eats. I don't. I put my napkin in my lap, and watch him eat, the small bites, the careful chewing.

"Spencer said you changed your mind."

He glances at me. "So did he, as I expect you heard." He laughs. "Perhaps he's not the fool I thought." He sounds amused.

"I don't understand you," I say. "Don't you care for anything?"

He takes another sip of wine, looking at me above the rim. "Would it make a difference if I did?"

I look at him, and wonder who he is.

He glances at the portrait on the wall. He looks at it, and slowly nods his head.

"Perhaps," he says, "the reason's there."

"Reason for what?"

He turns his wineglass in his hands, a careful motion, back and forth.

"I was spoiled as a child. Adored. Whatever I wanted, I could have."

"OK, but I . . ."

He lifts his hand to silence me.

266

"Which means that my legacy, dear Peter, is a sense of entitlement that some might call ambition, and a belief, not completely unfounded, in my own powers of persuasion. A legacy that also includes a rather pernicious ennui."

"Boredom, you mean?"

He nods. "Boredom. Spencer bores me. Dunster bores me. And so . . . I am perfectly willing to leave." He smiles, shrugging, a mock gesture of despair.

"Only because you didn't get the job."

"I suspect the job would bore me too. The pleasure for me is in the quest. Once the desired object is achieved . . ." Smiling as if he thinks I'll be amused.

"You mean like Cate."

"Perhaps."

"And me?"

He looks down at my plate. "Would you like more?" he asks even though he sees my plate's still full.

I shake my head. He helps himself.

"Mrs. MacQuire," I say. "You wanted her."

He looks at me. "When I first met her, yes. She had a certain presence. In some ways she reminded me of Mother. I liked that. I liked that very much. There are very few people I respect. In the beginning I respected her."

"Until she was dumb enough to fall in love with you?"

He smiles. "I wouldn't call it love. More like a craving. No. Not that."

"Rufus?"

His fork stops halfway to his mouth.

"She told you?" I hear amazement in his voice.

"We talked about it."

He lowers his fork, and slowly shakes his head, waiting a moment before he speaks.

"Not Rufus, but the fact she lost control. Frankly, I was disappointed. I'd expected more from her."

"To care as little as you?"

My voice is hard, but he laughs, a small soft bark of sound.

267

"Perhaps. But addiction isn't caring. She hoped to trap me with that baby."

"Maybe she wanted a baby."

"She wanted me. She always has."

"Not anymore."

He looks at me. "I'm glad to hear it." He doesn't sound glad. He sounds bored. I lean toward him.

"She cared for Cate, you know. Maybe not at first but in the end. And it didn't have to do with you."

"Didn't it? How do you know?"

His voice is smooth. I take a breath. A deep breath.

"Because I've read Cate's journal."

I wait for him to show surprise. To ask me something. Instead he smiles.

"I hoped you had."

I stare at him.

"That's why I left it in your room."

"You!" My voice catches in my throat. "She did! She wrote a note!"

Eyes on me, he shakes his head. "I'm sorry," he says. "I hadn't meant to tell you."

That's what he says. I'm so angry that it's hard to breathe.

"You mean you wanted me to think she put it there?"

"Would you have accepted it from me?" He knows the answer; so do I. I look down at the table. "I wanted you to read it, Peter. To see how small a part you really played."

"You know what I thought, don't you? I thought at least she cared enough to leave . . ." My voice cracks. I clench my fists.

"That was my intention."

"Bullshit! You did it for yourself. To keep me quiet."

He shakes his head. "I know you, Peter. I knew that you were going to blame yourself, for everything. So when I found the journal afterward . . . among her things, I . . ."

I look at him, his eyes like velvet, dark as dreams. "Not

268

everything," I say. I say it slowly. I raise my hand, and hit the table. The table shakes. I see him flinch.

"I know what happened." I grip the table. My words come fast.

"You were on the bridge, with her, and she told you that she was leaving. Just after she'd been with me, and I'd said no. She told you, and you didn't like it. You threatened her, scared her, and she stepped back away from you and fell. You could have saved her but you didn't. You stood there. And then you walked away."

He looks at me. His eyes are dark. My stomach tightens.

"You didn't care enough to let her live."

He doesn't blink. He doesn't say a word.

"Admit it, damn it!"

Lifting his hand, he rubs his cheek. "Need I?"

Pushing back his chair, he rises.

"Shall we have dessert?"

He stands above me, looking down. When I don't answer, he takes our plates, and leaves the room. I sit there, rooted to my chair. I sit there, listening. A clock chimes in the hall, and on the wall his mother looks at me. In silence. She tells me nothing. There are still so many things I'll never know.

He comes back with a bowl of berries, a jar of cream. He sets them on the table.

"We'll have coffee later, shall we?" His voice is smooth, no different than it was before.

He spoons the berries onto flowered plates. The cream is thick, the berries sweet. They don't need sugar. Our spoons click against the china.

"Your paper," he says. "How's it coming?"

"It isn't."

"Perhaps we'll call it written."

"What do you mean by that?" I say, and Manning shrugs.

"I suppose I meant you've learned a lot from all that's happened. More than you'd ever learn from writing such a paper."

269

"So you think Cate's death was a tragedy?"

"No, Peter, I do not. As you should know, tragedy, in the Shakespearean sense, requires a hero of some stature, a hero with a tragic flaw."

"In Shakespeare maybe, but this is real life. I mean, she's dead! That's not enough?"

He shakes his head. "Not for tragedy, Peter, and I expect you don't need me to tell you that. I expect you know now very well what she was like." He looks at me and, for a long moment, doesn't speak. "And others, too." His voice is soft. He looks at me, and smiles, a slow smile that spreads like sunlight. I see the shadows gather at the corners of his mouth, in the creases by his eyes.

He smiles. And there is something in that smile that gets to me. I'm not sure what. Maybe only what that smile used to mean. The promise in it. The promise in him.

And I think, suddenly, that maybe in real life tragic heroes don't have to die.

I look at him. His eyes are dark. In his eyes I see the night.

I put my spoon down on my plate.

"Have you ever cared for ANYONE?" I say it loud.

He doesn't answer. I answer for him.

"You don't know how!"

He bows his head.

"But you do, don't you."

His voice is soft. It's not a question. I look away, remembering how I cared for him.

He looks at me.

"That's what I saw when I first met you. I saw, in you, what might have been. I saw a chance to try again."

"That's not caring."

"I also saw you needed help. And I did help you, Peter." He pauses. "Perhaps that troubles you the most."

I look down at the floor. "That night," I say. A whisper.

270

"That night helped neither of us. I mean what came before."

"And after?"

"That night, Peter, I lost control. I don't like to lose control."

I don't say anything.

"Look at me," he says, and there is something in his voice.

I look. His eyes are on me.

"You need to know I've cared for you as much as I have ever cared for anyone."

He doesn't smile. He looks at me. The breeze blows, and light plays across his face, and in his eyes I see myself. And I think, all these years, that's what it's been. He's looked at me, seeing only a reflection of himself.

I should be angry, but what I am is sad. And strangely, mostly sad for him.

I shake my head. "You don't know what caring is." I say it softly. "It's all as if. You can't care, and you can't hurt, and you can't grow. It's like you're trapped. Inside yourself."

His mouth twists. He smiles, shrugging with his hands.

His palms are smooth. Unlined. Untouched.

They are just about the last to arrive. Standing on the school steps, I see them coming past the lions at the gate, and walking quickly up the hill. The wind blows, scattering sunlight through the leaves. The sky is blue. The air smells clean, and full of promise. I think of when I stood here last.

Judith holds her hand to her head to keep her hat from blowing off. A white hat with a rust-colored ribbon around the brim. She grins when she sees me. My father, in a blue, gold-buttoned blazer, smiles.

"Do we look the part?" says Judith, her voice breathless from the climb.

They stand in front of me. I see a muscle working in my father's jaw, the tilt of Judith's head.

And there between them, I see Bets.

She looks up at me. She doesn't smile. She scratches a bug bite on her arm. Her hair is brown except where sunlight hits it. Brown and curly. Just like mine.

All I can do is stare at her.

She wears a blue dress with red balloons. Too short, it billows in the wind. Her knees are bony; her legs are long.

I want to pick her up, and squeeze her. I don't. I don't do anything but stare.

"They kidnapped me," she says in the same hoarse voice that I remember. Her eyes are bright, and very clear.

There's a big lump in my throat. I cough, hoping it will go away.

"Was it hard? To kidnap you, I mean?"

"Easy," she says. She grins. "I helped."

My eyes sting. "I can't believe you're here," I say. Blinking fast, I shake my head.

She holds her arm up. "Touch me," she says.

I touch her arm, and when I do, she grins again.

"See?" she says. "I'm real."

I have to laugh. "I guess you are."

Judith gives me a quick kiss on the cheek. "She's not bad either . . . for a kid," she says. "At least not half so bad as you."

Bets giggles. "She's awful," she says. "She teases all the time."

Judith grins. "You hold your own," she says to Bets. She grins at me. "She'll do all right."

It's hard to talk. I shrug and smile. I can't stop smiling.

"So," says my father. He clears his throat, shifting his weight from side to side. "You all prepared?"

I nod. "I guess."

I look around. The quad is full, and people are settling in their chairs.

It's almost time.

"Aren't you scared?" says Bets. "Dad says you have to stand up all by yourself."

I look at her. I still can't quite believe she's here.

"Not really," I say. I'm really not. I don't know why.

"So what are you going to talk about?" asks Judith.

"Stuff," I say. "Stars and things."

"Stars?" says my father. I hear his knuckles start to crack. I have to smile. He slides his hands into his pockets.

"The Big Bang theory," I say. "You know, the origins of the universe. We studied it in Physics this year, and I've been thinking . . . how it might connect to us."

My father blinks. "To us?" Thinking I mean him and me.

"To people. I mean, if you think of us as stars."

"I'm not a star!" says Bets.

I look at her. "Pretend," I say. "Pretend that first we were all together in a great big ball like this." I clench my fist. "And then . . . BAM!" I open my hand. Her eyes go wide. "There's a big explosion, and we all start floating into space."

Her forehead wrinkles. "You mean like this?" She waves her hands. "We just start flying apart?"

I nod. "You know how stars look like they're standing still? Well, now they've figured out they're not. All this time they've been moving away from each other, out and out and out. Like if you put polka dots on that balloon" — I poke a red balloon that's on her dress — "and blow the balloon up really big, the dots will move apart."

Bets looks at me. "That's sad," she says.

"So, kiddo, what's the point?" says Judith.

My father clears his throat again. "I'm afraid," he says, "I . . ."

Bets tugs my sleeve. "Forever?"

I look at her, and shake my head. "That's the thing," I say. I smile. "They used to think so, but now they don't. Not anymore. They've figured out that if there's enough density between the stars, they'll start to come together again."

She doesn't smile. "What's density?" she says.

"Something that's there that you can't see. No one can. But it's there. It's heavy, like gravity, and it pulls things back together."

"Invisible glue?"

"Sort of. Yeah."

Bets is quiet while she thinks. She nods her head.

"I like that story."

"It's not a story. It's true."

"It is too a story. People aren't stars!"

"That part's pretend."

"I like that, kiddo," says Judith. "I like that very much."

"I don't," says Bets. "I think it's stupid."

"Listen, Bets. I'm really talking about people. About what connects them. Us. How I'm connected to this school. To Dunster. I have to talk about the school. You know, what it's meant to me. I've been here six years, and now I'm leaving, but I figure I'll always be connected to it, to these people, even if I don't come back. Even if I never see them."

"But what connects you?"

I shrug. "Lots of things. Things that happened. Feelings. Stuff like that."

"Invisible things, you mean?"

"Mostly," I say. I look at her. "You're getting pretty smart."

She grins, pleased. She looks at me.

"Are we connected?"

"What do you think?"

I see her thinking. "You're my brother," she says slowly.

"Right."

"So we're connected?"

"Right again."

"It's more than that, though."

"I think so."

She looks at me. "Like invisible glue?"

I nod my head.

"Forever?" says Bets.

274

I grin. "You got it," I say.

"No," Bets says. She giggles. "I've got you."

She's never been shy. Flinging her arms around my waist, she squeezes tight.

"My God, you're strong!" I gasp, pretending that it's hard to breathe. Her laugh explodes against my stomach. I feel her breath. She won't let go.

I hold her close. Her skin is cool. Her hair is soft. She smells of summer, sun and flowers.

I hear my father clear his throat, and, holding Bets, I smile at him. He smiles too, and so does Judith. I see them smiling. I see their eyes are filled with tears.

The bells ring, echoing off the brick walls of the building around the quad. The quad is filled with sunlight, with people, parents, sitting in rows of folding chairs.

I should be nervous, but I'm not. My black robe flapping, I climb the stand. I smell the roses, and hear the water splashing in the fountain.

I look out over a sea of faces. Everyone is here. All five MacQuires in a row. Mrs. MacQuire next to Coach, and then the children, like stepping stones. When they see me looking, all five wave. I see Thurston, Snickers, Mary. Even Timothy leans against the farthest wall, and in the front row Spencer waits. Everyone but Manning. I don't know where he is, or why he hasn't come. I don't suppose I'll ever know. I don't suppose it matters either. Not anymore.

The wind blows, gusting. Programs flap, and dresses rustle. Above the quad clouds race across blue sky, small white clouds that miss the sun. I see their shadows though, moving across green grass, along pink walls before they disappear. I see them. And I think of Cate.

The wind sings through the cloisters, and slowly the bells' echoes die away. Spencer, in the front row, nods. The speakers hum, and, smoothing my notes down with my hand, I look up, to the far left near the chapel where Bets sits with

Judith and my father. She sits between them, one leg slowly swinging back and forth. Too far away to see their faces, but I see *them*, their faces turned in my direction.

I clear my throat. "Commencement," I say. My voice comes loud.

And I begin.